"ME GRANDAD
'AD AN ELEPHANT!"

UNESCO COLLECTION OF REPRESENTATIVE WORKS

INDIAN SERIES

THIS BOOK HAS BEEN ACCEPTED

IN THE INDIAN SERIES

OF THE TRANSLATIONS COLLECTION

OF THE UNITED NATIONS

EDUCATIONAL, SCIENTIFIC AND

CULTURAL ORGANIZATION

(UNESCO)

*

TO SHAHINA AND ANEEZ, DAVID AND MICHAEL

"ME GRANDAD 'AD AN ELEPHANT!"

THREE STORIES OF MUSLIM LIFE IN SOUTH INDIA

BY VAIKOM MUHAMMAD

BASHEER

*

TRANSLATED FROM THE MALAYALAM

BY R·E·ASHER AND

ACHAMMA

COILPARAMPIL

CHANDERSEKARAN

*

EDINBURGH UNIVERSITY PRESS

1980

© UNESCO 1980
Vaikom Muhammad Basheer
Edinburgh University Press
22 George Square, Edinburgh

ISBN 0 85224 386 3 (Hardback)
ISBN 0 85224 408 8 (Paperback)

Set in Monotype Barbou by
Speedspools, Edinburgh
and printed in Great Britain by
The Pitman Press
Bath

*

CONTENTS

*

VAIKOM MUHAMMAD BA'SHEER

INTRODUCTION

Born some sixty-five years ago in the small village of Thalayolaparambu, near Vaikom in southern Kerala, Vaikom Muhammad Basheer is one of India's outstanding living writers. Some of his earliest writings, including poems, were in English, but his most important works, which can be roughly and hesitatingly classified as prose fiction, are in Malayalam. Among the official languages of the country, Malayalam is near the bottom of the list as regards the number of people speaking it, there being not many more than twenty million. However, the reading public is relatively large, partly because of the exceptionally high level of literacy in all age groups and both sexes and partly because of an unusually widespread interest in literature.

Kerala differs from most other Indian states in a number of ways. One factor that needs to be kept in mind is the considerable mixture of religious groups; for along with the Hindu majority there are significant and vocal Muslim and Christian minorities. Some Christian groups can trace their origin back to a period that antedates by some centuries the beginnings of extensive European missionary activity in India—back, indeed, to the time of St Thomas. Similarly, there is a tradition among Muslims, first mentioned by a historian of the sixteenth century, that Islam was introduced to the Malabar coast during the lifetime of the Prophet Muhammad himself by the conversion of the Hindu raja, Cheruman Perumal.

Unique, then, in some respects, Kerala nevertheless shares many characteristics with other regions of India in its cultural development. Thus, early literature in Malayalam, as in other Indian languages, is almost exclusively in verse and concerned above all with religious themes. The widespread use of prose for creative purposes in Indian literature follows the arrival of Europeans into the subcontinent, and the very beginnings of prose fiction cannot convincingly be traced back further than the early decades of the nineteenth century. What is sometimes regarded as the first novel in an Indian language (Bengali) appeared in 1801 and it was not until the second half of the century that the new genre showed real signs of establishing itself in all the major languages of India. Malayalam, with its first original novel not appearing until 1887, was relatively late in the field but has made particularly rapid strides since then.

Contemporary writers in Kerala have a certain tendency to set their novels and short stories in the author's own community. Although Basheer has occasionally chosen Hindus or Christians as the heroes and heroines of his stories, he is fairly representative of this tendency. Furthermore, one might say that the tales with the most unreservedly Muslim setting have the most universal appeal.

For the selection that makes up this volume we have chosen three such stories of Muslim families in Kerala, *Childhood Friend*, *'Me Grandad 'ad an Elephant!'* and *Pattumma's Goat*, first published in 1944, 1951 and 1959 respectively (and now respectively in their 16th, 10th and 6th impressions). The first of the three had a very considerable critical success when it was first published and it was sufficient to establish its author as a major literary figure in Kerala. The second made possibly an even greater impact and has been translated into all the major languages of India. Over 100,000 copies of the original Malayalam version have been sold. One may perhaps justifiably assume that it was above all because of these two books that

Basheer achieved in 1970 the rare distinction of being elected a Fellow of the Sahitya Akademi (Academy of Letters) of India.

It is a common pursuit in certain critical circles to seek western influences in Asian prose fiction, as if a novel or short story written by anyone other than a European or an American must necessarily be derivative. It is true, admittedly, that some of Kerala's most original writers acknowledge their debt to Zola, Maupassant, Chekov, and others. Basheer, however, is conscious of no such influence and it would be a fruitless task to try and find one. In fact there is in all respects no neat way of pigeon-holing his writings.

Thus, critics have been unable to decide whether he writes short novels or long short stories. Basheer himself exercises the artist's prerogative of not involving himself in such discussions. He may be supposed to have committed himself to some classification of his works by publishing some of them as separate books (these, presumably, are novels) and some along with others as a collection (these, one might guess, are short stories). Yet one notices that, whereas earlier impressions of *Childhood Friend* and *Pattumma's Goat* carried the word 'novel' on the main title page, the most recent ones do not. Is this perhaps a hint that we should not regard the question as being one of real consequence?

There is a further difficulty of deciding whether Basheer writes prose fiction or autobiography. Of the three books included between these covers, the relative proportions vary considerably. *Pattumma's Goat*, we are assured, is entirely true and the names of the characters are the real names of the members of the author's family who are portrayed in its pages. *Childhood Friend* is, in a certain sense of the word, ninety or ninety-five per cent 'true' and is based on an episode in Basheer's own life. However, like any great work of art, it transcends the distinction between truth and fiction. There is no profit (or loss) for the reader in equating the hero, Majid, with the young Basheer. In

'*Me Grandad 'ad an Elephant!*' Basheer has drawn here and there for character on people he has known, but the percentage of crude historical fact remains low.

Basheer is not a prolific writer, for he is not readily satisfied with what he has written and spends much time revising and refining, seeking the right word, pruning. The most notable exception is *Pattumma's Goat*, which, as the rather eccentric introduction makes clear, was published in the form of its first draft, unchanged. There can be little doubt that this represents the right approach to this relatively light-weight book, which depends for its success on a sense of fun that a careful revision could too easily have obscured.

Pattumma's Goat and its introduction show the author as something of an individualist. As a literary figure, too, he stands somewhat apart from his contemporaries. Unlike the other major novelists of his day in Kerala, he is not readily classified as a 'socialist-realist' writer. It is not that he is uninterested in social reform. One of his ideas in writing '*Me Grandad 'ad an Elephant!*', for instance, was (as he has explained in a letter written a few years ago) 'to project the glory of the bygone days of Islam and at the same time to point out the failure of present-day Muslims to adjust to the modern life because of this mythical past. Every beggar and every butcher even now claims that he is a direct descendant of Akbar the Great. The elephant is the symbol of that obvious past'. However, suggestions of a need for social change, even when they appear, are always entirely secondary to his main purpose and are never obtrusive.

As will be seen, the three stories in this volume are very different, having in common little more than their Kerala Muslim setting. One reason for our selection additional to those already given is the fact that, as a recent volume of reminiscences makes clear, Basheer has made a conscious attempt in the course of his literary career to produce an Islamic literature in Malayalam. This, however, as has already been suggested above, is far from meaning that his writing will hold no attraction for non-Muslims. It is part of the appeal of his work that what is to most of us a rather exotic background helps rather than hinders our appreciation of the universality of the emotions he depicts.

Different as types of narrative, our stories also vary stylistically. They share an avoidance of any sort of linguistic pedantry—a tendency that is perhaps over-simplistically stated by Basheer when he summarises his approach with the words, 'What I have put down in writing is the way I talk in conversation' (see below, p. 184, in his fictionalised account of an argument he had with one of his brothers about what constitutes good writing). One implication of these words is certainly not misleading, namely that Basheer's style is far removed from the magnificently complex structures that characterise platform speeches in Malayalam and many types of writing, including literary criticism. There is, however, more to Basheer's writing than an attempt to keep reasonably close to colloquial language. Within this general tendency, the style of his books varies with the subject. The extremely short and staccato sentences that characterise *Childhood Friend* are not matched in the other two books, particularly *Pattumma's Goat*. It is as if the author sensed that the more profound the emotions he wishes to convey, the simpler and more stark the language used must be. Paradoxically, perhaps, the simpler the structure of sentences he uses, the slower is the pace of the story. This, too, may be taken to be part of his purpose, for the deep feelings he is concerned with in *Childhood Friend* would be less readily conveyed to the reader in a runaway narrative.

The most complex of the three books stylistically and structurally is *'Me Grandad 'ad an Elephant!'*. This is not unrelated to Basheer's concern here to do more than narrate a story in a straightforward and uncomplicated manner. Alongside the charming love story, there are the implied criticisms of outdated Muslim customs that have no basis in the teaching of the Prophet Muhammad, an appeal to live in the present, an absorbing account of old beliefs and traditions and an abundance of comedy. These various strands are intertwined in such a way as to be inseparable. Similarly—and with a related purpose—the different chapters of the book are linked by repetitions and part repetitions of phrases that have been used earlier. Particularly important are the chapter headings, which are the source of some of the partly repeated phrases and which also provide clues to the different themes of the book.

Like his books, Basheer's life has been very varied, particularly the early part, which was full of vicissitudes. As a young man he served a nine-month jail sentence for taking part in the 'salt satyagraha' and he was again imprisoned in 1942, this time on a sedition charge brought because of certain political pamphlets he wrote. Like Majid in *Childhood Friend*, he spent several years wandering all over India. During this time he took whatever job came his way, becoming—among other things—teacher, proof-reader, mill hand, hotel boy. Now he lives a comparatively quiet and uneventful life in an attractive house on the southern edge of Beypore, with his wife Fabi, whom he married relatively late in life, his daughter Shahina and his son Aneez. When his children were very young, there was also a remarkable cat, which became famous throughout Kerala through being made the leading character in one of his books. Unfortunately, as the heroine of *'Me Grandad 'ad an Elephant!'* would tell us, a few years ago the wind blew and its leaf fell from Sidrat al-Muntaha, the great tree in Paradise.

Something of Basheer's life before marriage can be learned from *Pattumma's Goat* and the introduction to it. Not the least remarkable feature of this book is the fact that it was written at a time when he was suffering from such extreme depression that he feared for his sanity. Yet even this he was able to see as having its humorous side.

Altogether Mr Basheer is a remarkable man. Lucky are

those who can call on him in Beypore to enjoy his conversation, his skill as a raconteur and his cooking. He has the status of a patriarch (though a very human one) and is known to journalists, who can depend on him to provide interesting copy, as 'the Sultan of Beypore'.

The Translation

This translation is based on the most recently revised version of the three books, which the author kindly made available to the translators ahead of publication. Alterations to *Pattumma's Goat*, apart from the removal of one sentence and the addition of one phrase, are limited to a handful of spelling changes. Only one page in *'Me Grandad 'ad an Elephant!'* has been significantly rewritten. Quite considerable revisions, however, have been made in *Childhood Friend* and we are grateful to Mr Basheer for making it possible to incorporate these in our English version.

All the familiar problems that face a translator wishing to put into English a story with an Indian setting and written in an Indian language have been encountered here, along with some less common ones.

Cultural items, in the realms of dress and food, for example, do not always have a ready English equivalent. In some cases we have made do with an approximate equivalent; in others we have seen no alternative to using a transliterated form (ignoring all diacritics that a pedant might properly require). All such forms are italicised on their first appearance, the only exceptions being words (not necessarily part of most English-speakers' active vocabulary stock) that are to be found in the Oxford English Dictionary—such as 'jambu' and 'pandal'.

A few remarks on specific items of dress may be appropriate. One 'bisexual' garment is the cloth worn in Kerala to cover the lower half of the body. For this garment as worn by men we have used the reasonably familiar term 'dhoti', but, at the risk of seeming inconsistent, have introduced a romanisation of the Malayalam word, *mundu*, when it is described as being worn by a woman. For the long-sleeved, long-waisted blouse worn by Muslim women in Kerala we have kept the Malayalam *kuppayam*, above all because it is an important feature of an incident in one of the stories that, in the view of some people, no self-respecting Muslim lady should wear a 'blouse', that is to say one with short sleeves and allowing a view of the wearer's midriff.

There is little overlap in Malayalam between the set of kinship terms used by Muslims and those used by other communities. Part of the special flavour of Basheer's stories for a Malayali reader lies in his use of *bapa* as a term of address and reference for 'father' and *umma* for 'mother'. It has seemed to us best to keep this in almost all cases. We have been rather more sparing in the use of *uppuppa* for 'grandfather' and have used English equivalents for all other terms but one, and this only in one story. The reason for the exception is that one of the turns of the plot of *'Me Grandad 'ad an Elephant!'* only makes sense if Aisha is seen to be using the exclusively Muslim term *ikkakka* to refer to her 'elder brother'.

A cultural feature of a different kind, but also in the field of the use of kinship terms, concerns the convention that one does not address or refer to one's elders and betters in the family by name, but by the term of family relationship. We have followed this convention, even though it may on occasion seem strained. Otherwise, if the need to show respect to older members of the family had not prevented Abu (on p. 188) from using their names to refer to them, he might have said: 'That's because Kochunni owes Abdul-khadar some money. When he saw Anumma, Abdulkhadar said that, if he didn't get the money back right away, he'd file a suit! The first defendant would be Kochunni, the second would be Pattumma, the third Khadija'.

In *"Me Grandad 'ad an Elephant!"* in particular, Basheer uses a good amount of Islamic terminology that is no more familiar to the non-Muslim Malayali reader than it would be to the average non-Muslim speaker of English. He does this, of course, not with a view to unnecessarily bewildering the reader, but for a clear artistic purpose. Given that the context or a gloss written into the narrative by the author means that there is hardly any even slightly annoying obscurity, we have followed the original in this respect in our translation, only on rare occasions taking the presumptuous step of writing in a gloss not provided in the Malayalam text. We have considered it especially appropriate to follow Basheer in using Arabic terms to refer to the Deity and to His Prophet. Thus, as a synonym for 'God' we have not only 'Allah' but also 'Rabb'.

One Muslim feature we have sacrificed entirely. The dialect of Malayalam spoken by Muslims (particularly those who have not had the opportunity to advance very far up the educational ladder) is quite distinct from other dialects, as regards pronunciation, grammar and vocabulary. In the conversational passages of his stories, Basheer faithfully represents all aspects of this dialect. It would naturally have been possible to choose some 'non-standard' dialect of English for these dialogue sections. We decided against this for two reasons. Firstly, and more importantly, there is no specifically and exclusively Muslim dialect of English. The only choice, therefore, would have been some regional variety. Yet there would have been no motivation for choosing one such variety in preference to another, and whatever had been chosen would have had an entirely different flavour and impact from the original. Secondly, we share Shaw's consciousness (as expressed in a note to the first act of *Pygmalion*) of the difficulties of setting down English dialect forms intelligibly with the limited resources of ordinary orthography and hence copy his discretion by abandoning any such 'desperate attempt'. It has nevertheless been necessary to make one or two exceptions to this rule in *'Me Grandad 'ad an Elephant!'*, since the better-educated Aisha tries to improve Kunjupattumma's pronunciation along with teaching her to read and write.

Hence we have had to indicate here and there by devices of spelling that certain characters in the story speak with an uneducated accent. We have followed the author in symbolising this in the title too.

Other minor points, such as the substitution of a Latin phrase for a Sanskrit one, seem to need no explanation.

One problem, however, we found admitted of no really satisfactory solution. In the last chapter of *'Me Grandad 'ad an Elephant!'* we find some rude and uninhibited urchins claiming that the famous *aana* ('elephant') of the title was in reality no such thing, but a small insect for which the name in Malayalam is *kuẕiy-aana*. The English equivalent is 'ant-lion', which, regrettably, does not allow the necessary pun. We have made the best of a bad job by inventing the term 'elephant ant'. The reader is warned that, to the best of our knowledge, there is no such insect. One similar, and repeated, allusion to the elephant of the book's title we have ignored. The name by which the heroine's grandfather is known is Anamakkar, literally 'Elephant Makkar' (for did he not own an elephant?). The relative clumsiness of this expression as compared with the Malayalam form spoke against its use.

For those who like to be in a position to turn up an explanation of the meaning of unfamiliar words, we have appended a glossary. We hope that most readers will find it quite superfluous.

Further Reading

The literature of Malayalam, like that of most of the major languages of South Asia, deserves to be more widely known than is in fact the case. Interested readers may care to look at one or another of the substantial number of book-length accounts of Malayalam literature that have appeared in English during the past decade or so. All are by Malayalis, though all but one were first written in English.

All Indian literatures followed new directions as a result of the impact of the knowledge of European culture that western contacts brought. These developments are necessarily one of the topics in all histories of the literature and are the theme of K.M. George's *Western Influence on Malayalam Language and Literature* (New Delhi, Sahitya Akademi 1972). One very valuable feature of the same author's *A Survey of Malayalam Literature* (Bombay, Asia Publishing House 1968) is the hundred pages devoted to translations from modern literature, both poems and short stories.

P.K. Parameswaran Nair's *History of Malayalam Literature* (translated by E.M.J. Venniyoor; New Delhi, Sahitya Akademi 1967) is more informative in terms of works and writers discussed, but as a result can devote less space to translated extracts. The most readable account is Krishna Chaitanya's *A History of Malayalam Literature* (New Delhi, Orient Longman 1971), which devotes three-fifths of its 500-plus pages to the present century. Translated extracts (mainly of poetry) amount to eighty pages and the book has the further advantage of making frequent—and appropriate—comparisons with European literatures. A single area of modern literature is discussed by Verghese Ittiavira in *Social Novels in Malayalam* (Bangalore, The Christian Institute for the Study of Religion and Society 1968), which devotes a whole chapter to Basheer.

For a more detailed discussion of Basheer's writing than has been possible in this introduction, the following essays may be consulted: 'Vaikom Muhammad Basheer' in Edwin Gerow and Margery D. Lang (eds.) *Studies in the Language and Culture of South Asia* (Seattle and London, University of Washington Press 1973) 19–47; 'Three Novelists of Kerala' in T.W. Clark (ed.) *The Novel in India: its Birth and Development* (London, Allen & Unwin 1970) 226–34; 'Aspects de la littérature en prose dans le sud de l'Inde' in *Bulletin de l'Ecole Française d'Extrême-Orient*, Tome LIX (1972) 160–77; 'On translating Basheer' in Puthusseri Ramachandran (ed.) *Pratibhaanam: Dr P.K.*

Narayana Pillai Felicitation Volume (Trivandrum, University of Kerala 1972) 175–84.

English translations of Malayalam novels are not yet as large in number as one might hope. Outside India only one has appeared so far, namely Thakazhi Sivasankara Pillai's *Chemmeen* (translated by Narayana Menon; London, Gollancz, and New York, Harper 1962). Read along with these stories by Basheer it will, apart from its intrinsic merits, give some small idea of the variety of writing in Malayalam today. *Chemmeen* and the present volume are both included in the Indian Series of the Unesco Collection of Representative Works, as is Thakazhi's *Scavenger's Son* (translated by R. E. Asher; New Delhi, Orient Paperbacks 1975).

R·E·ASHER
University of Edinburgh, Scotland
November
1979

CHILDHOOD FRIEND

1)

Although Suhra and Majid have been friends from their childhood, there is something unusual about this affectionate relationship, in that before they became acquainted they were bitter enemies. What was the reason for this enmity? They were neighbours; the two families were on good terms. But Suhra and Majid were implacable foes. Suhra was seven and Majid nine. They were in the habit of making faces and trying to frighten each other.

And then came the mango season. Ripe mangoes started falling from the young tree near Suhra's house. She did not get a single one. When she ran up on hearing a mango fall, it would be to see that Majid had already picked it up and was taking a bite. He would not give it to her. Even if he pretended to be willing to give her one, it would be one he had already bitten into. Even then, when she stretched out her hand, he would say, 'Bite my elbow!' and poke his elbow in front of her face. In addition to that, when he saw her, he would try to frighten her by glaring at her and sticking out his tongue.

Suhra is not in the least frightened by this. She does the same to him. But as far as mangoes are concerned, she always comes off worse. Why isn't she getting any mangoes? Whether the wind is blowing or not, Suhra will stand under the tree, but nothing falls, not even a leaf. She knows there are plenty of ripe mangoes on the tree. If none falls, the only thing to do is to climb up. But there are lots of red ants. They will bite you to death! Even if there were none of those big ants, how could she—a girl—possibly climb a tree?

One day, while she was standing there with her mouth watering, something fell down with a bang through the branches.

Wow! Suhra ran up. Overjoyed, she was about to pick it up. But she stopped short; it was a tiny coconut! Had anyone seen how she was taken in? No; but how can a small coconut fall from a mango tree? She looked all around. Then she saw! She was wild. Him!

Majid, a victorious expression on his face, made some meaningless teasing sounds. 'Joogjoogoo! Joogjoogoo!' he shouted and came to the foot of the tree. He did not stop at that, but rolled his eyes and stuck out his tongue as far as it would go. It was a fearsome sight!

If any girl in the village saw that, she would quake with fright and run off shouting, 'Help!' Many have. But Suhra does not run! That is not all. With her head to one side, she stands there, sticking out her tongue and rolling her eyes!

That made Majid furious. Is this little, insignificant girl trying to frighten a big boy? He came a bit closer. His eyes became bigger, his eyebrows arched, his nostrils widened; he made a terrible sound: 'Grrr!'

Majid was stunned. A slip of a girl! A mere areca-nut dealer's daughter. Why is she not afraid of a timber-merchant's son? Females should fear males, whatever their age. Majid went up very close. She did not budge an inch. Majid's dignity was gone; he got really wild. How dare she?

'Hey, you, what's your name?' he asked angrily, as he grabbed her by the wrist. Not that he doesn't know. He knows it well. He had to ask something, didn't he? He was a man after all. So he asked.

All this was done as if he was going to eat her up. Her tiny teeth and all her ten sharp nails were itching. For a moment she was not sure what she wanted to do. Should she bite a

piece out of his arm or should she scratch him all over? To
say 'Hey, you'! Even her father and mother have not
addressed her in this way. Why should this dirty boy, who
glares at her, refuses to give her a mango and offers her his
elbow to bite, address her like this? She stepped up to him
angrily. With the sharp nails of her left hand she scratched
him as hard as she could on his right arm!

Majid squirmed as if he had been scratched with burning
spikes. He let go of her wrist and cried out 'Help!' in spite
of himself. . . . He had not expected that. Anyway, he
decided to scratch her in return. But he had bitten off all his
nails. So all that was left was to punch her or bite her; but
he had a feeling that she might do the same to him. . . .
After all, she scratched him. If people came to know that
she had also punched him, it would be a big disgrace. He
did nothing. Defeated, he stood there like a prize fool.

Suhra grinned at him. Majid did not move. Pulling a face,
she made fun of him and said, 'Help!'

Even then, Majid did not move. He was wondering what
he could say right away to cover up the disgrace that had
befallen him, and how he could get his own back on Suhra.
He was a man, after all. . . . But . . . what can he say? It
must be something overwhelming! . . . But he could not
think of anything. He looked around distractedly: through
the banana trees he could see Suhra's house, which was
thatched with straw and had mud-faced walls; through the
coconut palms he could see his own house with its tiled
roof and whitewashed walls. This gave him an idea. With
a view to making Suhra feel small he said, 'My house has
a tiled roof!'

What is there to be so proud about in this? Her house is
thatched with straw. What is there to be ashamed of in
that? She again pulled a face and made fun of him, saying,
'Help!'

Majid then said something more: Suhra's bapa is a mere
areca-nut dealer, whereas his bapa is a big timber-
merchant. Even in that she did not see anything to be proud

) 3 (

of. Suhra stood there looking up at the mango tree without showing any sign of being aware that there was a worm called Majid beside her.

Majid was on the verge of tears. What a disgrace! What a rebuff! It was absolutely unbearable for him. He wanted to bray like a donkey. If he cried, he would feel better! The next moment, however, he had an inspiration! There was one remarkable thing he could do that nobody else was capable of, and in that he could outdo Suhra. Airing his assumed superiority in this respect, he proclaimed to the earth and to the heavens, 'I know how to climb the mango tree!'

Suhra's eyes did not move. To know how to climb the mango tree! Isn't that something great? She was non-plussed. If he were to climb up the tree, would he give her any mangoes? Suppose he would not. . . . She decided to establish her rights straight away. Pointing to two big, ripe mangoes that could easily be reached if one climbed the tree, Suhra said very seriously, 'I saw those two big ones first.'

Majid kept quiet.

Why is he keeping quiet? It must be because he is scared of the ants! So she said, 'Oh, the ants will bite you!'

Majid did not like either her tone or her expression at all. He became cross. Ants! Never mind ants; even if it were covered with scorpions, he would climb up! She saw the two big ones first, did she? . . . Majid hitched up his dhoti and laboriously climbed the tree. Though he had grazed the skin on his chest and he was bitten all over by the ants, he plucked the two mangoes that Suhra had seen and came down triumphant.

Suhra ran up: eagerly and anxiously she stretched out her hand.

'Give them to me!'

Majid kept quiet. He stood there with his lips stretched tight together.

'Give them to me; I saw them first!'

Majid looked at her mockingly.

'Did you really?' He started walking. He sniffed the mangoes and talked to himself as he did so.

'Mm . . . what a lovely smell!'

Suhra became angry. She was fuming. She was hurt. . . . Her eyes filled with tears. She began to sob.

He came back. This was the time to establish his superiority. He held out the mangoes. In spite of her eagerness, she made no move to take them. Majid put both the mangoes in front of her. She did not pick them up. She could not believe her eyes! Was he so unselfish? She could not bring herself to believe it. She put both her hands behind her back; tears falling from her eyes, she stood there.

Showing great concern, he declared, 'If you want, I'll get you some more!'

Suhra's heart melted. If she wished, he would get her some more! How unselfish! How brave! Such a nice boy! Was it right to scratch him? With great modesty, ready to be unselfish, she said, 'I want only one.'

That truly unselfish person said, very graciously, 'You can have all of them!'

'I want only one.'

She picked up one of them and offered it to Majid. He said he didn't want it. She insisted and said she would cry if he didn't take it!

Majid took it. It was while the juice was falling on their chests, as they were taking bites from the mangoes, that Suhra saw the ants that had bitten into his back. It pained her. Standing very close to him, she carefully picked them all off one by one and threw them down. When her nails touched Majid's body, he felt something.

Though she did not scratch Majid any more that day, for a long time she continued to scratch and pinch him. If she said, 'I'll scratch you!' Majid shook with fright. It was by means of a trick, but with her knowledge and full consent, that Majid cut off her nails—her sharpest weapons.

2)

One morning Suhra, accompanied by Majid, was bringing some shoots from flowering plants that they had collected from round about to make a garden in Majid's front yard. It was Suhra who was carrying the plants. Majid was walking ahead in grand style. After all, he was a man!

In his hand there was an open penknife. He was talking about all the great things he was going to do in the future. Suhra could only feel joy and amazement, while saying 'Yes' occasionally to show she was listening. Majid's dreams were incomparable: a beautiful world bathed in golden light. Although Majid is the sole ruler, Suhra is his consort. There is no gainsaying that! She would start to cry: her nails would stretch out. This gave Majid a burning sensation. To avoid experiencing it, Majid was very careful how he talked. Still, at times he forgot.

Majid is a slave to imagination. In time to come he will have a tall mansion built. All its walls will be of gold. Its floor will be of rubies. What sort of roof will it have? . . . He cannot think of anything. Is this not because Suhra is failing to pay proper attention? If only she would say 'Yes' or nod her head now and again, he would know right away what to say next!

'Hey, Suhra!'

'What is it, Majid?'

'Why don't you pay attention?'

'I am paying attention. Why do you say "Hey" to me?'

She stepped forward angrily. Her scratch made him squirm! He turned around with the penknife. She threatened him with the nails of her outstretched hands and with her fierce glare.

'I'll scratch you again!'

The recollection of the earlier scratchings and pinchings made Majid's blood run cold. . . . Suhra with her nails is a terror. If only she did not have those nails! But she had had nails as long as he can remember. Nor does she hesitate to use them. In view of that, is it wise to provoke her? Very innocently he asked, as if Suhra had scratched him for no reason, 'Suhra, why did you scratch me?'

'Why did you say, "Hey, Suhra"?'

Majid assumed an air of bewilderment.

'When was that? I didn't say that! You must have been dreaming.'

When she saw the expression on his face, Suhra really felt bad! Did Majid actually say it? Maybe she had imagined it. Then it was unpardonable of her to scratch him.... Four marks, red and swollen. Are they not the signs of her hard-heartedness?

Tears came to her eyes.

Pretending not to notice, Majid walked along the village path spread with white sand and said to himself, 'Even if I don't do anything, bapa and umma beat me and scold me. Then there are others who just pinch and scratch me, simply for the pleasure of doing it. When I die, they will say, "If only that poor Majid were here—we could at least pinch him!" ...'

After this, Majid slowly turned round. Great! Two streams of tears on Suhra's cheeks.... He was happy.

As if to take part in his joy, the morning sun looks over the top of the hill and smiles down on the village on its slope, immersing it in a golden light. The river that divides to encompass the hill and the village and then further along becomes one again looks like melted gold. ... In the chirping of the birds that breaks the silence of the village, Majid hears the echo of immeasurable joy.

In Suhra's heart alone there is no joy: she had committed an unforgivable offence! Did she not scratch Majid for no reason? The more she thinks about it, the more her heart aches. ... Those four marks, red and swollen, on Majid's back! How can she wipe out her mistake?

Reminding him of the mansion he had spoken of, and as if nothing had happened, Suhra asked softly, 'And that mansion?'

Majid kept quiet. After a while he asked, 'Are you paying attention?'

Filled with remorse she said, repeating the word as if to prove her readiness, 'Yes, yes, yes! I am paying attention!'

'You know!' he continued. 'The mansion will be on top of that hill!'

If it is, they will be able to see the whole village. Not only that, they will be able to see those two rivers joining together and flowing as a bigger one into the distance. Have not Majid and Suhra climbed the hill along with the other children of the village many times to see this? The mansion Majid is going to create there will be a wonderful one.

'I say!' she called to Majid. Then she asked anxiously, 'How tall will that mansion be?'

Is there any limit to height? Majid said, 'Very!'

Being unable to work out how tall 'very' was, Suhra asked, 'As tall as a banana tree?'

'A banana tree!' He did not much care for that. A house the height of a banana tree!

'Pooh!' he said and looked at Suhra.

'As tall as a coconut tree?' she asked.

Because Majid made fun of that also, Suhra raised her face to the sky and asked hesitantly, 'As high as the sky?'

'Yes,' Majid agreed. 'It will be as high as the sky!'

She had another question.

'Are you going to live there alone?'

'No!' Majid remembered the Arabian stories and said, 'Me and a princess!'

A princess? There is no-one like that in their part of the world. Still. . . .

'Who is that girl?'

As if it was a secret, Majid said, 'There is one!'

When she heard that, Suhra's face fell. She was both angry and sad. She put down all the flower shoots; her eyes overflowed with tears, as she said, 'Get your princess to carry these.'

Majid asked, 'Why don't you carry them?'

She burst out crying.

'I'm not coming with you; get your princess to carry them.'

What a turn of events! It touched his heart. He went near and sat in front of her.

'Suhra, you are my—'

'?'

'P – r – i – n – c – e – s – s.'

Her face lit up.

'You're joking.'

'On my honour!'

She was happy. She can live in that mansion with Majid. It will be fun! She stood there smiling through her tears. Majid was about to cut her nails.

'Don't.'

Suhra smiled through her tears as the full moon shines through light rain.

'Don't cut my nails!' She pouted her lips. 'If you say anything, I shall have to pinch you!'

'Are you going to pinch me, Suhra?'

'Yes I am! Always, always I shall pinch you.'

She gritted her teeth and arched her eyebrows and was about to pinch him.

Shaking, Majid got up.

As if to remind her how great her offence was, Majid said, 'A princess should not pinch!'

If a princess pinches, it will be a great sin! Not quite convinced, Suhra asked, 'On your honour?'

Majid swore it was so.

'On my honour; she shouldn't pinch!'

She stood there perplexed. If a princess should not pinch, what need had she for fingernails? As if she were making a great sacrifice, she stretched out both her hands and gave her consent.

'Very well then. Cut them off!'

Happy, Majid sat down in front of Suhra.

Majid cut off all the ten sharp, spiky nails, and then got up. They went and made the garden. Along the sides of the vast front yard of his house Majid dug small holes. Suhra put one shoot in each, filled them up and watered them. They set one with twisting leaves, one with yellow leaves and one with leaves like the tail of a cock, repeating the sequence until the work was completed. In the corner they planted a shoeflower. When Suhra put it in the hole they had prepared, there was a red flower on it that had begun to wilt.

Every morning Suhra would go to Majid's house and water the plants.

Once Suhra's umma asked her teasingly, 'Suhra, why do you water somebody or other's plants?'

Suhra said, 'It's not somebody or other.'

That evening Suhra and Majid were standing in the yard. Pointing to the sprouting plants, Majid asked aloud, 'Suhra, are all these yours?'

'Why, are they yours?'

Majid laughed at her.

'You would like to own them!'

Could she do other than get angry? She scratched him! Because the nails were not long enough, Majid said, 'Scratch again! It feels good!'

Suhra looked at her nails and burst out crying.

'Then I'll bite you.'

She was about to bite him on his wrist! Seeing no other way out, Majid swore in the name of the Koran.

'By the thirty parts of the holy Mushaf, I tell you that a princess should not bite!'

With tears falling from her eyes, Suhra asked, 'Not anyone?'

Smiling, Majid said, 'Not anyone!'

3)

Suhra was very good at arithmetic. The teacher used to praise her and beat Majid. When it came to arithmetic, he used to be all confused. However he might try, nothing would come out right.

'Number one blockhead!' is what the teacher calls him. This is what he calls out even when taking the roll. Nobody has any complaints about this. Majid *is* a blockhead. So from among the children he will answer loudly, 'Pre . . . sent.'

Once the schoolmaster asked Majid, 'What do one and one make?' Now it is a fact well known the world over that one and one make two. But Majid produced a remarkable solution to the question that caused the teacher to burst out laughing. The whole class laughed. The solution he gave became his nickname. Before answering, Majid reflected: as two rivers join together and flow as a broader river, so two ones joined together become a broader 'one'! Having calculated thus, he announced proudly, 'A rather big one!'

For finding a new theory in arithmetic Majid was made to stand on the bench.

'A rather big one!' They all looked at him and laughed. Majid still did not agree that one and one make two. So the teacher gave him six strokes of the cane on the palm of his hand and asked him to add all of them together and consider them as just one big one.

After that, when his classmates saw him, they would say to one another, 'A rather big one!'

This teasing and the reason for it pained Majid very much. What he said is the truth. But why did nobody believe it? Maybe it's wrong. Maybe Majid is a blockhead. Unable to bear his sadness, Majid went and complained to his umma. His mother advised him to tell all his troubles to God.

'Rabb al-Alamin will not refuse anybody's prayer, my son!'

Accordingly, that tender heart prayed fervently to the ruler of the universe, 'Oh Rabb, please make my sums come out right!'

That was Majid's first prayer. Day and night he would

pray. Still all his sums went wrong. He got caned many times. The palm of his hand was always throbbing. He could not bear it. He told Suhra all about it. That was after many disagreements. After becoming the 'rather big one' Majid never used to talk to Suhra. She would look at him from the next bench. Majid would turn away his face. In the end Majid spoke. Suhra smiled. She moved to another seat. Finally she sat right next to Majid at the end of the bench. From then on Majid stopped getting caned. He got all his sums right!

The schoolmaster was amazed.

'Remarkable!' he said. 'I was wrong in thinking your head is completely made of wood!'

Such flattery from the teacher wiped out Majid's nickname. The children would say enviously, 'Majid is top of the class!'

When she heard that, Suhra would smile. No-one else understood the significance of this. The secret of Majid's getting all his sums right lay hidden in Suhra's smile.

When all the children stood up in pairs facing each other to do the sums, Majid's left eye would be on Suhra's slate. Majid would copy what she wrote. Even if she had finished doing the sums, she would not sit down. Majid had to sit down first!

On their way home from school, Suhra would tease Majid when no-one else could hear. Suhra would think of many things and smile. Then she would whisper, 'A rather big one.'

Then all the anger within him would come out in one word: 'Princess!'

With a sad, sweet laugh like the tinkling of a silver bell, she would look at her fingers. All the nails were cut beautifully. In school she is a very good example for cleanliness and neatness. On Majid's clothes there are always ink-marks and other stains.

He climbs all the mango trees in the area. He enjoys holding on to the small branches at the very top of the tree and looking at the expanse of the earth over the leaves that spread out before him. He is eager to see the world on the other side of the horizon. When he stands like that at the top of the tree, lost in his imagination, Suhra will call out from below and ask, 'Can you see Mecca?'

In answer to that, Majid will melodiously recite these lines believed to be from the song of the eagles that fly close to the skies:

'I see Mecca,
I see the mosque at Medina!'

4)

Majid went to Suhra's ear-piercing ceremony secretly and in great pain.

He was in bed after his initiation. It was during the holidays. Majid's circumcision ceremony was an event that enlivened the whole village. There were fireworks and feasting. Majid was brought on the back of an elephant to the sound of a band and by the light of portable gas lamps! Then there was the feasting. More than a thousand people took part. The initiation took place before the feast. . . . The whole day Majid was afraid. Something will be cut off! What is it? Will he die? He was weak from fright. He felt he would not live through the day. He had no idea what was going to happen. All Muslim men are initiated. There is not one who is not. Still. . . . 'How do they do this initiation?' Majid asked Suhra.

She knew nothing about it!

All she could do was to console him by saying, 'Whatever it is, you won't die.' Anyhow, Majid was very anxious. . . . As the impressive tones of the *Takbir* or Creed, 'Allah akbar', resounded in the pandal, Majid's bapa took him and left him in a small room. . . . There was an upturned mortar spread with a white cloth, and in front of it a standing lamp with eleven wicks was burning. Apart from the barber—the 'Ossan' who carries out the rite—there were ten or a dozen men in the room. They took off his shirt and his dhoti. They made him sit on the mortar wearing no more than when he was born. He wondered what they were going to do.

They blindfolded him and held his hands, legs and head firmly. He could not move. The only sound he could hear was 'Allah akbar'. Majid was sweating profusely. Somewhere in all that confusion he experienced a slight pain on the part of his body where his thighs met. A sensation like the tearing of the dried film of an areca-nut leaf. Just for a moment. Soon everything was over and there was the sprinkling of water. He was left with a blistering, burning feeling.

They laid Majid on his bed. There were pillows for his head and his legs. In the commotion Majid took a look. . . . It was not exactly like dipping your finger into a bottle of red ink, but rather like having a circle of ink at the end of the finger from the mouth of the bottle without actually touching the ink. . . . Just a faint sign of bleeding. . . . The next day Majid said so much to Suhra.

She asked from the other side of the window, 'Were you scared, Majid?'

'What, me!' Lying on his bed, Majid bragged, 'I wasn't afraid at all!'

Then Suhra told him about her ear-piercing. Within ten or twelve days her ear-piercing will take place!

'You won't be able to come, Majid!'

'I shall,' said Majid.

But when the day came, Majid could not move. He heard first Suhra's umma and then Suhra coming and inviting his family. After some time he also saw Suhra near the window. Her face was pale with anxiety; but her eyes were shining.

'Today is my ear-piercing.'

Without saying anything, Majid smiled. The smile passed to her too. Majid looked at those beautiful ears. He wondered if it would hurt or not, when they made a line of holes in them. When he asked her, she said, 'I don't know; come and see!'

Then she ran off.

Majid wanted to go, but he could not get up from where he was lying. Still, after a while he got up when no-one was looking. It was hell! Like lifting a heavy grinding-stone! The pain of a thousand wounds.... It seemed to go right to his very heart.... Without anyone seeing, Majid slowly made his way outside, bandy-legged. He crawled along the edge of the canal, climbed up to the yard and reached Suhra's house. There were no great celebrations or crowds to be seen. Majid thought it was because they were not rich. If they had been rich, there would have been drums and fireworks and feasting.

As soon as she saw Majid, Suhra's mother ran out to him. 'My dear boy, why did you come?'

Majid said with difficulty, 'To see the ear-piercing.'

Then Suhra came out too. Her face was flushed and her eyes were red. Both ears were pierced from top to bottom and tied with black thread. The right ear had eleven holes and the left one ten. Majid knew that when the ears healed, the threads would be taken out and silver halqats inserted instead. Then later on, for her marriage, gold ones would take the place of the silver ones.

Majid asked Suhra, 'Did it hurt very much?'

Suhra smiled through her pain, as she said, 'A little bit!'

By this time people had come there in search of Majid. Two people carried him back to his house and laid him on his bed.

That incident caused a great row. Bapa scolded Majid. He scolded Majid's umma. He also scolded Suhra's bapa and umma. With that it ended.

Majid was healed first. That day he was taken to the mosque, after being bathed, dressed in new clothes and perfumed. It was a great occasion. Suhra made fun of the way he went all dressed up.

'Oh, so posh!' she said. 'As though you were going to get married...!'

5)

Suhra and Majid were promoted that year.

It was from the last class in the village school. An incident took place that shattered Suhra's dreams of going to the town school to continue her studies. Majid saw death for the first time; Suhra became fatherless.

As a result, she and her two sisters and umma had no-one to support them. All they had was a plot of land and a small house. Her bapa had supported the family with what he made from the areca-nut business. He used to wear a white cap, a dhoti discoloured by the red sand, and a towel of a similar shade over his shoulder. His black eyes, set in a fair face with a black beard, were always smiling. He would walk with a slight stoop, with a sack folded under his arm. He would buy areca-nuts from the houses round about, fill the sack and carry it himself to the town, where he would sell them. He was a great conversationalist. He would tell Majid all about the places he had seen. True Muslims lived elsewhere. Those in that village were superstitious and hardhearted! If you wanted to see good people, you should go elsewhere.

'People around here think they are the only authentic Muslims! This is only because of their ignorance. God willing, by the time you finish your education and are grown up, things will have changed.'

His highest aim in life was to give Suhra a really good education.

'Then—' he would say, 'when she holds a good job, she will forget us all. She will feel ashamed to admit that I am her father.'

'That's true,' Majid would say with a sly look. 'Suhra is a very proud girl.'

Then Suhra, standing behind the door, would roll her eyes, grind her teeth and say harshly and yet quietly, 'A rather big one.'

In situations like this, Majid would punish her in a very

unusual way. He always used to have a rubber catapult on him. He would take a pebble from his waist and aim it at her ankle. It never missed.

When it hit her ankle, he would say, 'I scored a direct hit on that white mark on the corner of the door.'

Suhra would not move. One or two tear-drops would fall from her eyes. That was all. Suhra's umma, who saw none of this, would tell Majid, 'Aiming at one thing or another, Majid, you'll break all our pots and pans; we're not as well-off as you.'

'Oh, I shan't be coming here again to aim at things. I'm going away from this place!'

'Where to?'

'A six month's journey off!'

'And then,' Suhra would say, 'he'll come back home at nightfall!'

That is Suhra's opinion about Majid. Majid's opinion regarding Suhra is something quite different.

'When I come back after seeing the world, Suhra will be an important official. Then this young lady will act as though she has never seen me!'

As if she was seeing a future distant and satisfying, a hint of a smile would appear on her face.

After long thought she would say, 'You are the one who is going to study and become a big official. We have no money.'

Suhra's bapa would say, 'Allah will give us the money. We shall all three come back together from the town school. Every day, after selling the areca-nuts, I'll come and stand in front of the school.'

But that was not to be. He came back wet in the rain and was laid up two or three days with fever. The third night he died. Majid, too, was there by his death-bed. Those two eyes like the glass chimney of a paraffin lamp blackened by the smoke when the light has gone out.... That motionless body devoid of light and warmth!

The body was buried the next day. That evening Majid

was standing as usual under the mango tree, waiting for Suhra. Weighed down by sorrow, she came slowly to him. When Majid looked at her face, she burst out crying. Majid could not say anything. His tears flowed down on her head and hers on his chest.

The moon shone bright over the darkened coconut trees.

6)

From the threshold of her house Suhra watched Majid being taken by his bapa to be admitted to the town school. Both have umbrellas. Majid's is a new one. His shirt, dhoti and cap are new. She saw them go along the village street and disappear in the distance.

In the evening, after returning from school, Majid made his way to their meeting place, beneath the mango tree. His new text-book was in his hand. Very proudly he showed it to Suhra, who ran up eagerly.

'There are lots of pictures.'

She took it and was flicking through the pages. Majid described all the wonderful sights in the town two miles away and finally told her about the school.

'Right in the middle of the town. Seven big buildings, whitewashed and tiled. Not like the school here. A very big garden! . . . All sorts of plants! I'll bring seeds of each kind! . . . Then the playground. Oh, it's a sight to be seen!'

'And so many students!' Majid continued. 'No end of them!' The headmaster is a fat man with gold-rimmed specs. He always has a cane in his hand; and my teacher has only one eye! There are forty-two pupils in my class—fourteen of them girls!'

Majid stopped short. He was shocked to see Suhra's tears on the book! . . .

'Suhra!' Majid exclaimed. He did not understand the reason for her tears.

'Why are you crying?' Majid asked again and again.

In the end she looked up and said softly, 'I want to study also!'

Suhra wants to study also!... Is there any way it can be managed? Majid racked his brains. In his head there was a sound like the chirping of a cricket. Finally he found a way.

'Whatever I learn, said Majid, 'I'll teach you every day.'

Although they came away agreed on that, Majid found an even better way. Majid comes from a well-to-do family. Why don't they send Suhra to school also? He was afraid to speak about it to his bapa. He would speak to his umma, he decided.

That night, after dinner, bapa was getting some betel-leaf ready for chewing. Umma was cutting the areca-nut to go with it.

His heart beating fast, Majid went and sat near umma and called to her softly, 'Umma!'

His mother asked him lovingly, 'What is it, my son?'

'Why don't we send Suhra to study also?' Majid said softly.

For some time nobody said anything. Bapa folded up the betel-leaf and put it in his mouth. He added the areca-nut and began to chew. Then from the brass betel-box that shone like pure gold he took a small silver box and opened it. A sharp fragrance spread everywhere. He took out some specially prepared tobacco, placed it on the palm of his hand and put it in his mouth. He moved the whole lot into the hollow of his cheek and then spat into the yard.

'Can't you spit into this?' umma asked, moving a spittoon towards him. 'It will look like blood on the leaves of those plants.'

'So what!' bapa said in a derisive tone and lay down in the easy chair. In the strong light of the hurricane-lamp, which was brighter than day, the buttons on bapa's flannel shirt glittered. He arched his dark eyebrows. He furrowed his smooth, brown forehead. Looking through the round lenses of his gold-rimmed spectacles, he came out with his opinion regarding Majid.

'Look! Let this fellow go somewhere. Let him go around

the country and learn how people like us live. You under-stand?—No!'

'He's started again! If he says anything, immediately it's either go away or leave the country!... But why do you always say this?'

'He's got no brains!'

'Others have plenty of brains!'

Umma's sharp tongue! Would bapa let it pass?

'What he's got is your brains! You understand?—No!'

'Oh, so nowadays my brains are no good! It is Rabb's will.'

'Otherwise, do you think he'd get such an idea? All told, my brothers and sisters have twenty-six children; all your brothers and sisters together have forty-one, with appetites like the demon Vaka! When any of this lot come and eat here all the time, do I say anything?—No!'

'In the name of all the saints! What I have to put up with!'

'You call on a thousand saints! Will that give you brains? —No! Can you understand what I'm saying?—No!'

'Write it down and show me!'

Umma, who cannot read, said this.

When he heard it, bapa burst out laughing. Umma's white kuppayam was spattered red from the betel he was chewing.

'You'd better go!' bapa ordered. 'Go and change your kuppayam. You understand?—No!'

Umma went off, and came back after changing her kuppayam.

'Write it!' bapa continued. 'Did your bapa learn how to write?—No! Of course not! Did your brothers learn?—No!'

Will umma let that pass? Hardly! 'Oh, all your people learnt a great deal!'

For a long time bapa had nothing to say by way of a reply. Bapa never learnt how to write. Neither bapa's bapa nor bapa's umma learnt how to write. Because umma reminded him of that, bapa got angry.

'If you talk too much,' bapa bawled, 'I'll kick the life out of you! You understand?—No!'

If umma had made any sort of reply to that, there would right away have been a real rumpus. He would have picked up the betel-box and flung it into the yard; he would have beaten umma; he would have beaten Majid; he would have beaten Majid's sisters. Not only that, he would have up-rooted all Majid's plants. . . . So umma said nothing. Because she did not say anything, bapa asked, 'What's up? You've lost your tongue?—No!'

Umma asked very calmly, 'Why do you say all this? Majid only asked. By the grace of Rabb and the saints we have enough for all we need. Now that Suhra's bapa is dead, they have no-one. What harm is there if we send her to school too?'

Majid waited anxiously. The gold ornaments on umma's neck and in her ears shone.

'Yes, we have enough for all we need! Did your bapa acquire all that wealth? And did you bring it as dowry?'

'Now we've got on to the subject of my dowry! You didn't marry me for nothing! They gave you a full thousand rupees, and on top of that no end of golden ornaments for my neck, for my ears, for my wrists, for my ankles; then there was the jewelled belt. Or have you forgotten?'

'Hm!' Bapa twisted his moustache. 'A thousand miserable rupees! Even if they gave your weight in rupees, would anybody marry a brainless creature like you?—No!'

'Right, then you go and marry somebody with brains!'

'I'll do just that! For handsome men like me, there are people who are willing to give not one thousand, but ten thousand! You understand?—No!'

Umma did not say anything in answer to that! If he wants, bapa can marry any number of wives he chooses. Because umma did not say anything, bapa got wild.

'To hear her talk, we have enough for all we need!'

He said that as though he did not have a single cent. Majid knew the truth. In the whole area bapa is the most well-to-do. Each time when the coconuts are gathered, there will be a mountain of them. Each time after the harvest, they did not have enough room to store all the paddy. Added to all this, he made big profits in his timber business. Once after a deal he brought back nothing but gold sovereigns. He put all these gold coins in a pile on a sheet of white paper before a lantern, counted them and stacked them in rows, tied them in a bag, put this in a box and locked it. Before he locked the box, Majid played with the gold coins. Ever since, he had been unable to forget their yellow glitter or their clinking sound. When they are so rich, can't they send a poor girl to school?

'Don't say we don't have anything!' said umma. 'We do! In the whole area we are the best off! If we send Suhra to school as well, it will cost only as much as for Majid.'

Bapa got angry.

'If I say you have no brains, do you understand?—No! Do you know how many they come to altogether your blood relatives and mine?—No! Do you know what twenty-six and forty-one make?—No!'

'How many is it, Majid?' umma asked.

Majid's brain was in a whirl! He ran to fetch a pencil and a piece of paper.

Bapa laughed very sarcastically.

'There he goes, your brainy one!'

Majid brought the pencil and paper, wrote forty-one below twenty-six and, sweating profusely, started to add.

Then bapa said with a laugh, 'Sixty-seven.'

By that time Majid, too, had finished adding.

'That's right. Sixty-seven!' Majid agreed. Bapa bellowed, 'Get out!'

'Look!' bapa went on. 'That Suhra is a good girl. And she's clever. Still, if we send her to school, we must also send all those sixty-seven! Are we that well-off?'

Umma said nothing.

'He's still here.' Looking at Majid, he said again, 'Get out!'

Sadly, Majid went. When, standing at the window, he looked through the darkness towards Suhra's house, he saw her sitting on the verandah, deep in thought, resting her face in her hands and looking at the flame of the paraffin lamp.

7)

So Suhra's life went on aimlessly. Most of the time she was in Majid's house. She was well-liked by everyone there. Still, there was always a doleful look on her face. Majid's umma would always tell her not to be sad.

'I'm not at all sad,' Suhra would say with a smile. But she could not hide the heartache that was in her voice. It upset Majid also.

'I long to hear you laugh like you used to, Suhra!' he would say.

'Don't I laugh the way I used to?' she would ask.

'No. It's as if there were tears in your laughter now—'

'Oh, it must be because I'm grown up!'

After some time she added, 'We shouldn't have grown up!'

Is it because they are grown up that they experience sorrow and longings?

They were children. Without being aware of it they grew up! Suhra has become a fully-developed young woman; Majid is a young man with a moustache.

Suhra has many anxieties about her future. She and her mother and sister are without support. After the father's death, the responsibility that had been his fell to her.

She is only sixteen. But she has to support the family. For how long can they accept help from Majid's umma? For how long can they be dependent on the good nature of others? If Majid alone were involved, she would not feel so bad.

Suhra has nothing against Majid's bapa or umma or sisters. But there is something that she does not feel for them that she feels for Majid. When he is before her, all is well. It is when he is not there that she feels it. From the time when Majid goes to school in the morning until he returns in the evening, she has a kind of uneasiness. If Majid is not well, she cannot sleep. She always wants to be near Majid. She wants to take care of him day and night.

As if in answer to her wish, something happened to him: Majid got an infection in his right foot. It was during his fourth year at the town school. One day, when returning from school, he felt a pain in his foot. Majid limped back home. The next day the sole of his foot was seen to be festering. His whole body was aching and throbbing. Majid lay moaning on his bed. Everybody said that if they burst the boil, it would ease the pain! But if anybody went near him, he would cry aloud.

There was always a crowd there. On those rare occasions when the confusion caused by people coming to ask after his health subsided, Suhra would go into the room, make her way to Majid's feet and sit there blowing on the part that was infected. It was yellow in colour and looked like a big ripe guava beneath the skin of his foot. Majid could not bear the pain.

'Suhra, I'm going to die!' Majid cried pitifully.

What was there to be done? She had no idea. She felt like weeping. She took his right foot and held it against her cheek.

Lovingly she kissed the sole of the foot.

The first kiss! . . .

She got up and, stroking his burning forehead, bent down over Majid's face. Her hair, which was done up in a bun, loosened and fell over his chest. . . . He could feel her breath on his face. He was shaking as if an electric current had passed through his nerves. . . . Majid's face was lifted as though attracted by a magnet. His two arms encircled her neck. He pressed her to his chest.

'Suhra!'

'My own!'

Suhra's red lips rested on Majid's mouth.

Although there had been something from the very beginning of their lives, on that day for the first time, with the awakening of their emotions, they became really close.... They gave each other a thousand kisses: on the eyes, on the forehead, on the cheeks, on the neck, on the chest. . . . They shook all over. There was a soothing repose, a new relief. Something happened! What was it?

'The boil has burst!' Suhra whispered with a smile. It was like divine music.

Majid sat up. Wonderful!... The boil had burst! Majid looked at Suhra's loving face which was bent down because of her shyness.... The sweetness of those coral lips, the intoxication of those first kisses!

There was an indescribable coolness in the sole of the right foot that Suhra had kissed.

Suhra could not sleep that night. She was hot all over.... She was absolutely melting.

Suhra's life had a goal. But she was afraid to think of it coming to fruition.

So her days and nights passed in a state of hopeless uncertainty.

8)

Suhra loves Majid; and Majid Suhra. Both of them know this. Majid was deeply in love. But he was guided by challenging thoughts and high ideals. Majid was self-respect personified. He had a high estimation of his own worth. There was no life for him in his father's world; he knew nothing about the family's affairs. Majid was afraid even to talk to his bapa.

Bapa manages everything like a despot who does not accept anybody's opinion. If Majid needs anything, he will ask umma and get it. When he hears bapa's voice, there rises from Majid's heart a silent roar of protest. Protest against what? Majid is not certain. Is he not a good father? Does he not do everything for Majid? Then what is his failing?

Majid was more able to love Suhra's bapa than his own. Suhra was not afraid of her bapa. When she talks about her father, tears come to her eyes. . . . If Majid's bapa dies, will he cry? If umma dies, Majid will surely cry.

However that may be, Majid does not like to live there. Most of the time he is either outside the house or in his own room. So things were when something momentous happened.

At the time, Majid was studying in the penultimate class of the town school.

Harvesting and threshing had started. It was a very hot summer. On top of that it was the season of fasting! Because bapa fasts the whole day, drinking not even water and swallowing not even spittle, he gets angry and quarrels over the slightest thing.

One morning, before going to the field, bapa told Majid that the threshed and dried paddy was to be brought in by boat. If nobody was on the boat, the boatmen would sell some on the way! 'You are not fasting; as soon as you get back from school, come to the field. You'll come?—No!'

'I'll definitely come,' said Majid.

But Majid did not go. As usual, as soon as he got back from school he went to play. It was when he did not see bapa in the evening at the time of the breaking of the fast, that Majid remembered. . . . Bapa came when it was well after dark. The moment he saw Majid, bapa stormed. Furious, he struck Majid hard on the side of the face. Majid stood there stunned. He saw stars.

Bapa hit him again and again.

'Either you should mend your ways, or you should die. You understand?—No!'

Hearing the sound of the blows and the shouting, umma ran up and put her arms round Majid.

'Stop it, will you! Haven't you beaten him enough?'

'Get out of here!' bapa shouted. 'She doesn't hear,' he said, and he beat umma too. He also beat Majid's sisters, who ran up crying. He smashed the doors. He broke the dishes. . . !

Amid all this, Majid stood petrified.

'Get out! Come back after you've been around the country and learnt something. You understand?—No!' Shouting, bapa grabbed him by the neck and pushed him out into the yard. Majid fell flat on his face. He cut his lip and it started to bleed. When Majid got up, bapa again shouted angrily, 'Get out!'

The sound of it was enough to drive Majid to the other end of the earth.

Majid went away from that spot. He got to the gate and sat there. . . . He was unable to cry. Not even a single tear. A violent storm of protest raged in his heart. . . . No-one went to say a kind word or to console him.

In the house there was an oppressive silence! The lantern was burning with a harsh brightness. Yet it was like a dead house. . . . Nothing stirred.

In the vast world he was alone! Majid decided to go away, far from his home. But where would he go to? He had no money with him. He had nothing but the strength of his body. Still he would survive! He was a young man! He would go!

Majid went!

Before going, he walked towards Suhra. Under the mango tree where they usually sat, he stood in the solitude of the night.

From a distance he could hear Suhra's beautiful voice. Sitting in front of the paraffin lamp, she was reading the Koran. In the middle of it she raised her head and looked towards where the mango tree stood. Her eyes became still, as if she were listening for something. Her golden cheeks shone. Her blood-red lips parted slightly.

After sitting like that for some time, Suhra started reading again.

'Suhra!' Majid called; it was a call not from the lips but from the heart. He felt like calling her aloud; to take leave for the last time. But no!

Majid walked away. Like a madman. Leaving the village behind, passing by the city, he went on his way, beyond woods, hills and towns.

For seven years he travelled. Seven long years! During that time Majid knew nothing of what happened at home or what changes took place in Suhra's life. He sent no letters. Not because he didn't want to know: he didn't write, that was all. Suppose someone came to look for him?

He travelled! In different ways—on foot and by vehicles of various sorts; along with beggars, as the companion of mendicants, as the disciple of sanyasis, as a hotel worker, as an office clerk, along with political workers, the guest of rich men—so he lived, his status constantly changing. He mixed with men of various religions.

In those days Majid had no desire to earn money. He did not use the opportunities he had to do so. To see and to learn—this was his aim.

Majid saw: little villages and big towns; tiny streams and big rivers; small hills and huge mountain ranges; agricultural land with its rich soil and the wide expanse of deserts covered with white sand. Majid covered thousands upon thousands of miles. To see what? To hear what? . . .

People are the same everywhere: the only difference is in language and dress. All are men and women. . . . They are born, grow, mate, reproduce. Then death. That's all. The grim struggle that fills the time between birth and death is everywhere. Will everything end with death? So, dejected, he went back to the place he had left. For what? To marry Suhra and spend his life somewhere quietly!

But what met Majid there were changes that stunned him.

Either because he had suffered frequent losses in his business, or because he signed a document which he was told was a petition to the government to get a bridge built but which was actually an I.O.U. for a huge amount, all bapa's property had gone to pay off his debts. . . . Even the place they lived in was mortgaged. Majid's parents have become very old; his two sisters have grown up and passed the age when they should have been married. Above all, Suhra is now a married woman! . . .

It happened a year before Majid came back! It was a butcher from somewhere in the town who married her.

Suhra had not waited for Majid. 'Life is full of selfish deeds!' Majid concluded.

Whatever the case, the people from round about went to see Majid. Seeing all the luggage that it took four or five people to carry, everybody thought that Majid must have a lot of money. What he really had was a great many books and around ten rupees!

Those days Majid got invited all over the place. Every day he had to go as guest to two or three different houses. Although he had already taken his fill, they would force him to eat.

Then in a month they learned the truth. Majid was just a poor member of that family that had sunk into poverty! No more than a pauper!

'What did he come back for?' That was the question people asked. 'He has come after seven years, empty-handed!'

Contemptuous looks and words of derision were directed at Majid. Because of that he avoided going out. He was always at home in his old room. . . . That room had many stories to tell. He used it while he was going to school. It was there that Majid's 'initiation ceremony' took place. It was in this room that he was laid up with the infection in his foot.

He lay there in the old easy chair and looked out.

There was not enough to eat in the house! Bapa would take to the market the rope that Majid's sisters made from the coconut fibre, sell it and buy something to bring back. Umma would give Majid a big part of it. Then she would say tenderly, 'My boy, you have lost weight since you got back. Do you know how I reared you? Because your colour wasn't good enough, I made you drink a lot of milk mixed with powdered gold!'

Cheerless, Majid would sit there. What was to be done? He had no money. No way of getting away either. There was no-one to help.

Majid got thinner day by day. Because he had no other work to do, he once again made a garden—this time on his own.

He spread white sand in a square in front of the house, and round the four sides he planted some shrubs. The boundary on one side was the shoeflower that Suhra had put in with her own hands. It had grown into a tree. When Majid came back, there were flowers on it. Bright red flowers that bloomed continuously, like blood splashed on a forest of green leaves.

He would sit at its foot in an easy chair, reading. But he did not really read. He would lie there with the book open in his lap.

'What are you thinking of, my son?' umma would enquire.

Softly, Majid would say, 'Oh, nothing!'

Umma, too, would be deep in thought. Then she would say to herself, 'Everything is Allah's will!'

Majid's two sisters would fight with each other for the privilege of watering his beloved plants to please him; finally they would come together to Majid and say, 'Elder brother, I watered the plants today!'

Majid would pacify them by saying, 'You can each have an equal share of the flowers.'

'His mother's plants!' bapa would say. 'I spent all my wealth to educate him. Then, after going off for seven years, this is all he has got: a garden to comfort me in my old age! I'll pull up the whole lot and throw them away! Did you hear what I said?—No!'

Umma would say, 'At least you got the yard cleaned!'

) 30 (

Bapa would ask, as he crushed some hardened lime and put it on a dried-up betel-leaf, 'Did you hear what I said?— No!'

'What?'

'Go and get a little bit of tobacco from somewhere.'

Putting an old piece of cloth on her head, umma would go next door in her torn, dirty kuppayam for a bit of tobacco.

Memories would fly through Majid's mind like clouds across the sky. Poverty is a dreadful disease. It destroys the body, the mind and the soul. Millions of men and women from all sections of society are destroyed in this way in body, mind and soul.

Such pictures would fill his mind. Why does he remember only those ugly, loathsome pictures? Life is bright and beautiful!—But he cannot forget the mud and filth that clings to its face! The ugliness and wretchedness of life!

Those without food, those without clothes, those without shelter, those without limbs—an unending procession of desperate people. . . . Day and night he sees it. He would rather not remember all this.

But how can he forget? His head is always in a whirl. His heart is always throbbing.

When he thinks of Suhra, tears fill his eyes. He would like to see her once. But she is someone else's wife! Still, he must see her, at least from a distance. Not to complain; not to say harsh words; simply to see her! To hear that voice.

She has forgotten Majid. But can Majid ever forget her?

In the loneliness of the night Majid goes and sits beneath the mango tree which has blessed them with so many fruits. He is not waiting for anyone. Who is there to wait for?

'If she learns that I have returned,' thought Majid, 'she will never, never come!'

9)

Suhra came!

Learning that Majid had returned, she came, with the anxiousness of one in love, panting as she ran. But Majid had no desire to see her. He was all confused. He was weary and unable to move.

Majid heard Suhra's question, 'Where is he?' and umma's reply, 'In the garden!' His heart was beating fast. Motionless, Majid lay on the chair.

The garden was immersed in the light of the evening sun. The bees were buzzing among the flowers. Leaves rustled in the fragrant breeze. Like a statue in the golden sun, Majid lay there in the chair. The sound of Suhra's footsteps came nearer and nearer.

'Oh, a new garden!'

Suhra's sad voice behind him. . . ! Majid's heart ached. It was not just an ache; his heart throbbed and ached as if pierced by blunt and hardened thorns.

Suhra, ill-at-ease and distressed, asked, as if she were about to burst out crying, 'Do you know me?'

Complete silence. He could not utter a word. Memories. . . . Tears came to Majid's eyes.

She asked again, 'Are you angry with me?'

Slowly Majid turned and looked. His heart burned.

Suhra had changed completely! . . . Sunken cheeks, swollen joints on her fingers, nails worn down, extremely pale, the black threads in her ears hidden by her hair. . . .

They looked at each other. For a long, long time neither of them was able to say anything.

Slowly the sun disappeared. The darkness spread over all, eliminating the changes that had taken place. They were not aware of anything. The full moon looked down from the peak of the hill and immersed in white the two arms of the river which embraced the village.

Breaking the silence of the village, a love song rose from somewhere far off. Some lover, thinking of his beloved, sang sad and sweet:

    'You who dwell
      in the lotus garden,
    Sharing the abode
      of the five-hued parrot,
    Is it enough for me
      to see your flowery face,
    Or has the time come
      to fulfil my desire?
    Has my beloved come close
      at last,
    Or has some misfortune
      befallen her?
    You who dwell
      in the lotus garden. . . !'

The unknown singer repeated the words again and again.

Finally Majid whispered, 'Suhra!'

As if from the very heart of the past she answered, 'Oh!'

'What went wrong?' Majid asked.

'Nothing,' she said.

'Then why are you so run down?'

Suhra made no reply to this. With a long sigh she said, 'I got to know only yesterday . . . that you had come back.'

With a hint of complaint, Majid asked, 'You thought I would never come back, didn't you?'

'Everybody thought so. I. . . .'

' Mm?'

'I was positive you would come back.'

'And then?'

'They decided everything. Nobody asked for my consent. Umma was burning with anxiety. It was many years since those of my age were married! Unless they gave jewelry and a dowry, nobody. . . .'

'You believed that there was not even one person who would be ready to marry you without taking jewelry and dowry—didn't you?'

'I was never without faith in you. Not for a moment did I

forget you. Every night and every day I thought of you and wept. I prayed that you would suffer no sickness, that you would meet with no accident. Every single day I prayed.'

'You thought I had forgotten you, didn't you, Suhra?'

'I did not think so. Why didn't you send any letters?'

'I just didn't send any: I wrote many, but didn't send them.'

'Every day I expected a letter. I kept thinking it would arrive today, or tomorrow.'

'Then how did this marriage take place?'

'I told you that nobody asked me. How long could I go on being a burden to others; I am a woman.'

'Hm!'

'Finally we mortgaged this house and the land that goes with it, had the jewelry and so on made, and the marriage took place.

'Why are you so run down?'

Suhra said nothing.

'Tell me, Suhra, why are you so run down?'

'Through worry!'

'Worry about what?'

'Mm?'

'Suhra!'

'Yes!'

'Tell me.'

Suhra burst out crying. Then slowly she told him about her husband.

'He is very short-tempered. He has another wife and two children. He says that I must come home and insist on getting my share of the family property. Don't I have two younger sisters? What am I to do? If ever he mentions it and I don't agree, he beats me. One time he kicked me in the stomach. I fell flat on my face. That day I broke my front tooth, see.'

She opened her mouth. In the middle of the whiteness there was a dark gap.

'Suhra!'

'Yes?'

'And then?'

'From going there till now, I haven't had even one meal that was enough to satisfy my hunger. Not for a moment have I enjoyed peace of mind. I am not a wife. Just a servant. I have to make money by beating out the fibre from coconut husks for someone. If I don't make as much as he expects, he beats me. He never gives me anything. When I was out—'

'Mm?'

'For four days in a row—'

'Mm?'

'I had to starve.'

So, slowly, Suhra began to talk. She had a lot to tell. Her heart held a lot of secrets. Sometimes she thought of taking her own life. She had just one wish:

'To see you once before I die.'

'You shouldn't worry in this way, thinking about death. You still have life ahead of you. You must believe that the future is bright.' When Majid said this, Suhra sighed.

She was sitting in front of the chair by Majid's feet. For a long time the two of them sat like that in silence, looking at the moonlit scene.

Finally Majid said, 'Suhra, go and eat and then have a good night's rest; sleep peacefully. I'll see you tomorrow.'

'I'm completely dead beat,' Suhra said as she got up.

'Are you that tired?' Majid asked, as he too got up.

'Worries!' said Suhra.

'You shouldn't worry. Go and sleep well.'

'Are you going anywhere tomorrow?'

'No.'

'I'll come in the morning,' Suhra said and walked away.

'Good,' said Majid.

Watching her as she walked between the coconut trees in the moonlight, Majid sat down again in the canvas chair. He was oblivious to the passing of time.

Umma came with a paraffin lamp in her hand. Seeing

Majid lying there half asleep, that fond mother asked, 'My boy, why are you sitting here so lifeless?'

'Oh, nothing.'

'My boy, did you see how awful Suhra looks. She was a lovely girl. It is all Rabb's will.'

'Who made her like that?'

Majid was angry and sad.

'My boy, come and eat something and then go to bed. Don't be sad thinking about things. God will set everything right.'

Majid did not sleep that night. Suhra, too, did not sleep that night. Between them, there were compounds and a stream. There were also two walls. Still they could not sleep. They were thinking of the future.

The future...?

10)

Suhra's looks underwent a sudden change; there was a new glow inside her; colour came to her face and brightness to her eyes. She would walk with her hair parted in the middle and tied so that it covered her ears. Women who lived nearby wondered why she was so changed.

'Suhra looks much better than when she came. Now, if she goes back, her husband won't even recognise her!'

Husband!

She was always in Majid's house. She also tended the plants and watered them. Majid's sisters would say, 'The plants have reached this stage because we looked after them!'

Suhra would ask them about the shoeflower tree.

'How about this one?'

'It's been here for a long, long time.'

Suhra does not dispute it! Everything has been there for a long, long, time.

A long time.

One day Majid asked her, 'When will you go again,

Suhra?'

She did not understand. Puzzled, she asked, 'Where?'

'To your husband's house.'

'Oh!' Her face fell. 'It is not me that he married.'

'Then who?'

'The gold ornaments I took with me,' she said, 'and the share I have in the family property. He sold all the gold. What is left is the share of the property. He knows there is no way to get hold of that.'

After some time she said very slowly, 'If the people round about object to you seeing me!—I'll go away!'

'Is this the way people talk?'

'It seems they do.'

She picked a rose, smelt it and put it in her hair.

'That shoeflower would suit you better!' said Majid.

Hearing that, Suhra laughed. Yet there was a look of sadness on her face.

'This shoeflower tree—do you remember?' she asked after some time.

'I've heard of it,' said Majid.

'Then you must have heard about the rather big one!'

'Yes, I have heard about it from the "princess"!'

Although they were very close, she would not come to know anything about those seven years in Majid's life. She wanted to go deep into those secrets, to know everything. She wanted to know about each man and woman he had met. When it came to women, Suhra would ask, 'How old was she? Was she dark or fair? Was she beautiful? Do you think of her often?'

Majid would answer all those questions. Still she was not satisfied. Isn't there something he hasn't said?

'To me—to me, you must tell only the truth; you hear?'

Majid laughed as he said, 'What a girl!'

'You reprobate!'

She would arch her eyebrows. She would lean forward to pinch him. Then she would smile. The dark gap in the middle of the beautiful, little, white teeth, her worn-down finger-nails, that old look of hers when she was about to pinch him—Majid felt as if the fine skin that covered his heart was being rubbed hard by something rough. . . .

'What's going on between this Majid and Suhra?'
The neighbours wanted to know!
'Why doesn't she go to her husband's house? All this is against the law of God.'
For Majid and Suhra to talk to each other was immoral! Would not the sky break apart and fall?
'What if her husband kicked her once? When he beat her, she might have lost a tooth! Still he's her husband!'

'Suhra!' Majid said one day. 'The neighbours are talking about us.'
'So?' she asked.
'Nothing; you must be careful, Suhra! You are a woman: your name must be free from stain.'
'Oh! Let it be stained! Let even my soul be stained—as long as you are the cause!'
Tears came to her eyes. Majid wanted to say something right away: it was a positive decision about Suhra; but how could he say it? What had he to offer Suhra? No house; no money. But he did have health and strength.
'Suhra,' said Majid, 'you needn't go to your husband's house again.'
'No.'
Majid told his mother about it. For a long time she did not say anything. Finally she told him that it was good that he should marry Suhra. But he had two sisters old enough to be married.
'We lost all that we had. But shouldn't we think of our self-respect and our obligations? My son, you must go somewhere and find husbands for them and make some money for the gold ornaments and dowry. . . . After giving these girls in marriage to someone, you too can marry.'

It is not enough that he find somebody; he has to make the money for gold ornaments and dowry!

'Wouldn't someone marry them without a dowry?' he asked.

'Who would, my son? We might be able to find some coolies or some recent converts. Is that good enough for us?... You must at least give them ornaments for the ears, neck and waist.'

Between the two of them Majid's sisters have forty-two holes in their ears. Why were all these holes made? What if there are no ornaments for the neck or for the waist? If only there were no dowry system!

'Umma, if only there was none of this ear piercing and so on! Why only in our community are there these stupid customs—stupid ways of dress and stupid ornaments...!'

Umma and bapa said nothing. Majid asked no further questions. Why blame them? They did these things according to the custom of their generation. They did not consider whether these things were necessary or not. To diverge even the slightest bit from the old customs—it was very difficult! But was this realistic in the circumstances?

Majid can no longer sleep at night. He is always thinking. He must give his sisters in marriage to someone.... They are filled with the restlessness of youth. They have desires and aspirations.... They have no clothes to wear; no food.... There are moments of weakness. Suppose they take a step in the wrong direction!

Majid became uneasy. There is a lot he wants to do: pay off the mortgage on the house, get his sisters married, do things that will make his parents happy. They are old. You cannot tell at what moment death will come. He must make their life pleasant.

He must marry Suhra. Then there are his sisters and his mother; he must do something for them also. But what is he to do? For everything, money is necessary. If he starts somewhere, he can go on. But the difficulty is to start. Did anyone ever accomplish anything in this world without ready money and without someone to help? He thought hard about it. What was he to do?

One day umma put forward an idea. There are rich and generous Muslims in distant cities. They do many things for the uplift of the community. They get destitute young women married; find work for the unemployed; start schools for free education; establish homes for the poor and the maimed—they do many such things, umma said.

'My boy, if only they know about our case, that'll be enough. The rest they will do! I'm sure of that; that fakir told me all about it!'

Some itinerant Muslim beggar has told her, that all the rich Muslims in other parts are the epitome of generosity. Umma has complete faith in it. In earlier days umma had given a helping hand to many who needed it. Perhaps bapa had done even more. Very often it happened that people deceived the two of them by talking of non-existent troubles. Umma did not understand that. Yet there are those who tell lies and those who tell the truth, are there not? When he appealed for help, suppose people were not able to believe Majid?

Without having to rely on someone's good will, what way was there to obtain money? Majid's mind was in a whirl. What work should he do? If he managed to get a job, then with application and knowledge of the ways of the world—

Anxious about the future, Majid prepared to leave. Bapa raised some money by selling all his possessions and gave it to him.

'I'll be back soon,' Majid told Suhra, as he outlined all his plans. 'I entrust everybody to your care.'

'I'll take care of them till you return.'

Suhra accepted the responsibility.

Firm in his resolve, Majid set off.

One evening, the western sky was glowing with a golden light.

Taking Majid's bedding and suitcase, a boy went to the

bus-stand. Majid took leave of everyone.

'I can't see very well,' bapa told him. 'Will you bring me back a pair of glasses?—No!'

'Yes, I will,' Majid said and went into his room. Suhra, apprehensive and on the verge of tears, was standing by the window.

'Just a word!' she said.

Majid smiled.

'Speak, princess!'

'You know—'

She could not complete it. At that moment they heard the bus-driver sound his horn. Umma came to the door.

'Hurry up, son, the bus is leaving!'

Majid was about to go. Tears flowed from Suhra's eyes.

'Shall I go then?' Majid asked.

Suhra bent her head in consent.

Majid set off into an unknown future.

He reached the gate and looked back. The picture he saw of Suhra and of the house would never fade from his mind. Resolutely Majid pressed on, driven forward by his earnest desires and by his sense of duty.

11)

Marry Suhra.

Before that, find husbands for his sisters. Save up enough for the dowry and the jewelry. For that he had to have some job. But . . . it was only despair that faced him. There was no work anywhere. Even if there were, he needed someone to recommend him. He would have to give a bribe. He needed certificates for the examinations he had passed. Without any of these it was not easy to obtain employment. Still he continued to search. He wandered around many cities.

Finally he managed to reach Mahanagari some fifteen hundred miles away from his home town. In the meantime four months had gone by.

There he got a job: not anything hard. It paid very well.

All that was required was that he work without rest. He would get forty per cent commission. It was the company owner himself who promised this.

He had a company cycle. All he had to do was to go around on it with his samples. He would be given a place to stay in very close to the company.

So Majid started to work. He arranged his samples in a small leather case and set off with his order book. He went round the town, got his orders and came back in the evening very happy!

In this way one month passed by. After taking enough for his outgoings, Majid sent home a hundred rupees. He also sent a pair of glasses for his father's failing sight and clothes for Suhra and the others.

Another month passed.

No-one is sure what is going to happen in the near future. No-one expects anything unpleasant. Nor had Majid expected anything. Yet there was an unforeseen accident.

It was a Monday. Majid remembers it particularly well. High noon. Hanging his leather case on the lamp-bracket of his cycle as usual, he was cycling along the empty tarred road by the beach. It was a steep slope and he was riding pretty fast. The case swung from side to side, its handle came off and it got caught in the wheel! Majid was thrown from the cycle, hit some iron railings a distance away and fell into a deep gutter.

It was as if a mountain had fallen on top of him: he had a painful recollection of something being broken and shattered. Something had been cut and severed from him. Everything disappeared in blackness. . . . Everything was lost in the darkness of forgetfulness. . . . Sometimes the light of consciousness would flash like lightning on a stormy night. . . . Severe pain. . . . A strong smell of antiseptic. . . . The groaning of men in pain. . . . Some long tube-like thing that seemed alive went down his throat. . . . A hot liquid filled his stomach. . . . A strange feeling. . . . It was as if ages passed by while he went through all of this!

The things he remembers are very remote. Nothing is clear. Like white smoke, like silver clouds, they are flying very far away from Majid!... Is everything going to fade into oblivion?

No! He must live!... Life: severe and stabbing pain.... Still, he must live! Majid tried: it was as if he was using all his strength to raise and topple the mountain of oblivion that was pressing down on him.... Painfully he regained consciousness.

He gave a deep sigh. Slowly he opened his eyes. He was lying flat on his back. He was covered up to his neck with a white sheet.... Hospital!... He remembered everything.

The severe and stabbing pain! His right hip was burning. ... The pain seemed to go right up to his head.... Majid felt with his hand. He was heavily bandaged round his waist!

What had happened? Majid felt around once again. A cold shiver went through his bones.

An empty space!

He was bewildered. He was sweating profusely. He felt faint. A half of one leg had parted from him for ever.

He felt as if he was going down into a deep pit. Everything around him was turning.

Again Majid felt for his leg. Emptiness! There was nothing below! Unbearable pain! His right leg that received Suhra's first kiss!

Where has it gone?

He opened his eyes and sat up. Warm tears were streaming down his cheeks. Doctor, nurse and company manager approached the bed. Putting his cool hand on Majid's forehead, the company manager bent slowly over him:

'Mr Majid, I am deeply sorry. Don't let it distress you.'

'Hey, Suhra!'
'What is it, Majid?'
'Why don't you pay attention?'
'I *am* paying attention. Why do you say "Hey" to me?'
'Suhra!' Majid called out and woke up with a start. . . .
'Are you having a dream in the daytime?' the nurse asked.
Majid tried to smile.

Sixty-four days and sixty-four nights passed. With the help of a stick taller than himself Majid, along with the company manager, passed through the hospital gate into the crowded street.

Giving him fifty rupees, the company manager said, 'You should go home now. I'm sorry it ended this way.'

Tears came to Majid's eyes.

'Back home I have two sisters who are past the age when they should have been married,' he said. 'My parents are old. Everything we owned is mortgaged. I am the only man. Without finding some solution to the problems at home, I don't feel like going back. Moreover, in a state like this, why should I go and upset them?'

'What do you intend to do now?'

'I've no idea.'

'If there was a suitable job for you in my company—can you work as a clerk?'

'No. I'm bad at figures.'

So Majid was on his own once more. No matter. Many people in the world were on their own. What reason was there to be afraid?

Majid sent forty rupees home. In the letter he sent along with the money he said nothing about having lost his right leg. He just wrote that he was sick and laid up, and asked them not to write until they heard from him again.

Majid once again started his search for a job.

Using both his hands to support himself on the stick, he limped along on his one leg. . . . He would stop every four

steps; then he would set off again; he would stop and think
... then set off again. One or two months passed like this.
He had no fixed place to stay. He would sleep wherever
he got to by nightfall.

Finally he decided to see the rich people in one town he
came to and request their help. On enquiry he found out
that the most generous person was one Khan Bahadur. It
appeared that all the big buildings in the town were his.
People said that gold bars and such-like were gathering
mildew in his store rooms. He was a man with a lot of
influence and a big pull in government circles. He had just
spent tens of thousands of rupees on a banquet in honour
of the Governor. Anything was possible for him. . . .
Anything.

But the gatekeepers did not let Majid go in. Every day he
would come and stand at the gate of the mansion. A week
passed in that way. Finally the gatekeepers took pity on
him. Majid was led to the presence of Khan Bahadur.
Majid greeted him in the correct fashion. When one
Muslim meets another, they are supposed to say, 'As-
salamu alaikum.' Majid said it. But somehow Khan
Bahadur did not return this salutation. He showed no signs
of having heard it. Khan Bahadur was a fair, chubby man
of about fifty; his heavy, jewelled, gold rings shone, as he
stroked his beard and listened to Majid's sad story.

Finally Khan Bahadur said, 'In our community there are
many poor women who cannot be given in marriage; there
are many who do not have the means to buy food! Whatever I can, I do for everyone. Tell me, what more should
I do?'

Majid said nothing.

Khan Bahadur started to recount all the great things he
had done for the uplift of the community. He has had four
mosques built. The other millionaires have built only one
each. Moreover, he made a gift of a plot of land to the
community to build a school. If he had constructed a
building there and rented it out, how much money he

would have made every month! How much loss he sustains every year for the sake of the community!

'How much more should I do? Tell me.'

Majid said nothing.

Khan Bahadur sympathised with Majid for having lost his leg: 'Fate! What else is there to say?'

It's fate. It doesn't matter. In that case, what is there that does matter?

Leaning on the long stick, Majid, with sorrow in his heart, salamed him and slowly went out. As he was about to pass through the gateway, Khan Bahadur sent a servant after him with a rupee.

'You keep it and tell them you gave it to me,' he told the servant and walked on. Was that the right thing to do?

Why did Majid not take that one rupee? Does he not know that every day hundreds of poor people go to that millionaire and that he gives something to all of them. If Majid were a wealthy man, what would he have done? Would he have given half of his wealth to the first beggar who came to him? Would he have given more than a copper? Khan Bahadur gave him a rupee! Ought he not to have accepted it? In that place, Majid reflected, there are only five millionaires. The remainder is made up of three-quarters of a million common people of different kinds. They all manage to live. Occasionally some of them die. All that Majid has lost is part of one leg. There are some who have lost both legs. Or both arms. Even those who have lost both eyes go on living. Life brings both sorrow and happiness to both great and small. When one thinks of this, it is possible to smile. To weep also. Majid decided that there was no need to attach importance to anything. Was it not one's duty to make every effort necessary for well-being and happiness?

Four inches were worn off the end of Majid's stick. Calluses a quarter of an inch thick were raised on the palms of his hands. He sought work in many places. Going without food caused him to become very lean. Then he had a stroke of luck!

Majid obtained a job in a restaurant, washing dirty dishes. After getting up at four in the morning, he had to sit by the water-tap until eleven at night. He would wash one by one the dirty dishes that were brought in a large basket and then stack them in another basket. Someone else would take it away. By that time another man would have brought more dirty dishes. . . . That was his job. Anyway, he got enough to eat to fill his stomach. Every month he could send home the sum of five rupees.

The first letter he received from home contained the news that Suhra was rather unwell. She had lost a lot of weight. She coughed now and again. 'Here everyone is well. I long to see you!

Your own Suhra'

12)

Majid, too, is longing to see Suhra. When he does see her, and also umma, bapa, his sisters, Suhra's umma and sisters, the people from round about—what will they say?

Majid with his one and a half legs! . . . Will Suhra refer to him in those terms? . . . She would never do that. She would kiss the half leg that remained, with tears in her eyes. Those days of long ago. . . . When he thought of them, Majid smiled. A rather big one!

Majid had brought smiles to the faces of many people by telling those stories. Suhra, too, would become a topic of conversation. The other hotel employees were Majid's friends. When, after taking a bath and eating his fill, he lay down at night, Majid would recount his experiences and tell funny stories. Especially, he would tell funny stories. Everybody would laugh. Every night, when it was time to go to bed, Majid must talk of something or other. Did he not have a lot of things to talk about? Most of them went to sleep with a smile on their face.

When they had all gone to sleep, Majid would talk of this and that with Suhra. Fifteen hundred miles away . . . he would see Suhra! He would hear her cough! He would say a few words and comfort Suhra!

Night and day.

'Suhra, how do you feel now? Do you have a pain in your chest now?' he would say, and look into the washed dishes. Blisters on the palms of his hands had softened and burst. Physically he was very fit. He was able to face up to anything cheerfully. He took pride in what he got from honest toil. There would be some changes in his life. There were legs of wood or of rubber. Over them one could wear trousers and shoes. . . . The proprietor of the hotel had pointed this out. He sympathised with Majid. He would discover an island of comfort in the ocean of sorrow.

At night, when the others had gone to sleep, Majid would say to Suhra, 'Sleep, my dear Suhra, sleep!' But all Majid could see was the wide expanse of the starlit sky.

What could Suhra see?

Majid used to get up early. After completing his daily ablutions and drinking a cup of tea, he would start work. The city never slept. There was a constant hubbub—the mingled noise and bustle of people and traffic. It was while listening to all this that Majid washed and stacked the dishes.

Then, as life was going on in this way, another letter came.

The handwriting was not Suhra's!

Umma had got someone else to write. When he read it, it seemed to Majid that the uproar of the town suddenly stopped.

'Majid, my dear son, it is your own umma writing this for you to read.

'Our Suhra died the day before yesterday, early in the morning. It was at her house. She was lying with her head in my lap. It was near her bapa's grave in the precincts of the mosque that Suhra was buried.

'So our only friend and helper has gone. Now all we have

after Allah is you.

'My son, on the 30th of last month our house and the land that goes with it were seized and sold for the creditors. They say we must vacate it at once. Where can I go with these two grown-up girls and bapa who is laid up sick?

'My son, it is a long time since I slept. Girls of your sisters' age have given birth three or four times. If anything bad happened to them. . . . My son, the Muslims in these parts are without pity. Although bapa and I pleaded with them, they say we must leave immediately.

'There are many kind, rich people of our Muslim community there. If you tell them, they will not fail to find a way out. You must not be shy about going to see them and speaking freely about everything.

'My dearest son, while Suhra was here, she was a consolation to me. Suhra said we must not upset you by telling you of all the troubles we have had here. That is why I have not written earlier. For the last two months Suhra was laid up. Consumption. There was no-one to give her medical treatment. Before she died she spoke your name. Time and again she asked if you had come.

'All is the will of Allah.'

For a while Majid was stunned.

It was as if all had become silent.

The world was full of emptiness.

No! . . . Nothing had happened to the world. The hubbub in the town was still there. The sun was shining. The wind was blowing. It was just that Majid was soaked in perspiration that had come out through all the pores of his skin. There was no help left. Had life then lost its meaning?

Majid began once again to wash the dishes and stack them carefully. Where would his parents and his sisters go?

Suhra!

Memories. . . . Words. . . . Actions. . . . Facial expressions. . . . Pictures. All these came rushing into his mind! Time and again before she died, she had asked if Majid had come.

Memories.

The final memory:

That day . . . Majid was setting off after taking leave. Suhra started to say something. Before she had finished, the bus-driver sounded his horn. . . . Umma came in. . . . Majid went out into the yard. Through the flower garden he came to the gate . . . looked back for a moment:

Golden clouds in the western sky. Trees, house, yard and flower garden immersed in the soft yellow light of the sun. . . .

His two sisters standing behind the door, showing just their faces. Bapa on the verandah leaning against the wall. Umma in the yard.

Standing in the garden with her hand on the shoeflower tree and with tears in her eyes—Suhra.

What she had started to say must have been still in her mind.

What was it that Suhra started to say?

'ME GRANDAD
'AD AN ELEPHANT!'

1. 'This is a lucky mole!'

2. 'That scoundrel Iblis!'

3. 'Where are the kings and others who boastfully said, "I . . . I"?'

4. Two old wooden sandals

5. The wind blew—the leaf did not fall!

6. The cry of a sparrow!

7. Silly booby!

8. 'I cannot bear false witness!'

9. 'Me heart is aching!'

10. A time of dreams

11. The new generation is talking

'ME GRANDAD
'AD AN ELEPHANT!'

1)   'This is a lucky mole!'

It is as if it happened thousands of years ago. For childhood is a long way off, is it not? Since then many things happened. Kunjupattumma can remember it all only as something pleasant. Laughter is much better than weeping.

Kunjupattumma has not hurt anybody. It could be said that she has not so much as hurt a fly. Among the Lord Rabb al-Alamin's creations she has no hatred for anything. From childhood on she has liked all living beings. It was an elephant that she started loving first. She has never seen it. Yet she loved it. This is how she hears about it.

At the time she was about seven years old. Or maybe eight. Not more than that. At that time she was served with a strict injunction. It was not from her bapa, but from her umma. The thing is simply this. Even though they are Muslims, she should not be friendly with the neighbours' children! In short, she should not have anything to do with them. What is the reason? Her mother told a world-renowned secret.

'My darling Kunjupattumma, you are the darling daughter of the darling daughter of Anamakkar. Yer grandad 'ad an elephant!—a huge tusker!!'

From that day on she has said to herself a hundred times, 'My darling elephant!' She grew up playing with it. That means she would play in the middle courtyard of that tiled building, thinking of it. She had gold ornaments on her neck, ears, arms and feet—and she dressed in a silk *mundu*.

She wore a silk *kuppayam*. Covering her head she had a head-shawl embroidered with gold and silver threads.

Though she is fair, there is one dark feature. Although she has not mentioned it to anyone, this pains her. On her cheek there is a small, black mole.

It was when she was fourteen years of age that she realised it was a lucky mole. At that time she received proposals of marriage one after the other. She doesn't know who is coming to marry her. What difference does it make who it is?

'Then I shall be able to chew betel-leaf,' Kunjupattumma told herself. It is not proper for unmarried Muslim girls to chew betel-leaf. Kunjupattumma is not sure whether Allah or Nabi have said anything regarding this. But according to custom it is not permissible. Also Muslim women should not go into the presence of strange men. When she was very young, Kunjupattumma did go. But it did not really count as going; it is merely that she has seen other men. She does not remember anything about anybody. Even if she does remember, it is only about women.

'Those women are all kafirs!' is all Kunjupattumma can say about them. In the world there are only two classes. Muslim and kafir. Whether they are men or women, after death all kafirs will go to hell. They are all fallen ones. If Muslims imitate them, they too will become lost souls worthy of hell. The kafirs Kunjupattumma saw were schoolmistresses. It was when her bapa took her to the river all dressed up that she has seen them. Kunjupattumma has also seen the children of the rich people who come from town on a vacation. Hardly a single one of them has as much gold jewelry as Kunjupattumma has! She has seen many of them looking at her enviously. She has also heard them asking, 'Who is that girl?' pointing at her as they do so. On all those occasions someone would say with great awe, 'It's Vattan Adima's daughter, Kunjupattumma; Anamakkar's daughter's daughter!'

Some would ask, 'Isn't she the daughter of our Kunjutachumma?'

The schoolmistresses gather round her saying, 'Give us a smile, Kunjupattumma.' Kunjupattumma likes them. Although they are kafirs, they smell nice. They all wear saris. They all have those small kuppayams known as blouses. Underneath the blouse they have a thin, tight bodice. What is more, they wear flowers on their head. Some will weave flowers into Kunjupattumma's hair. Some of them will pretend they are pinching the mole off her cheek. She does not enjoy any of this. She wants to be able to wear the same sort of sari and blouse, with the thin, tight bodice underneath. She mentioned this to her bapa. Then those teachers laughed. One of them said, 'When you grow up!'

How she wants to grow up! So a desire was born in her. She must grow up!

'Umma, when am I going to grow up?' she asked her mother.

When her umma asked why, she openly told her the truth. Then her umma put fear into her.

'We can't do anything like that, Kunjupattumma! That's the way the kafirs dress. We should distinguish ourselves from kafirs!'

'That's true, my dear,' her bapa said. 'We don't want that sort of thing!'

If we don't want that sort of thing, we don't want it! There is no going against bapa's words. Life is according to the precepts of Islam. Where Vattan Adima's name is mentioned, there is love and respect. He is a leader of the community; he is a trustee of the mosque. He is the tallest man in those parts. His head is always clean-shaven. His beard and moustache are cut in the manner ordained. The two ends of the moustache are twisted like a pair of horns. He wears only a dhoti. Hanging carelessly over his shoulder he will have a long stole. If at times its end happens to drag along the ground, those who are following a step or two behind will with great respect pick it up and hold it. Bapa will know nothing of this. He will just keep walking, tall and straight. Bapa will not miss his prayers even once. In the month of Ramazan he fasts all the thirty days. He gives *zakat*—the alms required by divine command. He would like to go on the *hajj*. But he will make this pilgrimage to Mecca only after Kunjupattumma's marriage.

So the matter of the marriage became pressing. In the house it is like a feast every day. Five to eight bundles of betel-leaves are needed. Yet Bapa is not much of a chewer.

Umma chews a lot. Umma needs a hundred tender betel-leaves a day. Umma's work consists of chewing and talking. Decked out in all her jewelry, wearing gold-threaded head-shawl and silk kuppayam and dressed in a double lower cloth also made of silk, she sits by the betel-box on a finely woven mat. She will not go barefoot. Umma walks only on wooden sandals. Both the toe-grips of umma's wooden sandals are made from the tusk of uppuppa's elephant. The sandals will always be close by her.

There will be lots of women to chew and listen to her talk. The topics are not many—either Kunjupattumma, or the seven aunts who are bapa's sisters. Mostly the subject is the black mole on Kunjupattumma's cheek.

'This is a lucky mole!' umma will say. 'It's not mere chance. She's the darling daughter of the darling daughter of Anamakkar!' That is not all: 'I gave birth to five,' umma will say, 'but God and the Prophet and the saints gave me only one.' Then she fondles Kunjupattumma's jewelry before going on with what she has to say. 'Tell me, my friend, don't you think this one at least should be well cared for?' What she says next is in a somewhat angry tone of voice: 'I tell you . . . even if her bapa's people don't take part in the wedding, Kunjupattumma's wedding will take place. She's the darling daughter of the darling daughter of Anamakkar!' When she has thus said what she has to say on this topic, umma will ask one of the women to say something.

'Say something!'

The women will talk. Once, as they were talking like this, Kunjupattumma heard from the women a piece of local news which disturbed her. It made her sad and angry.

The disturbing news that Kunjupattumma heard is this:

In the neighbourhood and in almost all the houses of the area, there are children of four or five years of age. A new generation is coming up! Kunjupattumma has nothing against that. But their names! Mere coolies, fishermen, common beggars—in fact in most of the Muslim houses of the area, there are Kunjupattummas, and Adimas, and Kunjutachummas, and Makkars!

Oh Creator of the Worlds! What can be done? Do they not have any shame or humility? . . . Could they not give some other names to their children? For Kunjupattumma had not understood one of the secrets of this world: the names of those who are rich and famous will be used by the poor, who are neither. This is a common thing. There is no law against the use of the names of people who have wealth and fame by those who have neither. They might obtain prosperity and renown as a result. Yet somehow that did not seem right to Kunjupattumma—because she was the only true Kunjupattumma in the world, her bapa was the only Vattan Adima, her umma the only Kunjutachumma and her uppuppa the only Anamakkar!

Whatever had in fact happened, Kunjupattumma was not going to excuse this practice. She made this clear to her mother within the hearing of the other women. She asked, angry and aggrieved, 'Why should they all take our names?'

Umma laughed. Kunjupattumma does not know what the other women thought. Umma said, 'The girl's about to be married! Do you hear what she asks?' Then umma touched the black mole on her cheek saying, 'You see this!' It was then that she understood. She has not heard that any of the little four- or five-year-old Kunjupattummas has a black mole on her cheek. When umma asked the other women about this, they confirmed it. Why do they not have one?

Umma asked, 'What colour is it, dear?'

The colour of a black mole is black. Kunjupattumma said, 'Black.'

'What colour was your uppuppa's elephant?' umma asked.

Kunjupattumma thought for a while. Ordinarily an elephant is black.

'Black!' she said.

'How about you?' umma asked.

Kunjupattumma is fair.

'Fair,' she said.

'Do you know why there is a black mole on your fair cheek?' umma asked.

Now Kunjupattumma understood the seriousness of the matter. All mysteries stood clearly revealed! She felt happy and proud. She said, ' Me grandad 'ad an elephant!'

Touching the wooden sandals, umma said, 'A huge tusker!'

2)   'That scoundrel Iblis!'

While the negotiations for Kunjupattumma's marriage were going on, Kunjupattumma heard a couple of things.

Uppuppa's huge tusker had killed six people! She felt unhappy about that, and she was angry with the elephant. She even went so far as to say, 'Naughty elephant!'

But the anger did not last very long, because all the six people the elephant had killed were kafir mahouts. It had not killed a single Muslim. But then she was not sure that it had ever had a Muslim mahout.

'It was a fine elephant!' said umma.

For it used to take fruit and jaggery from uppuppa's hand and eat them.

'Your bapa came to marry me on that elephant!' said umma.

Kunjupattumma wondered whether the boy who was coming to marry her . . . would come on an elephant.

To whom . . . why . . . is she being married? Kunjupattumma did not think of any such things. As soon as she is
married, bapa will go to Mecca for the hajj. It was in this
sacred place that Muhammad Nabi was born. There is a
holy shrine there called the Ka'ba. This is the world's first
mosque. It is very ancient. It was Ibrahim Nabi who
renovated it. Kunjuppattumma's bapa has not had any
mosque built. After he comes back from the hajj, bapa will
be called 'Haji Vattan Adima' or 'Vattan Adima Haji'.

'Are you going, umma?' Kunjupattumma asked.

'Where?'

'For the hajj.'

'Yes, I'm going!' said umma.

This is news.

'Then . . . you must take me too!' said Kunjupattumma.

Umma laughed and said, 'You must say that to your
husband!'

She felt shy and did not say any more. Who is coming to
marry her? Will he be young or old? Dark or fair? She has
no idea. Some man is coming.

If you are born a girl, you will be given in marriage to a
man. This is a custom that goes back to the time of Muhammad Nabi and his Companions, the As-habus. Even before
then, this must have been the custom. Long, long ago
Adam married Eve. Adam and Eve had no bapa or umma.
It was God, Rabb al-Alamin, who got them married. Adam
and Eve are the first parents of those who are now living
in this world and of those who are dead. Before them there
were no men on the earth. Kunjupattumma does not know
how many millions of years ago Adam and Eve lived on
this earth. After Adam the world has seen many prophets
. . . Noah, Abraham, David, Moses, Jesus, Muhammad.

Muhammad is the last prophet. There will be no more
prophets. With the prophet Muhammad everything has
been fulfilled.

Muhammad Nabi's eldest daughter was called Fatima.
Instead of Fatima some say Pattumma. Muhammad Nabi

got Fatima married to Caliph Ali.

Ali was very brave and valiant. Ali had a glittering sword called Dhualfiqar. During his last days, in accordance with the commandment of God Almighty, Ali threw this sword into the ocean. It cut the necks of all the fish. That is why a cut is seen on either side of the gullet of all fish. It is from that day that fish has become 'halal' to the Muslim and so can be lawfully eaten.

Kunjupattumma wondered whether the man who was coming to marry her would be a great hero. She had no idea. Whom should she ask? There is only one thing: ... do what you are told, accept what you are given—that is the duty of a Muslim girl. Kunjupattumma has realised this. What have Almighty God and his Messenger Muhammad laid down regarding this? Although she could not understand the meaning, she has read the Koran. Her bapa and umma have read it. Her uppuppa Anamakkar has also read the Koran. But nobody knows what it contains. If you make all the trees in the world into pens and all the oceans into ink and try to write the meaning of the Koran, you will find that before you finish one chapter, all the trees will be used up and all the oceans will be dry. The Koran is a holy book. Everything is in it. It was not written by anyone. The Lord God Almighty through his angel Gabriel sent it down to Muhammad Nabi. Nabi did not know how to read or write. Yet the Koran is in his mother tongue, which is Arabic. Kunjupattumma has heard that there is a country called Arabia. There are two holy places there called Mecca and Medina. Muhammad Nabi was born in Mecca, and he is buried in Medina.

When bapa and umma go for the hajj, they will go to Medina also. Will the man who marries her let Kunjupattumma go with them? Her thoughts went along these lines. Night and day she thought only about these things. Meanwhile, one day she noticed that her bapa was very agitated. His eyes were red. He laughed.

'They're playing with me!' said bapa. 'They're playing

with Vattan Adima! With the help of God, the Prophet and the saints, I'll teach them!'

At that time Kunjupattumma did not understand what it was all about. A new case has been filed against bapa. It has to do with the trusteeship of the mosque. It seems that bapa has no right to the management of the mosque.

Then who has the right? It is always the leader of the community who is the trustee. To be the leader one needs money. It is Kunjupattumma's bapa who is the richest man in the area. If there is more than one rich man, there will always be a dispute over the trusteeship. There will be fighting and killing. Then there is a court case. That is the way it goes. Wherever there is a mosque, there are court cases. Kunjupattumma knows that all this is the work of that scoundrel Iblis. If Iblis was not there, there would not have been any trouble in this world.

It was in the mosque that Kunjupattumma first heard about the scoundrel Iblis. It was not to pray that she went to the mosque. After all, a Muslim woman cannot go and pray in the mosque along with the men! It was to hear the evening sermon or 'wa'z' that she went to the mosque that day. An elder was giving the wa'z. In front of the mosque, but to one side, a pandal had been erected. It was for the women. If you sat there, you could not see anything. Kunjupattumma heard about the scoundrel Iblis (also known as Satan) while sitting in that pandal. The elder spoke about Iblis in a loud singing voice. Kunjupattumma remembers the whole thing very clearly.

In the beginning, the scoundrel Iblis was a leading angel. At the time when he was there in heaven in the holy presence of Rabb al-Alamin, an incident took place.

This was before the creation of the world. The story that has been handed down goes like this: Before all other living beings Allah created Muhammad. After that, countless ages passed by. Then He created the earth, sun, moon and stars. From three drops of Muhammad Nabi's sweat He created other living beings. Among them was Adam, the first man.

After creating him, God told all the other living beings, including *malak* (the angels) and *jinn* (the genii) to venerate Adam. Only the leading angel failed to carry out this command. The reason was that angels were created from fire, while in the creation of man in the form of Adam there was a lot of earth.

Is it right for one created from fire to venerate one who is made of earth? This was the argument put forward by that *malak*. Anyhow, God Almighty punished him for disobedience. He was driven out of heaven.

It is he who is the scoundrel Iblis, alias Satan!

Kunjupattumma knows something more about Iblis. With malice aforethought he tried to lead Adam and Eve astray down on earth. Since then he has been trying to lead astray all living beings, especially the Muslims, thus making them kafirs destined for hell. He goes about in many disguises. He speaks all languages. He can take any form. He wants to get people on his side. That is his intention. For that, too, there is a reason.

This is what Kunjupattumma has heard from her bapa. Muslims have a special way of dress. If it is a man, he must wrap his dhoti to the left. His head must be clean-shaven. His beard must be trimmed to a thin line, like a path going through a paddy field. If it is a woman, she must have her ears pierced for the special ornaments called halqats. They must wear a kuppayam and cover the head. They can comb the hair but cannot part it.

Once a Muslim youth went against these rules. He let his hair grow and had it cut and groomed.

Bapa sent for this boy and had the barber shave his head! Then he said, 'As long as I am alive, with the help of God Almighty and Nabi, I will not allow you to break the Muslim customs!'

For it is only those who are in league with Iblis who have their hair cut and groomed. So one must be careful. He will come and sit on the head. That is what a cap is for. If there is no cap, a turban will suffice.

But bapa does not wear a cap or tie a turban. He covers his head only when he prays. Will Iblis sit on bapa's head at other times? There is no reason for such a fear.

Will Iblis dare to come near Vattan Adima?

However, Kunjupattumma always covers her head. Umma also covers her head. Although they comb their hair, they do not part it like the kafirs.

There is a story bapa told about Iblis:

In the beginning, after creation, Allah asked the souls of all living beings, 'Who is your creator?'

All said, 'We don't have a creator.'

Allah punished every one of them. He punished them in different ways and for a long time.

Still none admitted that they had a creator.

In the end, Rabb al-Alamin gave all of them the punishment of hunger. So it is from that day on that hunger has existed. As soon as the punishment of hunger was meted out, all agreed, 'Allah is our creator!'

That agreement was put inside a stone. This stone will be taken as witness on the Day of Judgment, when souls will be brought to trial. The name of the stone is Hajar al-Aswad—the Black Stone. It is kept in the Ka'ba in Mecca. Those who go for the hajj touch it with their fingers and kiss it. Bapa and umma will not fail to do this. Will it be possible for Kunjupattumma to go for the hajj and kiss that stone? If anything goes wrong, it will be the work of Iblis. He often causes things to go wrong!

'Oh Lord Rabb al-Alamin!' Kunjupattumma will pray, 'Save us from the snares of that scoundrel Iblis!'

3)   'Where are the kings and others who
             boastfully said, "I . . . I"?'

Kunjupattumma is sitting all dressed up. She has reddened her hands and feet with henna and blackened her eyes with collyrium. She is in a wonderful state of anticipation.

Who is coming?

In the beginning she took marriage to be fun. She would be able to redden her lips by chewing betel-leaves and be grown-up. She would be able to wear gold halqats in her ears. She would be able to go for the hajj along with umma and bapa. But . . . will that man allow her to go?

However, none of the boys who came to marry her was good enough for Anamakkar's darling daughter's darling daughter. Some did not have enough money; some did not come from sufficiently high-class families.

In this way more and more days are going by. Kunjupattumma is getting older. All this time there is one small thing that she would like. It is not really clear. She feels a little uneasy in her mind. She would like to see the man she is going to marry beforehand. Just see him—nothing more.

But she could not tell anyone about this desire. Is it not bad? It is not fitting for Muslim women. Yet the wish gets stronger day by day. What can she do but simply sit and dream? There are five or six servants in the house. It is very noisy. Now and then will be heard the 'clop clop' of umma's wooden sandals. On the other side can be heard the sound of bapa's voice. Many men have gathered there. What are they talking about?

They are not matters that she understands. Court house, lawyers, opposing witnesses—and other such things. Sometimes the question of her wedding comes up. Every atom in her tries to listen. But she cannot move. If Kunjapattumma moves, the world will know. She is shy about it. If she so much as breathes, the sound will reverberate. And if she were to walk! There would be such a clinking and clanking and clattering! Why does one need so many ornaments? Maybe she could take a few off. But then nobody knows when some women will come to see the future bride.

All the women who came were covered with gold. All were very grand. What questions they ask! No end of doubts. . . . Some have looked into her mouth. Does she have a full set of teeth? Are any of them decayed?

None of her teeth has any defect. She has a full set of beautiful teeth.

Some others wanted to know if she was deaf; or whether she was well-informed. To find out they would ask various questions.

'Who made us?' one woman asked.

'Allah,' said Kunjupattumma.

'What are the signs of *qiyamat*?'

That means, 'What are the signs of the end of the world?' One day this world will be destroyed. There are some signs by which one can know about it in advance. Kunjupattumma will go into this in detail. . . . Those of low estate will rise. Those of high estate will go down. Evil will prevail. Faith in God will fade. Religions will disappear. Parents will not be obeyed. Teachers will not be respected. Old people will be mocked. Women will lose modesty and shame. Nobody will have respect for anyone. Nobody will believe anyone. Love will disappear. Jealousy will increase. Hardheartedness will be more prevalent. Kings and rulers will become very cruel. The desire to rule the whole world will increase. There will be terrible wars. . . . Even then the world will not be destroyed. Only Allah can destroy it. Very many years before qiyamat, men will fall into the confused state of forgetfulness. . . . Then one day, as soon as the sun is up, while men are in the midst of getting ready for their daily work, the people of the world will suddenly hear a long, protracted sound.

'Oh . . . what sound is this?' they will wonder. . . . It is the trumpet called Sur!

It is the angel Israfil who makes this sound. It comes from a pipe. That pipe has holes according to the number of all the living beings on the earth. . . . People who hear these sounds will come from different parts and gather in groups asking confusedly, 'Where is it coming from?'

These sounds will slowly increase until they become terrible as thunder. Living beings will wander around in a confused state of mind. The sounds will become more and more frightful. Men and other living creatures will start falling down dead singly and in groups. The earth will tremble and burst asunder. All the oceans will storm and foam and go over the land. Hills and mountains will burst into millions of pieces. Tempests will rage. Fire will be put out completely in the world. The sun, moon and stars will cool down and become dark. Everything will perish. Not a trace of the heavens or the earth will remain. In the end ... in the end there will only be Lord Rabb al-Alamin. Then he will say, 'Where are the kings and others who boastfully said, "I ... I"?'

Like this millions of ages will pass during which God alone will be. ... Again he will create the world. There will be sun, moon and stars. He will raise all souls to life again. Then punishment, salvation. . . . Kunjupattumma will recite all this in detail. She knows all of it by heart.

Asking questions like this, examining her, coming to see her ... on behalf of a son; or on behalf of a brother.

If only she had a brother. . . ! She too could go to some houses, ask questions and be a grand lady. She knows all that a Muslim lady should know. She can read the Koran in a singing tone. If one wants to touch the Koran, the body should be made clean. For that, either you should bathe; or you should do 'wuzu'. This is done by saying some Arabic words and washing the hands, mouth, nose, face, ears, the crown of the head; and the feet—three times each in pure water. Then she also knows how to pray: Subh, Zuhr, Asr, Maghrib, Isha—prayers for the five different parts of the day. Moreover, she knows all about 'Islam' (submission) and 'Iman' (faith). Nobody can excel her.

One of those fine ladies who came to see her asked, 'Who was Aisha Bibi?'

'Nabi's consort!' said Kunjupattumma.

Aisha Bibi was one of Muhammad's wives.

'Were Aisha Bibi's ears pierced?'

'Yes.'

'How many halqats did she have?'

Kunjupattumma replied, 'The angle Gabriel (Peace be upon him) brought a bunch of pearls from heaven and gave it to the Messenger of Allah. Nabi put them in Aisha Bibi's ears!'

It is not pearls Kunjupattumma has in her ears. In the two of them together she has twenty-one gold rings. On each of them there is a fine gold leaf. When the wind blows, these all move with a faint sound.

In the lobes of her ears are two gold pegs. From these hang two tiny gold leaves. On her neck are some gold chains and also a solid gold luffa fruit. She does not have a *tali* like her mother's. That will be worn only after marriage. On her wrists she has gold bangles that jingle. On one finger she has a ring. It is not like her father's, which is made of copper, for Muslim men cannot use pure gold.

The ring on Kunjupattumma's finger is of solid gold. It is set with a stone that is red like the eye of an elephant. There is a golden chain round her waist. On it are numerous ornaments and charms. Then she has big golden anklets. These are hollow and it is from inside them that most of the sound comes when she walks. She does not know what is inside them. Grains of gold, or sand . . . or something.

That is what makes the noise when she walks.

She just sits quietly. It is without feeling hungry that she eats. It is without feeling sleepy that she goes to bed.

On moonlit nights she stands in the centre courtyard. She feels slightly dejected. What is the reason for this? Kunjupattumma does not know. She thinks it is just a feeling. She has all that she wants. Then she looks up at the sky and tries to smile. Umma calls her in. She shouldn't stand there like that. Won't somebody see her?

'Who is there in the sky, umma?'

'Ifrit and jinn!' umma will say.

What if some invisible beings that fly through the skies see her?

The sky is not empty as it seems! Malak, jinn, Ifrit, Satan —not to mention that scoundrel Iblis, fly in the air. Suppose they see Kunjupattumma as they fly along like that—if they are fascinated by her, she might be possessed by them.

She comes indoors.

She does not object to being seen by men, angels, or demons. But after all, she is a Muslim lady.

She is a prisoner. Air and light are not for her. She is bursting. Her kuppayams do not fit her any more. She has waking dreams. They are not the sort she can tell to any-one. They disturb every atom of her being. Thus, through dreams, Kunjupattumma reached her twenty-first year. Then something decisive happened in her life.

Bapa took all her gold ornaments from her. He took umma's too. He was selling them all to enable him to conduct his court case.

Kunjupattumma's ears, neck, waist, wrist and ankles were empty. Every day bapa and his retinue are in the court-house. The case is proceeding. The outcome is something of a shock. Judgment goes against bapa.

Disgrace and defeat. It has come to this, that they have to leave.

Where will they go?

It was evening. The moon had come up early. Kunjupat-tumma bid farewell to the house where she was born and brought up. They departed. Bapa, tall and straight, in front; umma, with downcast face and tear-filled eyes, behind. Last of all came Kunjupattumma with no emotions whatever. While people watched, they entered the public road. Passing by the mosque, they reached the bank of the river.

Nothing has happened to the world. But . . . their past, present and future are all shattered. Yet . . . the river and the sands lie glittering in the moonlight. . . . People are bathing in the water. . . . On the sand some are sitting together and enjoying the fun of gossip. . . . Nothing has happened to the world.

Without knowing where, Kunjupattumma walked on, behind her umma and bapa. Her legs were weary; she was tired. Yet she found the world full of wonders, as they made their way along the now deserted road.

Through the moonlight she walked behind them. Where are they aiming for? Will this night never end?

4)   Two old wooden sandals

What Kunjupattumma felt was a kind of gratification. A gratification mingled with vengeance and protest. What had happend was a great disaster. Yet now she could see people, breathe clean air, stand in the sun, be bathed in the moonlight. She could run, jump, sing. Although she did not know any songs, she had the freedom to sing or to do anything. Let anyone come—malak, jinn or *ins*!

Oddly enough, nobody came! Who wants people with no money?

Kunjupattumma could not go on nourishing that sentiment for long. Even if she had no money, she had youth and beauty. Men started showing interest in her. Some winked at her. Some showed her coins.

She knows that all this is not for anything good. What can she do to them? She goes and sits under the tamarind tree or by the lily pond, where she will not attract anyone's attention.

It is a stretch of blue water full of white and red water-lilies. Round, glossy leaves that lie close to the water. A cool breeze caressing the flowers in full bloom.

There she sits.

The house is close by. Kunjupattumma has not begun to feel that it is a home. It is a little old house with walls of unplastered red stone that look as if they have been skinned. It has two rooms and a kitchen. It is thatched with straw. Here and there on this roof, paddy shoots have sprouted.

There are not many things inside the house. A few mats and pillows. A box to keep everybody's clothes in. Two or three oil lamps.

In the kitchen there are a few earthenware pots and some bowls to eat or drink from.

They are hard-pressed for something to eat and drink. They have not brought anything from the old house. They came away empty-handed. But somehow umma brought the two old sandals with their toe-grips made from the tusks of uppuppa's huge elephant. Kunjupattumma does not know whether umma had these in her hand when they left.

It is on these wooden sandals that umma moves around. She talks non-stop. There must be enough betel-leaf for her to keep her mouth full all the time.

Bapa has given up chewing. He became grey suddenly. He doesn't talk too much. He sits staring into space.

'All this is the will of God, of Nabi and of the saints,' bapa will say. 'I have never failed to pray five times a day. Not once have I missed fasting.'

Then why did things happen this way? Kunjupattumma does not think that anything has happened. If it has, who is to be blamed? She does not have the heart to blame bapa. Nor does she consider her umma, or her aunts and uncles responsible. How can she blame leaders of the community, though they bore false witness after touching the Koran? Kunjupattumma sees no fault in any human being. The real culprit is that scoundrel Iblis, otherwise known as Satan!

Every day Kunjupattumma prays, 'Oh Lord Rabb al-Alamin, protect us at least now from the molestations of the scoundrel Iblis!'

What else could she do? This is what that scoundrel did. The coconut plantations and paddy fields that Kunjupattumma's bapa controlled and enjoyed were not his alone. That big house and all the rest belonged to bapa and his seven sisters.

The seven sisters together filed a case against bapa saying, 'Unknown to anyone, our brother Vattan Adima took our umma in a bullock cart to the court-house and got her to will to him alone what was rightfully ours also!'

'Our dear umma willed it to me!' Kunjupattumma's bapa

argued. The case, which dragged on for many years, cost both sides a lot of money. Competent lawyers argued the case. To ensure victory, both sides promised offerings to all the mosques. In the mosques flags were raised; sandalwood paste was presented. Moreover, both parties had many worthy people as false witnesses. Slowly the case was developing in Vattan Adima's favour. Then it took an unexpected turn.

Vattan Adima's mother was insane! She was not in her right mind when she wrote the will. Is it possible to bring to the court someone who is dead and gone so that a matter can be cleared up? Witnesses came to testify that Vattan Adima's umma was insane! Moreover, it was argued, whether she was insane or not, weren't Vattan Adima's sisters entitled to his mother's property?

Kunjupattumma does not know much about that complicated court case. All she knows is that it was all the work of the scoundrel Iblis, alias Satan. However it might be, the case was decided against her bapa. For the 'trusteeship' case and the 'madness' case a large portion of his landed property was mortgaged. In the end, what was left to bapa was that small piece of land on the side of the road.

On it was the small straw-thatched house. It also had four areca-nut trees, nine coconut trees, a well, a tamarind tree and, on the boundary, a lily pond. Kunjupattumma was very happy when she saw this for the first time. It was the first time she had ever seen a lily pond. There were many flowers, both white and red. She would count them all. When she starts to count from one end, her umma or bapa or someone will call her for something. Somehow she has not been able to finish counting. But it is a beautiful sight. Yet in its beauty there is something frightening, something unpleasant. What this is, is not clear.

One day something happened there. Since then she has gone to the well in the neighbouring compound to take her bath. There is a house there, but nobody lives in it. Once in a while some people who come on vacation stay there.

Then she does not go there. The water from the well is nice and cool. By it stands a portia tree, up which there climbs a jasmine covered in white flowers. She picks a lot of these, but she does not wear them in her hair. She is not sure whether Muslim girls are allowed to wear flowers. But she likes jasmine flowers and so sits there and makes garlands with them. Just to sit there is a pleasure too. Nothing moves. There is no-one. In front, on a lower level, is the road. Beyond the road are paddy fields. Somewhere beyond the fields is the river. To go there and bathe, one has to go along the public road. How can a Muslim girl of marriage-able age go along the public road? Yet if she were to bathe by the well where they live, there is nothing to screen her from the public eye.

So one day Kunjupattumma decided to bathe in the water-lily pond. Nobody would see. It was afternoon time. The sun was shining bright. She went to the pond with her bath towel, took off her kuppayam somehow and put it on the grass. Then she wrapped the towel round her, took off her mundu and laid it on the kuppayam.

Slowly she got into the water. When the water came up to her chest, she dipped herself in the water. After dipping herself two or three times, she started soaping herself. When she chanced to look down into the water, she saw a long and wrinkled, thin, black thing coming quickly towards her!

'Oh God, a leech!'

Kunjupattumma lost no time in getting up on to the bank, where she started to dry herself. Something black on her thigh. . . . When she looked, she shook with nausea and fright. A leech was biting into her thigh! And with both ends!

'Umma! Bapa! Come quickly! It's biting me to death! Come quickly! Everybody come!'—Kunjupattumma wanted to cry out. But she had no clothes on. What could she do?

She stood there fuming. The leech was getting puffed up.

When it let go with one end and hung there full and bloated, it was more painful. When she moved, its smooth body rubbed against her naked thigh.... She stood there like that, gritting her teeth. When the leech fell down looking like a ball filled with blood, she jumped with pain!

There was blood on her thigh. Blood was trickling out also. She took a handful of water and washed away the blood that was on the thigh.

What could she do to the leech?

She was angry and revolted. She wanted to swear at it. What swear words should she use?

'Iblis, you drank all my blood,' she said, and thought of killing it. But it was impossible to do that. The leech had a bapa and an umma. She didn't know whether it was male or female.

Whatever it is, let it go. She will let it go back home.

'Leech, you shouldn't drink anyone's blood again. If you do, then when you die, God will put you in hell you know.' With those words she embarked on her good deed. She took a small stick and, without hurting it, slowly nudged the leech into the water. As though waiting for it to fall, a large murral made a grab at it and swallowed it whole.

When Kunjupattumma looked carefully, there was not one, but two: 'Husband and wife!' And not only that, 'The kids are also there!'—tiny little red youngsters, like red ink drops shining in the blue water.

'Tell me, fish, why did you swallow it whole? Isn't it a sin?'

Kunjupattumma did not feel that it was sinful for men to eat fish. She stood there looking at the murral family. There was absolutely no love in those eyes. Water was passing through the gills of both; these are 'the cuts made by Ali's sword Dhualfiqar!'

That fat murral is looking at her! If Kunjupattumma goes near it, it'll make a grab at her and swallow her whole!

Combing her hair dry, she viewed the lily pond.

All the flowers are white and red as before. . . . But underne'ath them are leeches that drink people's blood, and fish that swallow the leeches. The water-lilies stand there unconcerned. . . . The whole scene seems to be mocking and laughing at her. . . . As she was standing there, along came another inhabitant of the lily pond.

It is a big water-snake! Is it the poisonous sort? The underside is white. It crawled on to a lotus leaf and lay there with its head in the water. Suddenly, like a harpoon, it darted forward and caught something and then lifted its head. It was a poor baby fish. It didn't cry; it made no sound. It squirmed and shook its tail. Without any fuss the snake swallowed it and calmly lay down as before.

When Kunjupattumma looked more carefully, she saw some other residents too: tortoise, pallatti, carp, frog—all kinds of living things!

The water-lilies are smiling! All in all, the pond is outstandingly beautiful and frightening.

After this discovery Kunjupattumma goes to the water-lily pond as if she is going to a friend who loves and hates her.

She has nothing to do. Although there is a great deal of work to be done, she does not know how. She has a freedom she did not have before. But of what use is this freedom? She went to prepare some food, but she did not know how to make the fire. Umma is not good at that sort of thing either.

Bapa had to bring the food and prepare it.

'If you are born a woman, you should at least know how to make a fire,' he says.

When she hears that, Kunjupattumma blushes with shame. But bapa is saying it to umma. Walking with a 'clip, clop' on those old wooden sandals, umma says, 'I am the darling daughter of Anamakkar.'

Bapa makes no comment on this.

Umma will not eat unless someone pours water for her to wash her hands. She just sits there.

Bapa looks at her with anger. Meanwhile, Kunjupattumma pours water on her hands.

'Yer uppuppa 'ad an elephant; a huge tusker,' umma will say.

Bapa does not usually say anything; when umma talks too much, he will say softly, as if controlling a storm inside him, 'Oh, shut up!'

'If I don't,' umma will ask, 'what will you do? I am Anamakkar's darling daughter; I am licensed to say anything.'

Umma is licensed to say anything!

'Umma dear, please be calm,' Kunjupattumma will say.

'You unlawful child,' umma will say. 'This is all because you were born!'

So poor Iblis is not the culprit. Kunjupattumma will smile sadly. But she cannot smile for long. She is already possessed by fear—the fear that bapa is going to kill umma. When will this happen?

5)   The wind blew—the leaf did not fall!

Why do people become like this? Kunjupattumma thought hard, but she could not understand. How is it that, after a certain age, husband and wife cannot stand the sight of each other? Are all ummas and bapas like this? They are ready to bite and tear each other apart. When she watches that ... sometimes it amuses her. But she does not laugh. Altogether life has become a mess. There is no proper food. As for clothes, there is no need even to mention it. Wearing the same old things ... washing them ever so often ... they have all become grey. Who is to be blamed for all of this?

The most interesting point is that they now have no-one to help them. Three living beings that no-one pays any attention to! In his days of glory, bapa had so many dependants! Any tramp in the area used to claim blood-relationship with them.

'A sort of maternal uncle.' Or else, 'a sort of paternal uncle.'

In the end, no 'sort of' anyone! Just the three of them. But these three. . . . Umma cannot stand the sight of bapa. She finds fault with him for everything and abuses him too. Nor does she do it quietly; passers-by can hear it. People all over the place make fun of them, laugh at them. But what can be done? Umma always tries to find some new name to ridicule him with. Thus umma labelled bapa, 'Shrimp-dealer Adima'.

Bapa has not done business in shrimps. He tries jobs for which he does not need to have much capital. At one point he got into the dried-fish business. But he did not like it. The men smelt; the surroundings also smelt. There were dried flat-fish, shark, mackerel, sardine—things like this. Bapa piled them all into a basket and carried them on his head to a distant market. When he came back, he brought rice and other things and also fish for curry. Formerly Kunjupattumma used to eat fish and meat. Then eventually she stopped eating either.

It was after the murral swallowed the leech in the lily pond that she stopped eating fish. When bapa went out of the fish business and started selling mutton, she stopped eating meat also. Those eyes that do not close on the severed head. . . . Not that there is anything in them. But the sight of them upsets her. She has no objection to preparing fish or meat. The only thing is that she won't taste it. Somehow she learned to cook.

Early in the morning, by the time bapa has cleaned his teeth and finished his morning prayers, she will have got ready a cup of black tea. Bapa drinks it and walks away, tall and straight, reciting the 'Bismillah'. He will have with him two rupees in small change. With this money he goes to a distant market and buys bunches of bananas, yams, areca-nuts, coconuts or something for reselling.

Umma rises from sleep asking, 'Has shrimp-dealer Adima gone to change his gold?' By this time all the crows are busy cawing, day has broken and the sun is shining. Umma is not on good terms with God either. She does not say her prayers.

'I prayed a lot. What came of it? . . . Hey, you unlawful child, is the hot water ready?'

The water will have been heated. Kunjupattumma says, 'The hot water's ready, umma!'

If there is no hot water, umma will not bathe. So every day Kunjupattumma keeps the hot water ready. But umma finds fault with that also; either it is too hot; or it is not hot enough. After her bath, umma wants to wear clean clothes. She wants strong tea with plenty of milk and sugar, and some thick pattiri soaked in ghee. Whatever clothes they have—bapa's, umma's and her own—Kunjupattumma will have washed them before dusk and hung them out to dry. When umma has taken her bath, Kunjupattumma gives her her clothes. When it comes to tea and snacks . . . it will be tea without milk, sweetened with jaggery. Kunjupattumma has made the discovery that one can drink tea with salt instead of sweetening it. Umma does not like any of these things. Because there is no way of getting anything else, she gulps it down saying, 'You unlawful child, this is all because you were born!' During the first few days after they moved, umma used to bang the earthen bowl on the floor and break it. You need money to buy bowls every day. So bapa said on one occasion, 'From now on, give it to her only in coconut shells.'

Umma, who could not control her weeping, said, 'Are you listening, you blessed saints? Are you listening, Nabi? He says a coconut shell is good enough for Anamakkar's darling daughter!'

Even on that account, umma abuses Kunjupattumma.

'You are unlucky; your mole is a sign of bad luck!'

Is it possible to pinch off that black mole from her cheek?

Bapa's eyes become red with anger. He will call out softly, 'Hey, you, Kunjutachumma!' But there is a threat in those words. Umma will keep quiet. Then as soon as bapa goes out, umma starts again.

'Bastard! Bitch! Slut! You'll be bitten by a deadly snake! From the moment you were born. . . .'

So goes her abuse. The children walking in the street will jeer. Kunjupattumma will say, 'Please, umma, speak softly!'

'I will speak loudly. I am licensed to speak loudly!'

One day umma was talking about something in a loud voice. Bapa, who heard this as he was coming in, told her to keep quiet. Umma took no notice. Bapa told her again. With anger in his eyes, he went up to her.

Seeing this, umma laughed sarcastically and said in a singsong tone, 'Shrimp-dealer Adima has come to frighten Anamakkar's darling daughter!' Before she could finish saying this, something terrible happened.

With his right hand bapa caught umma by the throat. The grip on the throat became tighter. Umma's stare became fixed.

Between his teeth bapa said softly, 'I'll kill you!'

Bapa lifted umma by the neck with one hand as if she were a small child and then dropped her. He kicked both her wooden sandals outside. Umma lay there motionless!

All this happened in a flash. Kunjupattumma stood there petrified. It was as if the whole world had become dark and as if she had fallen into a deep pit. . . . See, bapa has killed umma! She could not make a sound. She stood there crying silently.

'There's no need to cry, child!' said bapa.

Kunjupattumma's weeping was uncontrollable. She stood there crying, crying bitterly. Oh Rabb al-Alamin! What is going to happen now? One calamity after another. There is no-one to help. Umma is gone. . . . Soon the police will handcuff bapa and take him away.

Now Kunjupattumma has no-one. . . . Umma's body. . . . Someone will wash it, cover it with a *kafan*, lay it in a *sanduq* and carry it to the burial ground chanting, 'La ilaha illallah! La ilaha illallah!' There she will be buried. . . . And then? . . . She was unable to think. Her eyes could not see. She cried aloud, 'Look what you have done, bapa!'

'My child,' said bapa. 'Don't cry. Go and sit on the

verandah.'

Somehow Kunjupattumma managed to get to the verandah and stood there holding on to the pillar. Without a
sound she cried and cried. She was unconsolable. As she
stood there, she thought of 'Sidrat al-Muntaha'.

It is in heaven. Sidrat al-Muntaha is the name of that huge
tree. She learned all this from the evening sermon she heard
at the mosque. On the leaves of that tree are written the
names of all living beings. When the wind blows, some of
these leaves will fall. The beings whose names are written
on these leaves will die. Of the leaves that fall, some are
dry, some green, and some tender. The leaf on which
umma's name is written. . . . While she was thinking of it,
she heard umma crying out from inside.

'Oh God,' umma was saying, 'I have no-one! Oh Mayyadin, I have no-one!'

All Kunjupattumma's sorrow has gone. She thought: The
wind blew—the leaf did not fall!

Kunjupattumma went in. Umma was sitting up. When she
saw Kunjupattumma, she started beating her chest and
crying.

'Please, umma, be calm!' Kunjupattumma said, as she
went up to her.

Then umma started speaking in a rhythmic fashion, more
like singing than talking, as she said, 'Rub me down!' she
said. 'In the name of the Prophet, rub me!'

Kunjupattumma did not know where to rub.

'Where, umma?' she asked.

'My neck, my legs, my arms,' umma replied.

'You move!' said bapa, and he went up to umma and
started rubbing her down. He told Kunjupattumma to go
and sit on the verandah. She did so.

From the verandah she heard them talking inside. At one
point umma asked, 'You want to kill me and marry again,
don't you?'

Kunjupattumma did not listen to what bapa said in reply.
She went outside and walked about. Then she heard bapa

saying rather loudly, 'Today we must all do *tawba*.'

To ask pardon of Rabb al-Alamin for the mistakes they have made. To promise not to repeat the same mistakes. That is a good thing. But there is no tawba book in the house. In almost all Muslim houses there will be one. It is in Arabic. Muslim leaders have had the Arabic written in Malayalam characters and printed. Bapa will borrow a copy from some house or other.

While Kunjupattumma was walking there, umma and bapa came out together on to the verandah. Umma was saying, 'I shall need oil, ointment, soap bark.'

Bapa agreed, and said to Kunjupattumma, 'My dear, get some water heated for umma to have a bath.'

He then went outside.

As Kunjupattumma was getting the water heated, bapa came back with the oil, ointment and soap bark. When umma started having the oil bath, bapa went out.

'Can I go and have a bath?' Kunjupattumma asked.

Umma consented! Kunjupattumma started off to the well with her bath towel, a change of clothes, a bucket and a rope.

Kunjupattumma did not know that setting off like this she was to start a new chapter in her life.

'Don't stay out long!' said umma.

'No; I'll be back right away,' she replied.

Even as she walked, she thought: Suppose the leaf had fallen when the wind blew. . . .

'Oh Rabb al-Alamin!' she prayed. 'Even if the wind blows, don't let our leaves fall!'

6)   The cry of a sparrow!

From the yard itself Kunjupattumma could hear the cry of a sparrow. As she walked further, she could see it also: two sparrows were pecking each other. One of them was crying bitterly!

What were they quarrelling about? Kunjupattumma made all kinds of noises: 'Shoo, shoo!' 'Hey, hey!' 'Brr!'—

and so on. And the two of them flew away.

As she set foot on the large wooden bridge by the lily pond to cross over into the next compound, she saw the sparrows in the tamarind tree pecking each other again. Not only that, one was crying. It was pleading for help like a chicken caught by a hawk. She felt very upset about it. She dropped the bucket and rope and ran towards them.

She tried to plead with them.

'Why are you quarrelling? Stop it!'

The sparrows took no notice. One was pecking the other fiercely. Although they are very small birds, see how they go at each other! This is the first time she has seen birds that are free quarrelling. When cockerels peck each other, somebody will take one of them away. If that is not done, one will be pecked to death.

'Don't you hear?' she said again. 'Stop it! Why are you pecking it?'

A squirrel, too, was interfering in this quarrel. It was sitting on the trunk of the tamarind tree making a chattering sound to try and stop them.

Kunjupattumma said, as if to the squirrel, 'They won't listen!'

A woodpecker called harshly as if to warn that it was not right for non-birds to interfere in matters concerning birds! Then it sat on the side of a coconut tree like a ball of red silk and started pecking away. The sparrows flew to another tree and started the quarrel again. The one that was getting the worse of it fell fluttering down and dropped into a dry ditch filled with dead leaves. It was lying there face downward with its two wings spread out, like a human being hugging the earth for the last time with his two outstretched arms.

'See!' said Kunjupattumma heart-broken, 'What an awful thing you have done!'

She went to the edge of the ditch. There was no way of getting down to the bird.

Is there any life left in it? If one gave a drop of water into its beak, it might live. Has the leaf on which its name is written fallen from the Sidrat al-Muntaha? How huge that tree must be! How numerous its leaves! All the leaves could not be of the same size. The one on which an ant's name is written will be a tiny one. It must be on a slightly bigger one that the sparrow's name is written. The one on which an elephant's name is written will be really big. The leaf bearing the name of her uppuppa's elephant must be lying dried up at the foot of Sidrat al-Muntaha. Could it have disintegrated and become part of the soil in heaven? Kunjupattumma does not know whether there is soil in heaven.

As she was about to climb down slowly, holding on to an uvaria tree that stood on the edge of the ditch, she fell crashing down along with the tree she was holding and the ground she was standing on.

'Oh my God!' she said as she fell. There was a bumping and a banging and a tearing. It was her left arm that was torn below the elbow. Blood was oozing out from the wound. She did not know anything of this at the time. She was all hot and flustered. Lying where she fell, she picked up the sparrow and then sat up. She thought it was already dead. Suppose she gave it a little water? Then she saw her arm bleeding.

Saying, 'Because of you my arm is torn,' she opened its beak slowly with the fingers of her left hand. With her right index finger she took a drop of blood and let it fall into its mouth. Then she arranged its wings carefully. She turned it over slowly, and when she saw the underside she said, much surprised, 'Oh Lord . . . it's the wife!' The skin on its belly was soft and pink. Through the feathers she clearly saw two tiny eggs. Like bapa trying to kill umma by strangling her. . . . Oh dear. . . .

'Why was the male sparrow pecking his wife to death?' she asked.

Then she realised that it was still alive. Its eyes were open. In them she saw the signs of life. Slowly she got up. At the time she did not notice a young man standing above her, on the edge of the ditch. She could see no way out and was frightened. If she walked along the ditch for some distance, she could get out into the field. But that was not proper. Because then she would have to walk along the public road. What was she to do? It was while she was standing there that she heard the sound of a voice. She didn't get scared. She fumed! Some strange man asking a question.

'Is the sparrow still alive?'

She did not say anything. Let him think that she had not heard. It was so embarrassing. She stood there with downcast eyes. Hundreds of ants had gathered round the blood that was on the dead leaves.

'Can't you get out?' Another question from above.

It was difficult to get out. But what could she say? She told the truth.

'It's difficult.'

'Is it difficult?'

'Yes.'

Was it proper to talk like this? What would people say? A Muslim girl of marriageable age talking to a man she has never seen or heard about! When she thought of that, Kunjupattumma got all worked up. As she was standing there, she saw pieces of earth falling down from the other side. He is coming down! . . . A young man dressed in a white shirt and a white dhoti. On his left wrist is a gold watch. His hair is well-groomed.

She could see only so much. He was coming down slowly, holding on to the uvaria tree. May he not fall the way she did! Lord take care of him. . . . She stood there filled with anxiety.

'I have never seen a girl like you before. What is the sparrow's name?' said the young man panting. He had a thin moustache and laughing eyes. Not as fair as she was. Thinking that he had asked for her name, she said, 'Kunjupattumma.'

'So your name is Kunjupattumma, then?'

'Yes.'

'That's good,' the young man said. 'Isn't it your blood that is all over these leaves?'

'Yes,' she said. Then she could feel the throbbing beneath her elbow. She turned her arm and looked at it. It was torn by some stone or stump. It was still bleeding.

'Let me see,' the young man said. 'Hold your arm up so that it won't bleed.'

Then he took out a handkerchief from his shirt pocket. He tore it into three strips and tied them together. After that he took a packet of cigarettes from his pocket, took a cigarette from it, removed the paper and put the tobacco in the palm of his hand.

'Lower your arm a little,' he said. She did so. He put the tobacco on the wound and pressed it slightly. She was afraid her breasts might touch this man's body and she bent her shoulders forward so as to avoid this. Then she noticed something that made her rather sad. To her sorrow he had no little finger on his left hand! It looked as though it had been cut off. . . . How had he lost it? . . . She did not ask.

'Does it burn?' he asked her.

'No.'

'Not even a little bit?'

'Slightly.'

'Hm. That doesn't matter. You should be careful not to wet your arm. After two or three days the wound will be healed.' With these words, the young man bandaged it neatly. After that he lit a cigarette and asked her with a smile, 'How will you get out?'

Kunjupattumma could not see a way. But she was not confused or afraid. It was like standing by the fire when it is cold. . . . Somehow that was how she felt.

'Let me see the sparrow.'

She opened her hand. The sparrow flew away with a small sound that showed gratitude or love—or something.

'Can you fly, Kunjupattumma?'

'No.'

'Then we'll make wings!' Saying this, the young man took Kunjupattumma's right hand and climbed on to the bank. As he was doing this, he encouraged her with such words as, 'Don't be afraid; come along.' She did not understand how she could climb up so effortlessly. In a sense it was a remarkable thing. When they got out, he said, 'Fine! Now you can go, Kunjupattumma,' and with a laugh disappeared into the ditch!

From that point Kunjupattumma moved as if in a dream. She felt as if every particle of her being glowed with happiness.

Taking the bucket, rope and clothes, she made her way into the neighbouring compound and went to the well. Before taking her bath, she picked a lot of jasmine flowers and put them together on a leaf. After that she took off her kuppayam, wrapped the bath towel round her and took off her mundu also. She let down her hair. Then she started to lower the bucket into the well. When it was about to touch the water, she thought of the young man and what he had said about not wetting her arm. It was almost like a miracle: at that moment she felt shy and confused; in her confusion she let the bucket and rope drop into the well. Hastily she grabbed her clothes, covered her breasts and squatted down! For that man had opened the door and come out.

'Oh . . . you are bathing, Kunjupattumma,' he said. 'I didn't know that. I wanted some water. I'll go away immediately. I just wanted a glass of water.'

'The bucket and rope fell into the well,' said Kunjupattumma softly.

'What? The bucket and rope. . . ?'

'Fell into the well.'

Then the young man laughed and looked into the well.

'How will you bathe now?' he asked. Kunjupattumma did not say anything. If she went back without the bucket and rope, umma would get angry.

The young man folded up his dhoti, climbed down into

the well and came back up with the bucket. He brought a glass, took some water and, as he was going off, said, 'Now you can bathe; don't get that cut wet.'

The young man went into the house and closed the door. Kunjupattumma put on her kuppayam, wrapped her mundu round her, picked up the bucket, rope and towel and walked slowly home. On reaching home, she drew water and took her bath. She thought of the young man: out of shyness or something her body and face were burning. Who is that man? How did he come to that house?

She could not eat that night. When asked, she said, 'I don't want anything!' When bapa asked, she said, 'My heart is aching!'

Even while they were all doing 'tawba' together, Kunjupattumma thought about the young stranger. When they were doing tawba, it was late at night. Sitting before the oil lamp, bapa recited from the Arabic book. With devotion she and umma repeated it. The three of them recited each word in three different tones. Three living beings were supplicating the creator of the world to pardon them.

Bapa began, 'Oh Almighty God . . . We come to thee, oh God, seeking forgiveness for all our small sins, for all our mortal sins, for sins committed in the open and for sins hidden from the sight of others. Repenting and fearful, we do tawba and return to thee, oh God.' Beginning like this, they go on to promise not to sin again, they beg to be saved from the snares of the scoundrel Iblis who diverts the heart from the right path. Then they say, 'Admit us all to the heaven which is Firdaus, to behold thy divine presence and the happiness of the revered Nabi with our two eyes and to partake of it. Grant us this grace, oh Lord!' They conclude by saying 'Amen.'

For a few days after that umma did not get too worked up. Then, although she used to say with love about Kunjupat-tumma, 'This is the child we got after long periods of prayer and painful waiting,' umma again started getting into a frenzy. She would swear and quarrel. She would abuse bapa also. To make bapa angry she would abuse Kunjupattumma. If Kunjupattumma said anything in reply, she would at once start with the same old thing.

'That's why nobody comes to marry you. You sit there and grow mouldy because you are unlucky. I was married at the age of fourteen. You are now twenty-two years old. Twenty-two!'

'Can't you keep quiet?' bapa would say. 'If the blessing of God is there, she will be married this year. I am on the look-out for a boy.'

'Oh, so somebody's going to marry her!'

In umma's opinion, nobody will come to marry Kunjupattumma.

'What will bring them here?'

Nothing. Is there anything to give as dowry? Are there any gold ornaments?

'Somebody will come!' bapa will say.

Who is it who is coming? It is a heart-burning question. What if somebody comes? There is no peace in the house. Always there is abuse and curses. Umma wants to give a hasty opinion about all and everything. She feels she should be consulted about everything that happens in the place. But nobody asks her opinion about anything. So she just sits and abuses people. Children who pass by make fun of umma. Then bapa has to interfere, or umma will go down to them on those old wooden sandals. She will abuse their fathers and grandfathers and all. She has a licence to do all this! She also wants a hand in the administration of the mosque. She thinks she should be consulted if they want to change the 'khatib' or the 'muqri' at the mosque. But nobody asks her. So umma sits and abuses everybody.

'Can't you keep quiet?' bapa will say.

'If I don't, what is shrimp-dealer Adima going to do about it?'

'What!' Bapa's tone and his look!... Kunjupattumma

will sit and shake: what is going to happen? Softly she will call, 'Bapa!'

Bapa will look at her sadly. Quietly he will go outside and walk around.

Once again umma and bapa cannot stand the sight of each other. . . . Why does it happen so? She will sit there and think about the young man. He is not to be seen. Where has he gone? Where did he come from? What is his name? What is his religion? She knows nothing about him, except that he is a fine man whom she has met once in her life. That face. That smile. That missing finger. . . . Somehow she will always remember that missing finger. That deserted house, the jasmine flowering by the well. There is nothing else in that spacious compound. Only the dried-up grass. Kunjupattumma untied what that unknown man had tied. When she looked, it was all dried up.

All this has become just a memory.

As the days passed like that, she heard that someone had bought that house and compound. Who was it? After two or three days she learnt to her great sorrow that it was someone from far away come on vacation. There are three people, all kafirs. An elderly man and an elderly woman, and a small kafir woman who is something of a show-off.

It pained Kunjupattumma deeply. She felt helpless. She was unlucky. With throbbing heart she would say to the Creator, 'Oh Rabb al-Alamin!'

Creator of the Universe! Simply that. She stood there bursting with longing.

What was she longing for?

7)   Silly booby!

One day at noon Kunjupattumma saw her neighbour, the kafir woman who was something of a show-off, by the lily pond taking off her sari and blouse.

That young woman was standing in her bodice and slip.

'Oh. A tight bodice under her kuppayam. . . . And under her mundu . . .,' Kunjupattumma thought to herself. Then suddenly she remembered.

'Oh my God! That small kafir woman's going to bath! The leeches'll bite her to death!'

Kunjupattumma ran out. Her hair came down. Yet she kept running. 'Don't bath! Don't bath!!' she called out. Panting she came up to the young woman.

Without showing any excitement, the young kafir woman said to Kunjupattumma, 'Booby! . . . You should say, "Don't bathe, don't bathe".'

Kunjupattumma said nothing. Right! Then let the leeches bite her to death! Hm. . . . So I should say, 'Don't bathe, don't bathe'! What if I say 'Don't bath, don't bath'? See the way she shows off!—Kunjupattumma thought. All kafir women must be like this! But then she thought of the old days; she pictured bapa taking her to the river all dressed up. During those days, all those kafir school-mistresses were really kind and friendly to her. Although like them this girl wore a sari . . . she was more of a swank than them. Kunjupattumma moved towards the edge of the lily pond to look at the murral.

'Oh . . . what fine hair!' the swank was saying. 'And a black mole! Beautiful!' And with this she put on her blouse and wrapped her sari and went up to Kunjupattumma. Then, very seriously, she asked, 'Sundari! Anyone so beautiful must be called Sundari. Is there any law against the public bathing in this lily pond?'

'My name is not Tunnari!'

'Tunnari you say!' The show-off laughed. 'Booby, you must say Sundari. Very well, what is your name?'

'Kunjupattumma.'

'Oh. A beautiful name! Fine. What happens if one bathes in this lily pond?'

'The leeches will bite you!'

'Male leech or female leech?'

'There were both husband and wife. One of them bit me and drank all my blood!' Kunjupattumma continued, 'Then the murral swallowed it whole. There are water-snakes and turtles too.' After that Kunjupattumma described with great excitement how the leech had bitten her. When she came to how it hung from her thigh, the show-off shivered and stared. She made a noise like the trumpeting of a small elephant. 'If it had been me,' the show-off said, 'I would have called out and got all and sundry to come. In the end I would have passed out!'

Kunjupattumma had not called out! Neither had she fainted. She was proud about that. She walked to the foot of the tamarind tree. Picking up a ripe tamarind, she shelled it and put some in her mouth.

The show-off went up to her and asked, 'Are you eating tamarind?'

'Yes.' Would all women like tamarind? Kunjupattumma was doubtful. Still she asked, 'Do you want some?'

'Give me a small piece!' When she said this, her mouth was watering, Kunjupattumma thought! She gave her a big piece. The show-off took it and ate it. Not the way ordinary women will eat. She didn't squint or show any reaction on her face! The swanky kafir woman swallowed it seed and all!

Kunjupattumma, wonderstruck, said, 'Shouldn't swallow!'

'What if I do?'

'It will sprout in the stomach and become a big tree!'

'I can digest even granite!' said the show-off. 'People say it's because of my age!' Kunjupattumma gave her a big piece and asked, 'How old are you?'

'Seventeen.'

'Umma says I am twenty-two,' said Kunjupattumma.

'And what does bapa say?'

Kunjupattumma did not reply.

'You booby, why don't you say something?'

'Why d'you ca' me booby?'

'Not like that, booby. You must ask, "Why do you call me booby?" Are you asking why I call you booby? I don't know. My ikkakka calls me "silly booby".'

Ikkakka! Why is this kafir calling her brother 'ikkakka'—
a term used only by Muslims?

'I had the impression that "silly booby" was a synonym
for "girl". My ikkakka calls me Luttapy too. He likes
making up names.'

'What's your ikkakka's name?'

'Nisar Ahmad!'

'Nisar Ahmad. . . . And what's your name?'

'Aisha,' said the show-off.

'What's your religion?'

That sari-wearing toff said, 'Muslim.'

Good God! 'Are you like us?' Kunjupattumma asked.

'No: we are genuine Muslims!'

Genuine Muslims. . . ! She has not had her ears pierced
for halqats. In the lobes of her ears there are two gold
earrings. What she is wearing is a sari. She has a blouse
instead of a kuppayam. Underneath that she has a tight
bodice.

'What did you say your name was?'

'Aisha. If you want, you can call me Aisha Bibi, or Begum
Aisha. At school they called me Aisha Bibi. At home my
bapa and umma call me Aisha. I told you that my ikkakka
calls me "Luttapy"—except when he calls me "Silly
booby".'

Aisha! It is the Prophet Muhammad's wife's name!

Kunjupattumma looked at her with disbelief. What kind
of Muslims are they?

'Who's that man with no beard and an unshaven head?'
Kunjupattumma asked.

Aisha said, mimicking Kunjupattumma a little to make fun
of her, 'Me bapa . . . and that woman in the sari's me umma.'
Then Aisha asked, 'Is that tall man your bapa?'

'Yes.'

'And the woman who talks day and night?'

'Umma.'

'Why does she talk so loud?' Aisha asked. 'The neighbours won't be able to sleep for the noise. Is it good for

Muslim women to be like this, lacking all restraint and moderation?'

Kunjupattumma did not say anything.

'Why does your umma come to the stream in front of our house to relieve herself?' Aisha asked.

'If it's noight we use the road outside the house. It's because it was daytime that she went to the stream!'

'That's great!... Is it nice to use the public road for that! Do all the people here use the public road...?'

'Yes,' said Kunjupattumma.

'Why don't you make latrines in the house?'

When Kunjupattumma did not reply, Aisha said, 'Another thing—you mustn't say "noight". Say "night".'

'Neight,' said Kunjupattumma.

'Not like that. "I" as in "white". Say it. Night.'

Kunjupattumma said, 'Night,' and then asked, 'Where's yer 'ouse?'

'You must ask, "Where is your home?" Let's suppose you asked in that way. What shall I say? I must speak the truth. We don't own a home. But we have a house in the town. We hold the mortgage on it. We cultivate the land. There are mango trees, guavas, jambus, jasmine, roses—and many other trees from which you can get fruits and flowers.

Then she described the house. 'It's a tiled house with two floors. There is a yellow wall around it. The gate is blue. There is electric light in every room. We also have a radio.'

'What is that?' Kunjupattumma asked. All the rest she understood. She had seen 'lectic light' that shines when you press a button. But she did not understand what radio was.

'It's like a box,' said Aisha. 'From that you can hear the news and songs.'

'Can you hear anything from Mecca?'

'Arabia, Turkey, Afghanistan, Russia, Africa, Madras, Germany, America, Singapore, Delhi, Karachi, Lahore, Mysore, England, Australia, Calcutta, Ceylon—you can hear from almost all the places in the world,' said Aisha.

Kunjupattumma did not really understand what it was.

Whatever it is, this girl is showing off too much.

'Do you have a tamarind tree at your house?' Kunjupat-tumma asked.

'No!'

So—isn't tamarind tree more important! Kunjupattumma asked another question.

'Silly booby. . . . Did you 'ave an elephant?'

'No!'

With great pride Kunjupattumma said, 'Me uppuppa 'ad an elephant!—a 'uge tusker!'

'My uppuppa had a bullock cart,' said Aisha. 'He used to carry things in it and make money. With that he educated my bapa up to M.A. . . . And what about your big tusker? Where is it?'

'It died—I mean, passed away!' Because it is a Muslim's elephant, one has to say 'passed away' or 'breathed its last'. One should use 'passed away' for a Muslim and 'died' for a kafir.

'Oh, is it dead?' Aisha asked.

'Yes!' said Kunjupattumma. 'It passed away. It killed four kafirs!'

'Only four? How many Muslims did it kill?'

'None. It was a fine elephant!'

'If that is the truth,' said Aisha laughing, 'in heaven that tusker will get four mansions made of gems and precious stones, pearls and rubies.'

This is because those who do good in this world will get many pleasures and comforts in the next. According to tradition, it is a good deed to kill a kafir.

'We were very well-off!' said Kunjupattumma.

'Then what happened?'

All she knows is that 'It's gone'.

'What does your bapa do?' Aisha asked.

'Business.'

'In what?'

'Oh, this and that.'

'What's your bapa's name?'

'Vattan Adima.'

'And your umma's?'

'Kunjutachumma.'

'My bapa is a college professor,' said Aisha. 'His name is Zainal Abidin. Umma's name is Hajara Bibi. Ikkakka is Nisar Ahmad. He is a poet. He writes poetry on the earth. His poems become trees, flowers, fruits and vegetables.' Aisha has a lot of things like this to say about Nisar Ahmad. She continued, 'He loves this earth with everything that is and could be on it. He's very clean and tidy; he's a . . . terrible man.'

Kunjupattumma was not interested in any of this. Especially those names. Zainal Abidin, Nisar Ahmad. . . . She has never heard such names. Makkar, Adima, Antu, Kochuparo, Kutti, Kutti Ali, Bava, Kunjalu, Pakkaru Kunju, Maidin, Avaran, Biran, Kunjikochu, Addilu—all these she has heard. But Nisar Ahmad. . . . Big red eyes, long, curled-up moustache, a chest covered in black hair, a thick neck, a tall frame—this is how she pictured him. She asked, 'When will your ikkakka come?'

'Tomorrow or the day after—anyway, tell your umma right away not to come so close to us to relieve herself. When ikkakka comes, there will be trouble!'

Kunjupattumma was shocked. How could she tell umma? How could she not tell her? She prayed silently, 'Oh God, don't let Tuttapy's ikkakka come! If he comes, there'll be trouble!'

That terrible man!

'Are you married?' Aisha asked.

'No,' said Kunjupattumma, 'I'm not married. Are you married, Tuttapy?'

'You silly booby! . . . It's Luttapy. No. I'll get married after I've completed my B.A. Even then it will be only after ikkakka's wedding. We have not so far been able to find a suitable girl for that great guy. Many proposals came. I told you, didn't I, that he was very clean and tidy? Not only the girl, but the house also should be tidy. Once he went to the house of a university-educated girl from where there was a proposal. The glass in which he was given water to drink smelt of fish. Because of that the proposal was turned down.'

'Doesn't your ikkakka eat fish?' Kunjupattumma asked.

'In general he's a vegetarian. Just once in a while he eats meat and fish. But then he washes with soap. He has ordered that the house must never stink of these! Not only that: the girl he marries should have certain qualities. She must know how to shave. She should be skilled in washing, painting, dancing and music, and should be well-read. Her skill in cooking should include biriyani, pattiri and meat, sambar, curry, aviyal, kalan, dry vegetable dishes, and all imaginable things to eat and drink. In addition to this, she should know how to till the ground, carry soil, prepare manure for plants and trees. Umma and bapa have told him to find a girl with all these qualities and marry her.'

When Kunjupattumma heard so much, Nisar Ahmad became more terrible in her imagination. She felt angry with him. She felt angry with Aisha also. Ikkakka said this, ikkakka said that. . . . Oh, blow her ikkakka!

Aisha continued, 'A man like my ikkakka. . . . Would you like to hear? One night ikkakka was lying on the easy chair, reading. His hand was in one end of the drawer. I hadn't noticed this and I pushed the drawer in with great force. I heard something crack. When I saw what it was— I almost fainted: the small finger on ikkakka's left hand was crushed!'

Kunjupattumma was flabbergasted. More than that, she grew pale!

'And then?' she asked.

'Oh,' said Aisha, 'ikkakka didn't move. He asked me to go and get the scissors. I brought them. Ikkakka cut off the smashed finger!' After giving this description of what happened, Aisha then said, 'I'm going. Would you like to come to our place?'

Kunjupattumma did not hear. She stood there numb.

Aisha asked again, 'Are you coming?'

'Where?'

'To my house, silly booby!'

'I'll ask umma and come.'

She went home and said to umma, 'Umma, those people next door are Muslims. Can I go there?'

'Don't give me that, you bitch!' umma said. 'Muslims! They're kafirs.'

'No, umma,' she said. 'They're Muslims. Look: their Aisha is standing under our tamarind tree.'

Umma looked. Umma saw! A woman dressed in a sari! No halqats in her ears! Umma said, 'Oh Mayyadin, oh you saints! Is she a Muslim?'

'Yes, umma. Talk quietly. Can I go to her house?'

'If you step outside our yard, you are no longer my daughter. Don't come back!'

Kunjupattumma went and told Aisha, 'I'll come to-morrow.'

'Why not today?'

'I have a few things to do,' said Kunjupattumma. 'I must draw water. When I come tomorrow, I'll bring some ripe tamarind.'

Aisha went off.

That night for a long time Kunjupattumma could not get to sleep. Earlier she had prayed to God not to let Aisha's ikkakka come. How could she ask for the opposite now? In the end she prayed, 'Oh, God, let Tuttapy's ikkakka....'

8)   'I cannot bear false witness!'

Umma said very confidently, 'They are not Muslims! It is I, Anamakkar's darling daughter, who am telling you—they are not Muslims!'

Kunjupattumma would look at bapa's face. Bapa would say nothing.

Umma would continue, 'Do you see the signs of qiyamat?'

Aisha and her father and mother are signs that the world is coming to an end!

'Look, that woman has flowers on her hair . . . flowers!'
Aisha wears flowers in her hair. Is that proper for a
Muslim?

'And did you ever see such a sight as that girl. She has
done her hair in two pigtails and brings them in front over
her shoulders!'

Aisha does many tricks with her hair: she's completely
crazy. She'll run, jump, skip, dance and sing. One day she
gave an ecstatic rendering of a song, while standing by the
lily pond. Kunjupattumma thought that she was entreating
God for something. Then she thought it could be a *'bayt'*
or *'qissa'*. She did not understand what it was. She too
lifted her hands in devotion and said 'Amen' at regular
intervals and then again at the end. Aisha did not laugh.
She pretended to cough. But later on Kunjupattumma
realised that she was trying to stifle her laughter.

'What were you singing?' she asked.

'Don't ask me,' said Aisha. 'I'm a complete ignoramus.
When that great guy comes, ask him. He's the one who
wrote it. Nobody knows in what language. He composed
it for the girls in our college to sing in a procession. And we
sang it for the procession.'

'When you were singing, I was saying "amen"!'

'I noticed!'

'Is it bad to say "amen"?'

'Silly booby, it can never be bad.'

'Then sing it again. It's beautiful.'

'Sit there in an attitude of meditation. Put everything else
out of your mind, and pay careful attention. Imagine this:
There is a big procession of college girls. They—I should
say we—are moving forward, carrying flags and singing!'

'All right.'

'Then listen!' And she sang:

'La . . . la . . . la . . .
Huttini halitta littapo
Sanjini balikka luttapi
Halitha manikka linjalo

Sankara bahana tulipi
Hanjini hilatta huttalo
Fanatta lakkidi jimbalo
Da . . . da . . . da!
La . . . la . . . la!'

Aisha then explained, 'I'm not sure that all of this is right. I suspect I have left out a few words. If that is the case, he'll beat us!'

'How will your ikkakka know about it?' Kunjupattumma asked.

'Are you asking how he'll know? Well! As soon as he comes, he'll call me and say, "Luttapy! Come here. Come and stand in this circle!" I shall stand in that circle. Ikkakka will say, "Sing!" If I don't sing, he'll cut me into two thousand pieces and feed me to two thousand birds. Then he'll shoot all those birds, fry them and eat them!'

'Shouldn't they be properly bled?'

Before such flesh is eaten, the creatures should be ritually bled in the name of Allah to make it halal.

'Booby!' Aisha said. 'I'm talking about what happens after killing a good girl like me! Do you have to do wuzu before stealing the Mushaf?'

It is not necessary to be externally clean to steal a holy book! Aisha says many things like this. Sometimes she brings newspapers and reads some disturbing news to Kunjupattumma. For Kunjupattumma to believe that the newspaper had such terrible news was. . . . She will just stand there showing her disbelief. Aisha will point to the news and read it again. It is all most surprising to Kunjupattumma. She will say so too. Once when she said so, Aisha asked her, 'Why didn't they send you to school?—You were so very rich.'

That's true. They really were rich. There was no difficulty for anything. If she had learnt to read and write then, . . . today she would have been better-informed than Aisha. . . . Everything would have been different from today. Why didn't bapa and umma do that?

That night she thought about it. Why wasn't she educated? Lying on the mat, she asked bapa through the darkness, 'Bapa, . . . wh . . . why didn't you send me to school?'

Bapa just sighed. Umma said, 'Are you asking why we didn't send you to school to become a kafir?'

If you learn to read and write . . . and if you are well-informed . . . it is not possible to live like a Muslim! Is this true?

The next day Kunjupattumma asked Aisha about it. Aisha laughed! See where ignorance leads. . . . People can increase their ignorance! Just as they can increase their knowledge. Depending on what you want, you can develop either the good or the bad.

'Look,' Aisha said, 'Muslims should be well-informed. Those who are ignorant are *hamkin*. Are Muslims ignorant?'

Is a Muslim a silly ass? Kunjupattumma knows well that he is not. Yet. . . .

'Shouldn't we act differently from kafirs?' she asked.

They should distinguish themselves from kafirs.

'That's right,' said Aisha. 'When a kafir walks with his feet, a Muslim should walk with his head. A kafir takes a bath and brushes his teeth, so a Muslim shouldn't do either. Because a kafir eats with his mouth, a Muslim. . . .'

'Please stop it, Tuttapy!' said Kunjupattumma, offended. 'Why do you tease me?'

'Booby, silly booby! In what Allah and Muhammad Nabi have commanded, there is nothing like this "acting differently"!'

'Who did Allah create in the very beginning?' Kunjupattumma asked.

'We can't tell,' said Aisha. 'But among men were Adam Nabi and Eve Bibi.'

'Wasn't it Muhammad Nabi?'

'Who told you this? What the Koran says is that it was Adam Nabi. That is what we must believe. We must not put our trust in myths and fables. We should live like Muslims. We should be good human beings. We should be clean and healthy. There should be beauty in our lives. We should not hurt others. We should be truthful. We should have faith in Allah and the Prophet. There are hundreds of things like these. We should act differently only in respect of evil, not try indiscriminately to "act differently" from others. Muslims are those who follow these precepts. If you are still doubtful, you can ask ikkakka when he comes.'

But as soon as Nisar Ahmad came, bapa took a butcher's knife to cut his head off. Umma was behind this.

Nisar Ahmad brought a forest with him. Kunjupattumma did not know how or from where he brought it. It consisted mainly of fruit trees. And a lot of young coconut trees. Within a day that barren compound turned into a beautiful garden. All the trees were planted in lines and evenly spaced.

The whole place was in a turmoil. Kunjupattumma was surprised to see Nisar Ahmad, his bapa and Aisha working together in the sun.

'Do you see that, umma!' Kunjupattumma called to her mother. Umma put on her wooden sandals and came clip-clopping to the door.

'Oh, they're crazy!' she said and went back inside. Kunjupattumma did not think so. The only thing was that she was surprised. She had not seen Muslims who worked on the land. She believed that trade was the only thing for them. If the necessity arose to dig or till—that was done by workmen. Doing this on your own. . . . She was seeing it for the first time.

She felt bad, because their own land also was uncultivated. There was ample space to grow many things. If only she had a brother! But she was helpless. Kunjupattumma had done certain things in anticipation of Nisar Ahmad's arrival. She swept up all the rubbish and burnt it. She swept up and threw away all the waste that was left in front of the kitchen from cleaning fish. She tidied up the whole house.

She burnt all the old and torn clothes that were hanging in front of the house. In addition to all his, she tidied herself up too. When she saw all this hustle and bustle, umma said, 'What's all the excitement about?'

The first thing that Nisar Ahmad asked when he saw Kunjupatumma was, 'Has the cut on your arm dried up?'

'Yes, it has,' said Kunjupattumma. He remembered it even after such a long period! She was surprised at that. Kunjupattumma was filled with confusion and bewilderment. She was not sure whether it was before or after Nisar Ahmad came there the second time. Although she could not remember *when* it was, she could remember clearly what he said and what he did.

Nisar Ahmad made a privy for Kunjupattumma's house. A ditch twelve feet long by four feet wide and a yard deep. It was Nisar Ahmad who dug it. Bapa could not help him in any way, as he did not know what to do. Kunjupattumma was unable to hear what they were talking about, since it was in a corner of the compound a good distance from the house. He was perspiring as he worked in the sun. Then bapa came and said, 'Would you get some water for him to drink?'

Kunjupattumma went indoors. With a small piece of soap she washed two bowls. She smelt them to see if they were clean enough. There was no smell. She brought the water and gave it to her father. Before drinking the water, Nisar Ahmad sniffed at the bowl discreetly. Only then did he drink it. Kunjupattumma can swear that he did that.

When the work on the privy was completed, Kunjupattumma went to look at it. A small ditch within a fenced enclosure. Over it, two planks. All the sand heaped up on one side. On the sand was a coconut-shell. 'After using the privy, you should put some sand over it. The coconut-shell is for that,' Aisha said. 'In time this ditch will be filled. Then we must make another.'

'Why didn't we think about it sooner,' bapa said. 'If there was one like this in every house, the whole place wouldn't smell so bad.'

After that incident, bapa liked Nisar Ahmad very much. Meantime his doubts increased. He had hundreds of questions. Isn't the end of the world approaching? Why do people become so proud and wicked?

'I don't know,' Nisar Ahmad would say. 'We know that if we are born, we shall die some day. I shall die. You will die. Everyone will die. Maybe the world too will perish one day. What of it? Let it perish when it will. Till then one must live happily. It is because people lack intelligence that they become proud and wicked. There must be someone to direct them in the right path. We must not think that people are bad, but try to make them better.'

Then bapa has another doubt.

'Is it possible to reform a cobra?'

'Why do you ask?'

'There are people as poisonous as cobras. I have also seen people who are like jackals, tigers, monkeys.'

'Doesn't man tame them and make them do as he wants?'

'Still . . . ?'

The two of them will sit quietly and think.

Once umma asked, 'Ayamad, why do you grow all these trees?'

Sitting behind the door, Kunjupattumma said to herself, 'It's not Ayamad; his name is Nisar Ahmad.'

'They are not just any old tree,' said Nisar Ahmad. 'In two or three years I'll give you mangoes, guavas, pineapples, papayas and so on.'

'Why hasn't your umma come to see us?' umma asked.

'Umma is scared after the other day's quarrel,' said Aisha. They all laughed.

It was the day after Nisar Ahmad came. When Kunjupattumma knew that he had come, she felt both happy and afraid. The heartache she had felt earlier increased. Not only that, she had no appetite. She started losing weight. Then it happened.

Nisar Ahmad and Aisha were watering the trees and

plants.

Watching them both, but not showing that she was, Kunjupattumma was in the front yard pulling out a few weeds. She did not know what time it was. The sun had come up over the tamarind tree. As usual umma went to use the small stream.

Nisar Ahmad called out, 'I say! Just a minute!'

Umma turned in a frenzy.

Nisar just told her that it was not proper to do that right in front of them.

'Do you know who you are talking to?' umma asked.

Kunjupattumma called out, 'Umma, come away!'

'What will you do to me?' umma asked Nisar Ahmad.

Nisar Ahmad laughed.

Umma was shaking with rage as she said, 'What's the idea, bawling out women without any reason?'

When bapa came, umma complained, 'They won't leave us alone! Oh Mayyadin! They won't leave us alone!'

'What's up?'

'He came and peeped! While I was squatting there, he came and peeped! Oh Mayyadin! They won't leave us alone!'

'Who?' Bapa's eyes blazed with anger.

'Him,' said umma.

'Which one?' Bapa came out brandishing a butcher's knife. 'I'll slit his throat; who is it?'

'That chap who has come to live next d . . . !' Before she could finish saying this, Nisar Ahmad came up and greeted them: 'Salam alaikum.'

Bapa looked at that well-groomed head and the dhoti wrapped to the right. He didn't seem to be a Muslim; yet bapa returned the salutation, though in great anger.

'Wa alaikum salam!'

'We are the people who live next door,' said Nisar Ahmad. 'There's bapa, umma, my sister and myself.'

'Are you Muslims?'

'Yes!'

'What sort of Muslims?'

'We'll talk about religion later. Let us be anybody you like: supposing we are Hindus, or Christians—is it proper to ... ?'

'If it isn't?'

'Bapa,' Kunjupattumma called from inside. 'Bapa!'

'What is it, my dear?'

'What umma says is. . . .' At that umma put her hand over Kunjupattumma's mouth. 'Bitch! Spare my honour! I'm your umma! Anamakkar's darling daughter!'

Kunjupattumma pushed her hand away.

'Umma's not telling the truth,' she said loudly.

'You bitch! Mayyadin! How could I have borne such a daughter!'

Bapa came in asking, 'What is it, my dear?'

'I cannot bear false witness!' Kunjupattumma said. 'What umma says is not true!'

'Kunjupattumma!' umma said. 'Yer uppuppa 'ad an elephant!—A 'uge tusker!'

'Even then, I can't bear false witness!'

'What is it, my dear?' bapa asked.

'Umma is not telling the truth,' said Kunjupattumma. 'He just stood there and said, "I say!" Then he asked whether it was proper for her to go so close to them to relieve herself. For that umma got mad. That's all that happened.'

'I have no-one!' said umma.

'Kunjutachumma! I'll cut you into pieces, little pieces!'

'You can kill me! Here's my neck. Mayyadin, here's my neck! Ye saints, here's my neck! I have no-one!'

Umma sat down and wept. Bapa went out and said very meekly to Nisar Ahmad, 'We are poor people! What do you want us to do?'

'We are also poor,' said Nisar Ahmad. 'We don't have a place of our own. The house we live in in town is rented. Now we've bought this place. My interest is in farming.'

'This house and compound that we live in are our own,' said bapa. 'But we don't have a proper place for this. See, the whole place is open. Most of the people here wait till it gets dark. For my wife and daughter to use the public road. . . . You see, we have seen better days. People who used to get up when they saw us don't do that any more! Can my wife and daughter go and squat among them on the public road?'

'The public thoroughfare is not a place for people to ease themselves,' said Nisar Ahmad.

'What else can they do?'

'They should make their own privies. It's not expensive. All we need is half a dozen plaited coconut leaves, half a dozen stakes and some rope. It's a matter of an hour's work with pick and shovel. There is no further difficulty for a year. Why don't people do this? In towns there is the question of space. That's not the case here. A beautiful village. A good river. More than enough space. Would you do something on the lines I suggest. Could you get half a dozen or so stakes, some rope, a spade and a few coconut leaves?'

'That's no problem.'

'Good! Get these things and let me know.'

Nisar Ahmad went back home. Straight away bapa went to fetch the things. Then umma said to Kunjupattumma, 'You're not my daughter!'

Kunjupattumma did not say anything.

'You're no child of mine!' said umma.

Kunjupattumma did not say anything.

'You bitch, have you lost your tongue?'

Kunjupattumma still did not say anything.

'Why don't you speak?' umma asked. 'Are you frightened you'll lose your bangles?'

'There are no bangles on my wrist!' said Kunjupattumma.

'Who matters most to you,' umma asked, 'your darling umma or him?'

Kunjupattumma did not reply.

'Where's all shrimp-dealer Adima's big talk gone now?' said umma. 'Just look! This shrimp-dealer agreed with all he said! What are these coconut leaves and stakes for? To make a tomb?'

Kunjupattumma kept quiet.

'Why did you stand witness for him?' umma asked.

Kunjupatumma kept quiet.

'Couldn't you spare your dear umma's honour?' umma asked.

'I cannot bear false witness!' said Kunjupattumma.

'What happens if you do; are you frightened you'll lose your necklace?'

'There's no necklace round my neck!'

'Then why did you have to let me down?'

'Suppose bapa had slit his throat with that knife?'

'What do we care?'

'If the police had taken bapa and beaten him to death?'

For some time umma did not say anything. After a while she said, 'Oh God, that's true!' and went up to Kunjupattumma.

'My darling daughter! You saved our family!... Why have you looked off colour for some days?'

'Me heart is aching, umma!'

'Oh God, is she possessed by some ifrit or jinni?'

9)   'Me heart is aching!'

Even Kunjupattumma does not know what has happened to her. Bapa got a string dedicated by the khatib in the mosque and hung it round her neck. In addition to that there was something presented by an elder, namely a 'charm' in the shape of a tiny suitcase hanging from her neck. Still the 'ifrit' did not leave her. One day Aisha came with a message from Nisar Ahmad. Kunjupattumma thought it was very kind of him and listened most attentively. But when she heard what Aisha said, Kunjupattumma realised that they were making fun of her.

'Get off with you, Tuttapy!' she said.

'This will get rid of any kind of Satan,' said Aisha. 'The ifrit will be driven away in no time! You must just walk with it hanging from your neck. It's that big leather suitcase of ikkakka's. Shall I bring it?'

Kunjupattumma said, 'Silly booby, don't tease me!'

Immediately she felt sad.

Aisha asked seriously, 'What has happened to you?'

'Me heart is aching!'

It's not just a sharp stab of pain, but a tight throbbing pain. She will feel like just sitting and crying: then she will want to laugh. She likes laughter better than tears. Not to laugh out loud, but to think of things and smile. Then she will want to burst into tears. When she sees Nisar Ahmad, her cheeks burn and her breasts feel tight and heavy. She would like to ask Nisar Ahmad as if offended, 'Why do you look at me?' But then, what if Nisar Ahmad does not look at her again? Not that he has looked at her really. She would like him to look at her. She will go and stand in a place where he can see her. 'I have come here to gather kindling, haven't I?' she will say to herself. She will always find some excuse to go next door. 'Fire' is a frequent excuse. If not that, then 'salt', and if not that, then Aisha. On whatever pretext she goes there, she never meets Nisar Ahmad at a convenient spot. He is either cleaning the yard or watering the trees. What is there that needs so much cleaning? It is nicely spread with golden sand. Around that are flowering shrubs. If he is not working, he is reading. 'What is he reading so much?' she would ask herself.

One day when she looked, Nisar Ahmad was lying down at the foot of a tree. There was a book on his stomach. He was just lying there.

Her heart glowed with a pleasant warmth. Nisar Ahmad was looking upwards at the sky. To the west he could see the clouds in their many colours. The glowing red was reflected on the backs of passing birds.

She was firm in her resolve. That day she wore white. The kuppayam that she had not worn for a long time lay tight on her body. The material she used to cover her head was very fine. She did not know why she dressed like that. She looked in the mirror for a long time. Her eyelids had a kind of dark splendour. The black mole on her cheek shone like a beauty spot. With her big clear eyes she looked at herself. She smiled. She wanted to cry. But she laughed.

Showing no expression on her face, she started to walk next door. Her heart was beating fast.

Nisar Ahmad's look fell on her. A very pleasant look!

She took some fire. Kunjupattumma did not stay to talk to Aisha or her umma. She went back home quickly. As she was going, Nisar Ahmad called her.

'I say!'

That call went through her soul like a flash of lightning. Unable to take one step forward, she stood there. She felt a burning sensation. She felt afraid, confused and happy.... With all these emotions she looked at him.

Nisar Ahmad got up and walked towards her.

'I need a light,' he said, and took the firebrand to light a cigarette.

'Kunjupattumma,' Nisar Ahmad said, 'you remember that sparrow? It came to me and asked how you were. I said, "She is walking around with a suitcase tied around her neck to drive away some Ifrit!"'

'Give me the firebrand!'

'Kunjupattumma!'

'Yes?'

'What has happened to you?'

'Me heart is aching!'

'Can you get rid of it by tying that thing round your neck?'

'Give me the firebrand!'

'Haven't you learned to read and write?'

'Nobody learnt me.'

'Ask Aisha to teach you from tomorrow, will you?'

'Tuttapy will play me up!'

'If Luttapy plays you up, I'll cut her into two thousand pieces....'

'No; please don't do anything to Tuttapy! Give me the

firebrand!'

'I'll tell Luttapy. All right?'

Somehow she managed to get the firebrand. She felt like running. But she walked away slowly. The world stood bathed in a new light. Everything seemed more beautiful. She felt love towards everything. When an ant bit her, Kunjupattumma said to it in spite of her pain, 'Don't bite everybody as you bit me!' She picked it up and put it on the ground. She felt the night most beautiful. Umma and bapa were fast asleep and snoring, but she could not get to sleep. She thought about Nisar Ahmad and smiled. She pretended to be offended. She pinched the pillow and asked, 'Did it hurt?' As she asked this question, her eyes filled with tears. The next moment she smiled. In the end she slept.

The next day, as she was standing outside after lunch, Aisha came with a big stick in her hand and two books under her arm and called to Kunjupattumma in a serious tone. She had no idea for what purpose Aisha took her to the foot of the tamarind tree and made a circle with the stick.

'Stand right in the centre!' she ordered.

'What for, Tuttapy?' Kunjupattumma asked as she stood in the circle.

'Stretch out your right hand!' Aisha ordered again.

'Are you going to beat me?'

'Stretch it out!'

Kunjupattumma stretched out her hand. Aisha put a pencil, a notebook and a reader into the hand.

'From today, I'm your teacher,' Aisha said.

Kunjupattumma laughed.

'My pupil should not have any secrets that I don't know about!' said Aisha. 'You must tell everything openly. Only after that will the lessons start! Just what is going on between that great guy who is my brother and you?'

'Don't tease me, Tuttapy!'

'Are you going to tell me openly, or are you going to get a beating? I'll cut you into four thousand pieces. Tell me.'

'Get off with you, Tuttapy!'

'Tell me!'

'What?'

'What's the relationship between my ikkakka and you?' she said, as if to hurt Kunjupattumma.

'Don't tease me, Tuttapy.'

Aisha kept quiet for some time and then asked, 'Do you know how to dance?'

She didn't know what dancing was.

'No,' she said.

'Do you know how to shave, wash, cook, paint ... or any such thing?'

'Don't tease me, Tuttapy! I don't know how. Why don't you teach me?'

'Then listen. There are no other such silly boobies in this world as men.'

'Don't talk like that, Tuttapy!'

Then Kunjupattumma found something to divert Aisha's attention. Two or three ants were dragging a dead fly over the grass.

'Tuttapy,' she said, 'a small leaf must just have fallen from that great tree, Sidrat al-Muntaha. Look there!'

'We are talking about a very serious matter,' said Aisha. 'Do you want to learn to read and write?'

'Yes, I do!'

'Good; then give a correct reply to what I ask: when did you make ikkakka's acquaintance?'

'Teach me to read and write, Tuttapy!'

'Wasn't it me with whom you made friends first?'

'No, Tuttapy,' said Kunjupattumma.

'What?' Aisha asked with some surprise. 'You say it wasn't me?'

'No. It wasn't you.'

'Tell me about it.'

'Before you all came, I used to go to your well to have a bath. One day a cock sparrow was pecking a hen sparrow to death. The hen sparrow fell into the ditch. When I went to look at it, I also fell in. My arm was torn and it bled a lot. I gave some blood to the sparrow. It had two eggs in its belly. Then your ikkakka. . . .'

'Ikkakka?'

'Yes. He was watching all this. He came down and bandaged my arm. He got me out of the ditch and asked me not to wet my arm while bathing.'

'What happened to the sparrow?'

'It flew away home.'

'I see,' Aisha said to herself. 'This is the wonderful thing that Kunjupattumma did!'

'What is it, Tuttapy?'

'Oh, nothing!' Aisha said. 'These silly boobies called men—'

'Don't, Tuttapy! Can we talk like that about them?'

'You'll be in a position where you have the authority to beat me. That's my fate, I think. "Even then Aisha Bibi is always smiling!" the world will say!'

'What do you mean, Tuttapy?'

'I'm going to teach you. Pay attention!'

Aisha wrote 'B' on the sand.

'Look carefully; see if there is one like this in the book!' she said, and lay back on the grass.

Kunjupattumma looked everywhere in the book. She couldn't find one! Finally she discovered one on the cover of the book.

Aisha sat up.

'That letter is called "B". What's it called?'

'B,' said Kunjupattumma.

'Say a word beginning with "B".'

'Balue.'

'Booby! Silly booby! You should say "value"!'

'Value!'

'Is there a "B" in that?'

'No.'

'Then think of another one.'

'Brinjal!'

'Good. . . .'

So Kunjupattumma began to learn to read and write. Night and day she worked hard at it. She didn't let umma or bapa know. She was aware that umma would scold her if she came to hear of it. Suddenly umma has started praying!! She prays a lot. She rarely gets up from her prayer-mat. She enquires about household matters while sitting there. Kunjupattumma studies sitting in the kitchen or on her bed. She constantly has doubts, and then she goes next door. One day Aisha's umma asked her something about the sparrow.

She blushed all over!

'See how she blushes!' said Aisha.

Then she wanted to cry. Aisha's umma laughed and stroked her head.

'Don't you comb your hair?' Aisha's umma asked.

'Umma says I'll become a kafir if I comb my hair like yours!' said Kunjupattumma.

Aisha's umma laughed. She took a comb, parted Kunjupattumma's hair in the middle and combed it. Her face was aflame. Aisha's umma did her hair beautifully.

Aisha brought some jasmine flowers and wove them into Kunjupattumma's hair.

'Will Iblis get on to my head?' Kunjupattumma asked.

'Go and ask the sparrow!'

'Don't be like that, Tuttapy!'

She went home feeling bashful and happy. As soon as umma saw her, she asked, 'You bitch, what have you done? What's that on your head?'

Kunjupattumma kept quiet.

Umma got up, unplaited her hair and threw away all the flowers.

'You needn't copy them. That girl's uppuppa only had a bullock. Do you understand? You are Anamakkar's darling daughter's darling daughter! Your uppuppa 'ad an elephant!—a 'uge tusker!'

Kunjupattumma did not say anything. The very same day

she got another piece of news. Her wedding will take place soon. Bapa is looking for a boy!

She was shocked. Her mouth was dry. She stood there pale-faced.

'Without my permission you will not step out of this yard!' said umma.

Her sight and hearing became blurred. 'Oh Rabb al-Alamin!' she said and fell senseless.

'Mayyadin! Nabi! What has happened to my darling daughter?' Umma jumped up. Bapa came in. He sprinkled water on her! He fanned her! A real commotion!

Kunjupattumma opened her eyes and sat up. She stared at umma and bapa: they are going to get her a husband without asking her and without finding out her opinion about it.

'My dear Kunjupattumma!' bapa called out.

She did not say anything.

'What has happened to my darling daughter?' umma asked.

Kunjupattumma did not say anything.

'Mayyadin, is she possessed by some devil?' said umma.

Kunjupattumma burst out laughing; she laughed without stopping. Then she wept; with aching heart she wept. It was far into the night, and the whole world was sleeping. Still she did not stop crying.

As she lay there, she looked through the window.

The stars looked like glittering dots caught in a huge, black, spider's web.

10)   A time of dreams

Day comes, followed by night. Kunjupattumma is not clearly aware of anything. She neither eats nor sleeps. It is all a dream. People come. They ask her questions. Is she awake, or asleep? Perhaps it was Aisha who asked her something. The question was repeated again and again. She was answering it. But again the same question came. With aching heart she replied loudly, 'Tuttapy, they are going to marry me off!'

Again tears. An ocean of tears. She is afloat in them. From one end of the dark world a red globe is rising. It is the dawn of a new day. But the crows do not caw. The birds do not chirp. Some people are talking. It is umma and bapa. Then someone else is there. It is not dawn! In a pit in the yard there are live coals. Around it burn small candles on earthenware dishes. Kunjupattumma is made to sit on a board close by. Nearby is a man with a cane in his hand.

It is the elder exorcising Satan!

For the first time in her life Kunjupattumma was angry; she was really angry. She wanted to trumpet like an elephant, roar like a tiger, jump up and tear everyone to pieces.

But she just sat there. It was a pleasant smell; over her head the elder was putting various things into the fire. Among them were incense and sandalwood. The elder was murmuring various incantations: *suh, fala, hala.* Exorcism of Satan! It is the famous cane that drives away ifrit, jinn, ruhani and many such evil spirits.

He will beat her with it. Holding her by the hair, he will beat her on the back, the thighs and all over. That is how evil spirits are exorcised. If they still do not go, they will put ground chilli in the eyes. They will put fire in the palms of the hands. Then the skin will burn. It will hurt from the top of the head to the soles of the feet. Let it hurt, then. Umma and bapa have given permission for her to be hurt.

'Bapa, tell him not to beat me!'

The elder did not say anything. Nor did bapa say anything. Nor did umma.

'Tuttapy, tell him they are going to beat me!' she said to herself. Who is she asking Aisha to tell?

'Say who it is!' the elder demanded. 'Say who you are possessed by!'

If she is possessed, she can say who it is! Is she really possessed?

The elder asked again. The third time it was the cane that

spoke. After that she does not remember very well. The elder beat her ten or twelve times. She cried. She cried aloud. She snatched the cane from his hand, broke it and put it into the fire. She wanted to run away somewhere. But she did not run. Nisar Ahmad was standing near the circle of fire!

Did Nisar Ahmad pick her up? Or did she run towards Nisar Ahmad?

It was Nisar Ahmad who took her through the verandah into the house and laid her on the mat. When she opened her eyes, it was broad daylight. Aisha was sitting by the mat. Aisha's umma was there too.

Kunjupattumma's umma brought a sort of paste that she had made and put it on her forehead. It was nice and cooling. The air that was coming out of her nostrils was as hot as fire.

Her bapa came into the room. Aisha and her umma had got up and moved away. Bapa asked, 'My dear, do you want some kanji?'

She doesn't want anything; she is neither hungry nor thirsty.

'It's many days since my daughter had anything to eat,' bapa said sadly. Oh . . . why should he be sad? She is about to die. The wind has started to blow! The wind has started to blow. . . . Will the leaf now fall? A real wind is blowing. Leaves are flying. Trees are swaying. It might be the wind of death. Is the world coming to an end? The angel Israfil might have started blowing the trumpet Sur. The end of the world might be at hand! Trees uprooted; mountains shattered into pieces. . . . Is the world going to be laid waste?

It is raining. There is the smell of new earth. People are going about talking and laughing. It is daytime. The cry of the hawk can be heard. It cannot be seen. Yet it is gliding in the sky without moving its wings. In the room, it is neither night nor day. She cannot move. It hurts all over, as if somebody is cutting her in pieces, into ten thousand small pieces. Maybe they are to be thrown to the birds. The birds will peck and swallow them and fly away in flocks. And then. . . ?

'Kunjupattumma!' Someone is calling. Who is it? She opened her eyes. Her inside was burning. Nisar Ahmad's bapa! He was standing in the room.

'Light and air must get into this room,' he said. 'Why have you closed that window?'

He opened the window. Light and air came in: how bright the light is!

'Kunjupattumma!' he called again. 'Yes!' she answered. Was it loud enough? He went to the verandah. He is saying something to bapa. What is it? No; she cannot keep her eyes open. It is better to sleep than to be awake. Sleep is like a piece of black paper. She is melting into it. But even that is impossible. Light! Somewhere there must be something to hold on to. It is not possible to live without a support. She is a tree standing upright in the ground. Her hair forms the roots. Her arms and legs are the tree's branches. Two birds are going to build their nests in it. What birds are they?

'Kunjupattumma!' Someone is trying to wake her up. Who is it? Somewhere she has heard that voice before. She opened her weary eyes. Who is it? Oh. . . . Nisar Ahmad!

'Kunjupattumma!' Nisar Ahmad called to her. Then he said, 'Sit up and drink this. It is bitter. But imagine it is sweet. Never mind the taste.'

She wanted to say that she did not want the medicine. But before she could say it, Nisar Ahmad sat her up. He got her to drink some black liquid from a white bowl. While he was doing this, he was talking. When she was about to respond, Nisar Ahmad was no longer there. Umma was making her drink some kanji.

'Do you want to do your hair like Aisha's mother's?' umma asked.

'I'm going to snuff it,' said Kunjupattumma.

'My darling daughter,' said umma. 'Don't talk like that. Your marriage is all fixed.'

'I don't want to be wed,' said Kunjupattumma. 'I'm going to snuff it!'

'You must say, "I'm going to die!"' said Aisha, as she came in smiling. Then she asked, 'Was the medicine sweet?'

'Get off with you, Tuttapy!'

'The silly booby will take medicine from only one person!'

'Don't tease me, Tuttapy!'

She just lay there. Her heart was full. She had become all sweetness. Her appetite had returned. She was hungry and thirsty. She could sit up without anybody's help. She could also walk slowly.

One day in the course of her recovery Aisha asked, 'Silly booby, do you know who you will be married to?'

'Don't tease me, Tuttapy!'

'But do you know who it is to be?'

11)   The new generation is talking

It was at night-time that Nisar Ahmad married Kunjupattumma. The same day at about four o'clock an amusing thing happened.

Bapa had gone to the mosque to ask the khatib to officiate at the *Nikah* or marriage service. Although they had informed most of the families in the area, they had not invited anybody. There was no feasting and no celebrations. Nisar Ahmad's bapa and umma wanted it this way. Specially cooked rice was being prepared for seven or eight people. They themselves had bought the wedding garments for the bride. Kunjupattumma did not even know what they were. Aisha had asked her to go there after her bath. Aisha came and took her along when she had taken her bath.

It was not the Kunjupattumma who went in that came back. She had on a slip and a bodice. She wore a blouse and a green sari. Her hair was done beautifully and had flowers in it. Her head was covered with one end of the sari. In addition to all that she was wearing a pair of slippers. She was made to walk a hundred times back and forth in the room, so that she would know how to walk properly, before she went back.

'Don't stoop,' said Nisar Ahmad. 'Stand straight and walk with dignity.'

When this was over, Kunjupattumma returned home.

She was radiant. The black mole sparkled. There were a lot of children on the road to see this wonderful sight. Umma was standing in the front yard in her wooden sandals. Kunjupattumma saw the signs of a small commotion. Some words were being exchanged. She did not hear anything distinctly.

Umma was saying to some children, 'What, you vagabonds!'

The vagabond Kunjupattummas and Kunjutachummas, Adimas and Makkars said, 'Gulugulugulu!'

What did you say, you vagabonds?' asked umma.

'Lullullu!' said the children.

Umma started getting all worked up and said, 'You'll be bitten by a deadly snake!'

'Memmemme!'

'You pigs!'

'Peppeppe!'

'I'll knock you flat!' said umma.

'Umma,' said Kunjupattumma from some way off. 'Leave them alone. You say something and their bapas will come and start a quarrel!'

'Let them come!' umma said, loud enough for the whole world to hear. 'Let them all see you! Let them see Anamakkar's darling daughter's darling daughter. Let them all see! Yer uppuppa 'ad an elephant!—a 'uge tusker.'

'It was an elephant ant,' said an eighteen-inch tall, dark Adima with a snotty nose and hands covered with scabs.

'Elephant ant! Elephant ant!'

Could Kunjutachumma ever live it down? The brave and valiant, authentic Anamakkar Sahib—his fine and terrible huge tusker that killed four kafirs . . . to say that it was a little elephant ant that digs into the dust by the side of walls and lies buried in the tiny holes like black bedbugs!

'Oh God!' Kunjutachumma prayed, beating her chest, 'Let a thunderbolt strike these vagabonds!'

Marvellous to relate, no thunderbolt struck them and no lightning burnt them. Nothing happened. In one voice they called out, 'Anamakkar's huge tusker . . . was an elephant ant . . . an elephant ant!'

Kunjutachumma felt faint. She had difficulty in breathing. Her whole life passed before her in a flash. She sat down, both hands on her head.

Kunjupattumma came and stood by her umma and asked the children, 'What is it, children?'

'Ngulu ngulu!' said the children.

'What?'

'Peppeppe!'

'What is it?'

'Elephant ant!' said the children. 'Elephant ant!'

'What elephant ant?' Kunjupattumma could make neither head nor tail of it. She supposed that some kids must have put an elephant ant in umma's ear. She sat by umma and asked, 'What is it, umma?'

Umma did not say anything. What was there to say? Her world lay shattered! What had she left to live for?

Kunjupattumma asked again. In the end umma, tearful and stammering, said, 'They s-s-say your uppuppa's . . . huge elephant . . . was an elephant ant! . . . an elephant ant!'

PATTUMMA'S GOAT

INTRODUCTION

The man who wrote the true story of 'Pattumma's Goat' was an ignorant bachelor. (Among bachelors there aren't any learned ones!) The one who is writing this introduction is a learned husband. (Three cheers for wives!) Nothing else is new. What I should have been saying is that I am living peacefully and joyfully. But there is no peace and no joy.

I am having a house built!

*

Oh! What is so difficult about it? Just have it built, illiterate bachelors might say (Poor things!). But listen! Right away a wife (Lucky husbands!), but there is no house to live in. How long can one roam about with suitcases and bedding, pots and pans? Why not build a house?

Right; I'll build a house! It was easy to come to this beautiful decision. How about a site to build it on?

*

There is a road that stretches from Cape Comorin to Delhi. Why Delhi? By the grace of God, you can go anywhere along this road. Suppose there is a towel spread out in some convenient spot by the edge of this road. Suppose there is also a fence on all four sides of this towel. Suppose also that northwards from the middle of the towel up to the road there is a strip burnt deep. If you put two small elephants in this part, you get a nice view of their backs. That means this is a sort of trough. To tell the whole truth, it is a place where they cut stones from!

*

On the south side of the towel, there is a drop of about six
feet. That is to say, the area beyond the towel is all low
paddy fields. Miles and miles of paddy fields!

There will be a pleasant breeze.

Our towel is spread on an area of about one eighth of an
acre. On the southern side there are four young coconut
trees. Calculating on the number of coconuts we got last
time, there is a possibility of getting about 365 coconuts a
year.

Picture the part of the towel that is not burnt as being
somewhat soiled and dark, for there are some small rocks
there. If you dig down, you can get good water. The house
is in the middle. On all four sides there should be walls. The
site is being levelled; the house is being built; the well is
being dug. We should consider ourselves lucky that we got
water at the first attempt and that the water was good.
Everything progresses well—by the grace of God.

*

There should be no difficulty over anything, for I was paid
four lakhs of rupees. It is not without reason that the
opposition in Kerala raised a fuss. Not at all. Some time ago
I wrote a book with the title 'Me Grandad 'ad an Elephant!'
As soon as it came out in book form, two remarkable things
happened. One, the Congress Government gave me five
hundred rupees or something, saying that it was the best
novel of those years. (Don't misunderstand this. It was not
the Congress Government of Kerala, but of Madras.) The
second remarkable thing was that the Communist Party
criticised the book unmercifully, saying that it was against
the ideals of communism. One of those who criticised it
was the Finance Minister of the Kerala Communist
administration, Mr Achuta Menon. After that, the book
was awarded the M.P. Paul Prize. After that, it was
selected by the Sahitya Akademi in New Delhi to be translated into fourteen or fifteen Indian languages. Although
this has no great significance, the President of the Sahitya

Akademi is Jawaharlal Nehru. Some time passed by like that and then the Communist Party came into power in Kerala. Whether to my good fortune or bad, 'Me Grandad 'ad an Elephant!' was prescribed as one of the texts for non-detailed study in school examinations. (After the revered Parasuraman made Kerala, this is the first such incident. That is to say, an incident when a Muslim's book was accepted as a non-detailed text. It was the Communist Government that did it. So this must be taken a wee bit seriously. So conveniently forget all the other books that were accepted and oppose this one!) So opposition started.

*

Let me record a pitiable truth. I did not request anyone to accept this book for non-detailed study. As a matter of fact, I was opposed to it. I had even drafted a letter to exempt this book from being prescribed for non-detailed study, when the Government order came. The reason is that the price of the book has to be reduced to a rupee and a half. And 25 per cent commission goes to the Government. If I consented to this, the Government would take about seventy-five thousand copies. I did not feel like consenting. At two rupees it had gone into a seventh impression. Moreover, paper had become very expensive. I thought it would end in a loss. But it was at the insistence of Mr Karoor Nilakanta Pillai that I agreed to it and sent a favourable reply to the Government. It was the Sahitya Pravarthaka Co-operative Society, Kottayam, that published it from the beginning. I think this is the first co-operative society of its kind in the world. Anyway, it is definitely the first one in India. Mr Karoor Nilakanta Pillai is its Secretary. If you wish to know how many copies of this book were sold, you can ask either the honourable Communist Government, or Mr Karoor.

*

The book had to face opposition. Some friends told me that Catholics were going to oppose it. I do not know what the reason is for the opposition. Anyway, everybody opposed it—the Catholic Congress, Praja Socialist Party, Congress, Muslim League. If what I saw in the papers is true, they all told plenty of lies about it. I am an old Congressman, a dutiful soldier who has taken a lot of beatings and punchings and gone to jail several times. When I hear talk of Congress, I think of Mahatma Gandhi, Indian Independence and the like. Congress, which is supposed to represent non-violence and truth, need not have stooped so low. I read in the papers that the Congress members in the Assembly said that the book was sold for eight annas. The Indian Congress need not have told that white lie. I mentioned above that the book was published by the Sahitya Pravarthaka Co-operative Society. They have given me royalties on a price of two rupees a copy for all of the seven impressions. Messrs Karoor Nilakanta Pillai, Vettoor Raman Nair, P. Kesava Dev and others—writers and members of the S.P. Co-operative Society—who know more about books as regards price and so on, made statements. I do not intend to quote them here. It is unfortunate that people think that, just because they get a few more votes than somebody else, they know everything.

I see in the papers that the opposition made me a Communist Party member. Great! I also see that, according to the opposition, this book will bring me four lakhs of rupees. Come to think of it, why do I need so much money? The opposition is requesting the Communist Government to consult with the Sahitya Pravarthaka Co-operative Society which published the book, and then to give them the amount they spent on it, give me about fifty thousand rupees and give the opposition the remaining three and a half lakhs or more. Long live the opposition!

'Oh Creator of the World! They know not what they do; forgive them!'

*

I completed the story 'Pattumma's Goat' on 27th April, 1954. I thought I would copy it out and publish it with an introduction. Days passed by as I kept putting it off till tomorrow.

Five years!

Up to now I have not copied out the story. Almost all that I have published before this, I have written and rewritten more than once. This is coming out without being copied, without any corrections, just as I wrote it. I read it through and did not feel it should be corrected or copied. It is a gay story. Still, when I wrote it, I was burning all over. I must forget the pain of the past. Write! So the mind. . . .

*

Yes . . . at that time my mind . . . like a tiny island that is starting to sink into a bottomless ocean. . . . I don't know whether that makes any sense or not. Anyway, the mind gets drowned in darkness filled with frightful dreams. I myself am the mind. When I look up, there is only a small patch of light. In darkness and in light. . . . Oh God! Where am I? What is true? What is false? Light! . . . Light. . . . I want only light. But, . . . darkness filled with terrible dreams . . . is approaching from all the eight directions, roaring and booming.

Will I drown in this for ever?

*

No! I won't let my life be thrown into disarray. I must get well! I must get well! Gathering all the strength I have, I must make a powerful effort!

Goodness. Keep the attention only on that! Concentration! . . . Let it be kept on that . . . that pinpoint. The mind . . . the mind . . . is breaking up into hundreds of thousands of pieces of darkness. . . . In each of those pieces . . . what is it that I see and hear?

*

Don't lose your reason; find out the cause. Everything has a cause. Courage . . . courage to try to find out. Superstition is comfortable. If you take refuge in that. . . ! This is nothing like that. All the beliefs you now have—from childhood . . . from days gone by . . . from before history began—analyse them all, and accept only what is good. Evil is a sickness. If you treat it, you can cure it. There is no sickness that you cannot cure. If you think there is one, it is through ignorance; never make ignorance a permanent abode.

When you think properly, what actually is wrong here?

*

Nothing. Turbulent thoughts. Sleepless nights. Hard-working days. I loathed the days, the nights, the work, the place and everything. No food, no sleep; just dreams. Nothing but fear!

What happened? Hopeless heartache. Talking incoherently. That is how I came under the treatment of Mr P.C. Govindan Nair. I was taken to Trichur in a car belonging to Kuttappan Nair, owner of the Krishnan Nair Watch Company, Ernakulam. It was Kuttappan Nair who was driving. In the car were artist Raghavan Nair, editor of 'Narmada', Mr M.P. Krishna Pillai, owner of the M.P. Studio, and Mr Perunna Thomas. You must remember that Vaidyaratnam P.C. Govindan Nair is a specialist in madness and related sicknesses. When I arrived at my destination, there were about thirty mad people there. They were in different stages, some in chains, some handcuffed. I think everyone was following the same treatment. I shall tell you about mine.

*

After bed coffee, I go to the latrine. After that, as soon as I get back from washing my hands, feet and face, they put some oil on my head. It is very cooling. (I have heard that Mr Perunna Thomas had this oil on his head and slept for three days or something like that.) He is staying with me to look after me. There are others, too, to look after me. Mr K. Parameswaran Nair, Mr M.M. Khadar and Mr Paremmal Vasudevan. Mr Parameswaran Nair runs the Shobhana Studios of Trichur. He is a very good photographer. He is also an actor and an art director. I call him Paramu. The only person who read the manuscript of this book is Paramu. In those days, his main occupation was to write letters. I would dictate; and Paramu would write. I used to write to all the people with whom I had even the slightest acquaintance. I used to dictate all those letters just to forget my heartache. Later it was introductions to books. That was how I came to write the introductions to the two books, 'Hunger' and 'Life's shadows'. During those days many interesting incidents took place. It was arranged that Mr Perunna Thomas would write down whatever I said or did from the time I got up to the time I went to bed. He was given a big fat notebook for the purpose. I spent ten or twelve days reading it. Then I tore it into small pieces and burnt it. I have told Paramu many funny stories. I remember them all very well even now. I had thought of including all that in this introduction. Let me digress a little. Any sickness can be cured. But for that, medicine alone is not enough. The patient must have the will, too. I had a hundred per cent will. I do not have time now to write all the details in this introduction. (Didn't I tell you I was going through the turmoil of getting a house built. Moreover, I have been promoted to the rank of husband. My wife's name is Fatimabi. She is the eldest daughter of Koyakutti, a teacher from Cheruvannore, near Calicut. I call her Fabi. I have narrated all the interesting incidents of my sickness to Fabi. When I have time, I shall set it all down on paper.) So we were talking about the oil. It is very cooling. Suppose twelve elephants ran amok. It is said that if you put some of this oil on the head of one of them, all the twelve will go to sleep! They put that on my head. Then they pour some sort of potion into my mouth. To get the full effect of the oil, I sit like that for half an hour. After that there is the medicinal bath. That, too, is cooling. I lie on my back on a bench. The medicinal bath will go on for at least an hour. It is after this that two famous treatments come.

I am lying on my back.

I can hear voices. Birds are chirping. I can hear motor horns. (Because it is near the national highway.) The sun is shining brightly. Meanwhile, a cone made from a jack-leaf is put into one of my nostrils. Then they pour about three ounces of liquid into it. I start to get a powerful burning sensation. Wow! Does it burn! The liquid in the right nostril explodes like an atom bomb and jumps out with a bang through the left nostril. By that time the sun has burnt out; there is no sound of people, birds or cars. The world is silent. Earth alone is left. By this time, they have put the cone into my left nostril and also poured the medicine into it. Wow! It really burns. With a crash and a bang the earth has been shattered into pieces.

In actual fact, of course, nothing has happened in the world. All the uproar took place inside my head. Just because I can see properly, they put some salve on my eyes. Something that is a thousand times stronger and that burns a thousand times more than what was poured into the nose, is put into my eyes. Wham! I can't see. Some kind person leads me by the hand and sits me beside a big copper pot. Then starts the bath. Wait! It isn't just a bath, but a continuous pouring of water. That is to say, some-one pours ice-cold water on my head. Anybody will start shivering within ten minutes. But this will go on for at least an hour. Luckily, by that time I can open my eyes. Yet that burning and fuming have not gone completely.

*

All this that I have just described will be repeated at four o'clock. In between I get potion, pills, medicinal ghee and such-like. The most interesting part of the treatment is what is done in the nose and the eyes. Within a few days I reduced the potency of the salve. This is how I did it: as soon as they put the salve on the eyes, I would open both of them. It is as if I said with all the courage and strength I could muster, 'Let's see who wins!' I would keep my eyes open. If air gets in for a minute, then it isn't too bad. For that one minute you must have strength and courage. That's all. During those days and even after that, I used to insist on rubbing salve on the eyes of all those who came to see me. I give the names of those whom I remember.

Against the names of those I am doubtful about I have written 'doubtful' in brackets. If they let me know, in the next edition I'll remove the brackets and the doubt, and, if they want, the name also.

K.PARAMESWARAN NAIR
PAREMMAL VASUDEVAN
PERUNNA THOMAS
M.A.KHADAR
GOVINDANATHA
 PANIKKAR
R.S.PRABHU
K.SANKARAN (AIYAR)
SATYAN
 ex-police inspector & film star
RAMU KARIAT
A.C.GEORGE
K.A.JABBAR
S.K.POTTEKKATT
TIKKODIYAN
P.BHASKARAN
N.V.KRISHNA WARRIOR
 (*doubtful*)
V.ABDULLA
M.ABDURAHIMAN

M.V.DEVAN
 (*doubtful*)
M.P.KRISHNA PILLAI
P.K.BALAKRISHNAN
D.M.POTTEKAT
K.A.RAJAN
KOCHAPPAN
JOSEPH MUNDASSERY
 (*doubtful*)
PONJIKKARA RAFI
VAYALAR RAMA VARMA
M.GOVINDAN
 (*doubtful*)
BHASKARAN NAIR,N.K.
K.K.THOMAS,B.A.,B.L.
PONKUNNAM VARKEY
 (*doubtful*)
FABI BASHEER
 (*doubtful*)

In addition to these I have also put salve on the eyes of some women. Now that I am married, I have forgotten their names. No matter how hard I try, I cannot remember them! Satis verborum!

*

It was during this period of treatment that I wrote the story 'Pattumma's Goat'. When I got tired after writing for about an hour, I used to go and interview some of the mad people. There was one madman, Padmanathan by name, who used to be with me like my beloved disciple. He used to call me 'Swamiji'. He believed that I was a brahmin. He used to bring a pot of clean water and sprinkle my room with it to purify it. He even purified the path I walked on. He was a Sanskrit pandit. He recited a lot of Sanskrit slokas to me.

Meanwhile, he would drink the tea that I had sipped at and he would smoke the beedi that I had puffed at. There have been two religious teachers with the name Shankara. He would talk to me about both of them. Then he would ask which of the two I was. I would say, 'My name is Vaikom Muhammad Basheer. I am a heathen!' He would ask, 'Swamiji, why do you hide?' Because he was rather afraid of salve, I would say, 'Let's put a little salve on our eyes.' Immediately he would go to purify another room.

Another one was always silent. He was a Christian. I think he was a Catholic. It was after I had tried for many days that he talked to me. Usually, after the treatment at four o'clock, he would go to the verandah on the eastern side, turn west and laugh twice. Then he would light a beedi and come away. When we became friends, this chap told me the secret of his life. I asked him, 'What was your job?'

'Soldier,' he said. 'Five years ago I died in Syria.'

'And then?' I asked.

'Now God has sent me down to Earth.'

I did not ask him why. Another one was a fat madman who had only one wish in life—to eat an elephant!

I said to him, 'Me grandad 'ad an elephant!'

'Did anyone eat it?'

'No,' I said. 'He is walking around outside.'

'Is it possible to catch him?'

'I don't know,' I said.

*

There are many funny stories like this to write. But there is no time. One thing I must say, before I let loose 'Pattumma's Goat'. Last November three gentlemen, by name V. Abdulla, M. Abdurahiman and Tikkodiyan had come to Thalayolaparambu from Calicut. They wanted to make the novel 'Me Grandad 'ad an Elephant!' into a play. They wanted to give the first performance for the Kerala Arts Festival. There was no time for delay.

Right.

I went along with them to Calicut, made it into a play, and their performance was first-rate. The play was a success. I did not go to see it, for I was spending my honeymoon at 'Chandrakantam', Mr S. K. Pottekkatt's house in Pudiyara, after marrying Fabi.

*

I shall now bring this introduction to a close. 'Pattumma's Goat' is not just a story. All the characters in it are still living, by the grace of God; I mentioned before that it is five years since I wrote it. Many new characters have come into being since then. You must remember that this is the story of my family. When I wrote the story, I purposely omitted some of the things in this introduction. Reminding you of that, I am letting loose Pattumma's goat before you.

Best wishes.

VAIKOM MUHAMMAD BASHEER
Thalayolaparambu
1st March
1959

1)

The story that I am about to relate is called 'Pattumma's Goat, or the Wisdom of Women'.

After leading a lonely existence for a long time, just wandering from one place to another, I came to live in my own house in Thalayolaparambu near Vaikom, ready to lose my temper at the slightest provocation. What a welcome awaited me! I was beside myself with rage. I was absolutely fuming. My house. . . . Whom should I blame for it all?

For ten or fifteen years I had not really stayed in my own house. I have a recollection of spending a few nights there once in a while. For me to stay in, and for nobody else, there is a small tiled building opposite the house, by the side of the public road. When it was being built, I had carried stones and sand on my head. I had really worked hard. I had done lots of things to make the place calm and beautiful. Along the edge of the courtyard, which was spread with white sand and surrounded by a stone wall, there were beautiful shrubs. I had got different varieties of jasmine to climb around the hibiscus tree. I had planted guavas in the corners of the courtyard. There were two ponds, one for drinking and one for bathing. There was a special privy just for me. The compound was filled with coconut palms and banana trees. I had planted and tended numerous other trees, among which were some good mangoes. By the roadside and all along the boundary a neat line of pineapples formed a hedge. Around the compound was a six-foot high fence of plaited coconut-palm leaves and thorns. At the front was a barred gate that was always kept locked. If they looked through it, passers-by could have a fine view of all the shrubs and flowers.

It was there that I had lived quietly on my own. My umma, that is to say my mother, would pass tea, snacks and meals to me over the top of the gate. Absolutely no-one was allowed to come in. I would sit there and write in comfort;

or I would read something. Or alternatively I would walk around carefully tending the plants and trees. Then one day I went off for a short trip. I was away for some three years, staying at the Shivagiri Ashram in Varkala, and in Madras, Ernakulam and Coimbatore. Then, when I come back, not feeling too well, I find that my next younger brother, Abdulkhadar, has rented out the small place I lived in! Excise Inspector Sri Ramankutti is comfortably installed there along with his cook. The gentleman in question liked the house very much. Nevertheless, he would give it back. But there was no way to get another house in the village. What was to be done?

Hm! That's how it happened that I took up my abode in the main house, at a time when what I needed was complete rest. I had to regain my health. There must be no trouble or noise that would disturb my peace of mind. Yet I was right in the very middle of trouble and noise.

My house is just a small building with a thatched roof. Who are all those who live in it?

There is my umma; my next younger brother Abdulkhadar, his wife Kunjanumma, their darling children Pattukkutti, Arifa and Subaida; the next younger brother after Abdulkhadar, namely Muhammad Hanifa, his wife Aishomma, their darling children Habibu Muhammad, Laila and Muhammad Rashid; Hanifa's younger sister Anumma, her husband Sulaiman, their darling child Saidu Muhammad; and lastly my youngest brother Abubakar.

So much for people. In addition to them, there are some cats that have come from somewhere or other to take refuge and live there under the protection of my umma; going in fear of these are hundreds of mice, which are always scampering about in the roof-space. Cawing and kicking up a racket as they perch on the roof-top are the crows. Besides all of these are the hundreds of fowls which are my mother's own property and which are the rulers of the house. With them are chickens without number. In the trees are the hawks and kites which swoop down and carry these off for food.

The house is always filled with noise. Rashid and Subaida have not started to crawl. When they are not feeding at the breast, they just cry. Arifa, who has begun to walk, pursues the occupation of crying very conscientiously. Laila and Saidu Muhammad, who are a little older, are excellent criers also. Abi and Pattukkutti (ah, yes! I must mention that the name Habibu Muhammad is for school only. At home he is called Abi, and what he himself says is 'Bi'. He and Pattukkutti are in standard one)—these two, then, are expert at crying and making nuisances of themselves. Children, cats, hens, women, kites, mice, crows—together they really create a din.

In the middle of all the confusion that I have outlined, what do I see turning up but a goat!

It's a nanny goat, bran-coloured, and very active. Very early in the morning it comes to my house, goes into the kitchen and has its breakfast. Then it goes right inside the house, steps on the bodies of the children lying asleep there and wakes them up, makes its way into the yard and starts to gobble up the jack-leaves that have fallen during he night.

The jack-tree by the edge of the compound is very old, but there are jack-fruits on it nevertheless. And it has enough leaves to satisfy any number of goats. Quickly eating up the jack-leaves, the goat passes to the foot of the jambu tree which stands to one side of the compound and there eats all the jambu fruits which have fallen to the ground. Then it looks upwards. The jambu fruits hang clustered thickly among the green leaves, like big drops of dew that have been dyed light red. What is to be done? The goat stands on its hind legs and tries to eat the fruits on the lowest branches. It cannot get at them! Who has pulled these low branches up and tied them out of reach?

While it is standing there in this way, a mellow jack-leaf will fall. The goat will run to the yard, pick it up with its tongue and munch it with relish. By that time umma, or

Kunjanumma, or Aishomma, or Anumma will have come with a broom to tidy up the compound. The goat will run into the house and poke around there.

Whose goat is it? How does it come to take such liberties? It goes everywhere! It does anything! Yet no-one says a single word. It is a house where nobody asks questions!

Once, when I was lounging in a canvas chair, I heard the sound of some-one in my room, tearing paper. I looked in through the small door. That goat was standing on my bed eating a book!

On top of a trunk there was one copy each of the new edition of two books, 'Childhood Friend' and 'Sounds'. There it was, making a meal of 'Childhood Friend'. Hold-it down with its two front feet, it was taking two or three pages at a time with its tongue and eating them. Well, let it eat! It's a fine goat.... And there is still 'Sounds' left. Will it have the nerve to eat that, too?

It did not have the slightest compunction. 'Childhood Friend' had been put away. At once it started on 'Sounds'. Within a couple of minutes it had eaten every bit. Then this goat started to eat my blanket. I at once jumped up and stepped forward.

'Hey beautiful, please don't eat that blanket. It's worth fifty rupees. I don't have another copy of that. But there are other things I've written. I'll get them all for you and let you have them free of charge.'

Then I chased the goat out. It ran to the foot of the jack-tree. Two or three leaves had fallen there. The dear old thing set about eating the lot.

I called to umma and asked, 'Whose is this goat?'

'It's Pattumma's,' said umma.

'So that's how it comes to have so much freedom!'

It's Pattumma's goat.... The matter became clear. Before daybreak Pattumma lets it loose.

She'll counsel it in such terms as these: 'My precious, before they sweep the compound and throw away all the jack-leaves, go and fill your belly with them.' Straightaway the goat crosses the public road to the house, and then the trouble starts!

This goat-owner Pattumma is my sister. She is the next one after Abdulkhadar—and she lives behind the market, some three hundred yards away. After getting tea and a snack ready for her husband Kochunni, she sends him off to do his trading. The fellow has tried his hand at many different kinds of trade. Now he is in the coir business. He doesn't get back till dusk.

After Kochunni has left, Pattumma washes all the pots and pans, stands them upside down to dry, and then comes straight to our house with her small daughter, Khadija. They come in their own individual way. Khadija follows behind, like a tail. Pattumma walks as if in a dream. After she gets to the house, her mood changes. Pattumma, too, becomes noisy. There is a reason for this! She is umma's eldest daughter. She therefore has a little bit more authority in the house than the others.

When Pattumma arrived and went inside, I listened a little, to see what was going to happen. For Pattumma's goat was there, and umma, and our younger sister, and the two sisters-in-law.

Pattumma went in and in a slightly authoritative tone asked our younger sister, umma and the sisters-in-law, 'Did anybody give my goat some kanji-water?'

'There's a hundred and one jobs to do. You and your goat!' said umma.

Pattumma asked her sisters-in-law something and then said to her younger sister in a slightly reproving tone, 'I know you of old!'

I do not know what Anumma said to that. Pattumma told umma about her troubles. She was full of complaints. Then she declared forcefully, 'None of you need do anything. Just wait till my goat produces a kid. Then we'll see!'

What is it that Pattumma is going to let them see when her goat brings forth a kid?

The jambu tree was laden with fruit. When I was looking

at it as I lay in the canvas chair, facing westwards, the refugee cats came up to me, mewing away. One of them, which was not very clean, jumped up and sat on my lap.

Why has it come and sat on my lap? We are not acquainted with each other. Yet to look at it, one would think it had quite a liking for me. Ah well, let it stay.... Meanwhile, as I look towards the road, I see a good number of girls walking by. They are high school students. They are all looking at me!

What is the reason?

A crow alighted on Pattumma's goat. The goat came and stood before me, carrying the crow. The crow turned its head on one side and looked at me as if to say, 'I don't remember having seen you before.'

Near me a number of hens were pecking away at something or other on the concrete paving. The crow flew down and stood on the edge of the group.

The hens looked as if to say, 'What right has it got to be here?' The crow showed absolutely no sense of fear. It began to peck away as if to say, 'I am the one who belongs here.'

A white cat came to join the assembly. The biggest black hen among them did not much care for it. It pecked the cat's head. The cat hissed a bit. Then with its tail in the air and its hairs standing on end, it stood there as if to say, 'We'll soon show whether we have any rights in this house or not. Just peck once more, if you dare!'

Then my youngest brother, Abubakar, clothes washed and ironed, hair combed and dressed, shoes creaking as he walked, joined the assembly and said in a gruff voice, 'Umma, did you see this?' His general behaviour makes him seem more like a mere Abu than an Abubakar. There is even talk that he is a leftist. He changes his clothes twice a day. Umma has told me that he has sixty pairs of sandals. He is as thin as a lath. But he is very noisy; he has a mania for cleanliness. As soon as I came, I turned him out. He was living in the room I had in the house as if he owned it. Long before, father had had that room added to the house for Abdulkhadar and me to study in. Right away I had turned Abdulkhadar out of the room. From then on he slept in the same room as umma. Abdulkhadar's hair has now turned grey. If you saw him you would think he is my elder brother. He has now had another room built on the same side of the house to match my old one. It is there that Hanifa and his wife and children spend the night. When I turned Abu out, he moved with his boxes, books, lamp and bedding to Hanifa's room.

As soon as they heard Abu, the cats ran away, the crow flew off, the hens scattered, Pattumma's goat ran over to where the women were, and the children stopped crying. The kites and the hawks quietly hid somewhere. Even the women stopped talking. The house became silent.

'Elder brother!' Abu bawled out, 'How can you permit all this? Cats, children, hens, crows, goats! Letting it become a place to feed and bring up a goat! I'll take care of the lot of them—Umma, bring me a stick and a catapult!'

Pattumma was immediately to be heard saying sorrowfully, 'Khadija, call our goat. It's plain we have no rights here. Let's go! Umma dear, we're leaving!'

'Let me also see whether I have any rights in this house,' Abu shouted. 'Today I'll turn Hanifa and his wife and kids out!'

I too started shouting.

'Watch it! We don't want to hear a sound from you in this house. I'll break every bone in your body! He's so skinny! And what a loud-mouth! Hey, Abu! Where will Hanifa and the rest of them go and live then?'

Abu said in a low voice, 'Let them build a house on elder brother's estate and live there.'

There is something in that. There has been talk about it. Hanifa had also spoken to me about this business of building a house. He had bought a piece of land, about three-quarters of an acre in size, two miles away on the side of a hill near the road. He had already planted banana and mango trees on it and plans to make a house there. It is from me that he expects to get all the necessary help and support! He has no ready cash. So he gets up early in the morning, at four o'clock, to go there and water the bananas, and by seven o'clock he comes home. After that he takes Abi and Laila and goes to bathe in the river. Father and children are very close. Laila and Abi have said that, when there is a house on their land, they will take me there. Saidu Muhammad has said exactly the same thing. For him, his mother Anumma and his father Sulaiman, a house is being built in the compound next to our house. All the woodwork for it has been completed. The stone has been delivered. Hanifa, on the other hand, has not done a thing.

'Look, Abu,' I said, 'I don't think Hanifa has any money.'

'Elder brother Hanifa is a real miser,' said Abu softly. 'He's rolling in money.'

'Get away with you!'

He took his catapult and went to take pot shots at some birds with a few round stones.

'Come, goat; he won't do anything,' said Pattumma soothingly as she came in my direction with the goat. Seeing Abu standing in the adjacent compound, Pattumma called out to him, 'Hey, Abu! You'd better watch your step! Don't you know that our eldest brother has come back?'

'I say, ikkakka, did you hear eldest sister say "Hey, Abu!" to me? What a nerve! Because you're here, she's showing off! Hm!'

Pattumma is several ahead of Abu in seniority within the family—and she shows a great lack of respect when she says 'Hey, Abu!' to him!

'In that case,' I said, 'We'll all call you Mr Abu! Buzz off!'

Pattumma came up to me. Then she looked all round. There was nobody there! Pattumma told me in confidence, 'Elder brother, nobody need know. If Anumma finds out, she'll pick a quarrel with me. From now on you don't need to give me anything in the form of money. It'll do if you have a pair of earrings made for Khadija. Hanifa, too, mustn't know. Nor second brother. Nor Abu. Nor umma.'

'Are the earrings to be of silver or of gold?' I asked in a low voice.

Pattumma looked all round and whispered, 'I'd like them to be gold! You won't tell anyone, will you?'

'Oh no,' I said. 'I'll keep it entirely to myself.'

So I entered into a secret compact with Pattumma.

'I want the earrings right away!' said Pattumma.

'I'll see about it,' I said.

There is a reason why these earrings are a matter of urgency. Right after I came, I had three small umbrellas brought from Ernakulam. These I gave to Abdulkhadar's daughter Pattukkutti, Hanifa's son Abi and Anumma's son Saidu Muhammad. I had not given an umbrella to Pattumma's daughter Khadija! Pattukkutti, Abi, Saidu Muhammad and Khadija were roughly the same age. They were equally mischievous and noisy. They were well-matched, too, when it came to crying. Yet Khadija was not given an umbrella! Why was that? To tell the truth, I had forgotten about her. Never mind; there would be a pair of golden earrings for her!

At the opportunity offered by Pattumma going off to do some housework or other, Anumma slowly came up to me. She was pregnant. Pattumma had not been to school, whereas Anumma had. So her way of talking was not like Pattumma's. Anumma whispered, 'Elder brother, from now on you don't need to give me anything in the form of money. All I ask is that you buy me some pots and pans. Those, too, I don't want now. It'll do when we flit. Don't tell elder sister about this.'

That means, in short, that Pattumma must not know. If she knew, she would say, 'That'll do; that's enough of your sneaky ways! You're an educated woman! Didn't you take everything from elder brother when I wasn't there?'

That is why this secret of the pots and pans must not pass from one ear to another. I gave my signature to the agreement that I would buy the household utensils for Anumma and that I would keep it secret. Then, as I sat there quietly, my peace was shattered.

'You stupid twit, you stupid twit! I won't take you with me!'

It was Laila's voice. Who was it she was shouting at like this? I did not have to wait long. Unable to bear the insult, Saidu Muhammad came up to me, his eyes filled with tears.

He was stark naked.

Very much put out, he said, 'Uncle, Laila called me a stupid twit!'

For a male person to be called a stupid twit! And that, too, by a girl!

'Go and fetch the stick!'

Saidu Muhammad went for the stick.

'Hey, Laila! Come here!' I shouted.

She did so. Stark naked. On seeing the stick brought by Saidu Muhammad, she said, 'We won't take you with us, uncle.'

'That doesn't matter!' I said and took the stick from Saidu Muhammad. Laila started to howl.

'Mummy, mummy!'

'Mummy' was what Laila called her umma. I said, 'Call your mummy! Call your bapa! Call your uppuppa! I'll beat the lot of them!'

By uppuppa I mean grandfather. Laila's umma's bapa. (Bapa, of course, is our word for father.) The aforesaid lives near Hanifa's banana plantation. Somewhere in that area there is going to be a railway station. Then the place will fetch whatever you care to ask. In addition, the area will improve. It was with that purpose in view that Laila's uppuppa got Hanifa to buy the place.

'Please don't beat Mummy!' said Laila. 'Please don't beat bapa! Please don't beat uppuppa!'

'Then in future you shouldn't call people "stupid twit".'

'I won't.'

'When your bapa builds a house, will you take Saidu

Muhammad there? Will you take your uncle?'

Tears in her eyes, she said, 'I'll take everybody.'

Phew! So that case was closed. As compensation I gave Saidu Muhummad a couple of sweets and a nice banana. I kept a good stock of this sort of thing—tomatoes, pineapples, sweets and several varieties of banana. It was only the sweets that I paid good money for. They were useful for stopping the children's crying. The rest of the items my brothers and Kochunni and Sulaiman bought for me. I need plenty of fruits. The whole lot were kept on the table. I caught Saidu Muhammad standing on a box, helping himself to some. He felt sad at being caught red-handed. He started to cry. From then on, in order not to provide an opportunity for him to cry, I now keep these things carefully inside the box. When she saw Saidu Muhammad eating sweets and bananas, Laila too began to cry. I gave two sweets and a banana to her also. I gave the same quantity to Arifa, who was attracted by the smell. I also sent two sweets each for Subaida and Rashid. Then I got Anumma to bring me a glass of tea, lit a beedi and, with a sigh of relief, lay back on the canvas chair with a book.

While I was lying there, my umma came up. She is either sixty-seven or seventy-seven. She has not lost any teeth. She gets up at six o'clock in the morning. She then fetches the coconut leaves that have been steeped in the streams to make them pliable and plaits them. When that is done, she spreads them all out in the compound. This is so that they will be drying from the moment the sun rises. After seeing to that, she draws the water that is needed for the house. She comes carrying a large pot in each arm. She scolds Pattumma, Anumma, Aishomma and Kunjanumma; she makes a fair amount of noise; she is fully occupied with housework until ten o'clock at night. Pattumma is not in the house every night. But there are three women apart from her. Why does umma work? Can't she just take things easy? Umma has answers ready for such questions: 'None of them knows a thing. They haven't learnt how to look after the house.' Fine, then let them all learn. Hand over all these chores to them. Then, too, she has an answer: 'What do you know about running a house? You're just a single person with only one stomach to think of.'

If this argument fails to convince, she says, 'Don't they all have children? Who is to look after them?'

'One of them should look after the kids,' I tell her. 'The rest can do the work.'

'It's all right for you to talk like that. You're a single person with only one stomach to think of. Let me have a bit of money.'

Our conversations always end with her trying to get money out of me. That is not to my advantage. So, whatever umma carries, whatever I see her dragging along, I keep quiet. Why should I unnecessarily cause umma to ask for money?

On this occasion, as soon as umma came, she said in a low voice, 'I say, give me ten rupees.'

When I looked at her as if to ask what advice I had given to make her ask this, umma went on in a low voice, 'Don't let Abdulkhadar know. Or Hanifa. Or Anumma, or Pattumma.'

I asked in a conspiratorial tone, 'Do you have any objection to Kunjanumma or Aishomma knowing?'

Umma was annoyed.

'That'll do. Give me it, if you're going to. There's no need for anybody to know.'

I, too, was slightly annoyed.

'Since I got back, how much money have I given around this house? How much money have you taken, both in public and without witnesses?' I asked.

'I'm not saying you haven't given anything. I've just got to have ten rupees now,' said umma in a confidential tone.

'Where is all the money I've given already? It's not all that long ago, is it? Where is it all?'

'Speak softly!' said umma, very softly. 'Abdulkhadar got it all.'

'I've already given him money separately! That cripple! Wait till I see him.'

When he was a boy, he became paralysed from the neck down. Bapa spent several thousands of rupees on treatment. In the end, he was left with a sort of lameness in his right leg. His right leg is very thin. Otherwise he is very robust. He supports himself with a steel stick when he walks.

Keeping her voice down, umma said, 'Don't say anything to him. Isn't he the one who looks after all these dependants? If it were not for him, you'd see what would happen. And you just a single person with only one stomach to think of. In all those places you've been to, how much money have you spent?'

'I've already paid the penalty for that. I've spent a lot of money here also.'

'Keep your voice down. Nobody said you didn't. Just give me ten rupees now without anybody knowing.'

'What about all the money I gave you so far without anybody knowing? How did Abdulkhadar get that? How did he come to know this secret?'

'Keep your voice down! Abu and Pattukkutti went and told him!'

'I'll tell you a secret. Don't tell anybody else. All I've got at present is a five-rupee note. I've no other money at all!' I said in a very low voice.

'Let's have it!' said umma immediately.

After looking all round, I went into the room and fetched the money and a banana. Pattumma's goat had got the smell of the banana and came right away. I peeled the banana and ate it. Seeing me eat something, umma's refugee cats came up. So did the hens that went around under umma's care. The goat stood there expecting something further. I looked this way and that. There was no-one. Neither man nor beast. Just the hens, Pattumma's goat and the cats. Very furtively, I handed the five-rupee note over to umma. Umma looked this way and that. There being neither man nor beast, umma folded it, tied it in the end of her cloth and stuffed it out of sight. Then she sat there as if nothing had happened.

'So, what's all the news?' I asked.

'You know, I'm so old now. Who knows when I shall die? I've one wish—to live with you after you've got married,' said umma.

'If I want to live quietly somewhere, will they let me! Pattumma! Anumma!' I shouted. 'Come quickly! Get my suitcase and my bedding. Send for a coolie!'

They both ran up.

'What's this?' Anumma asked.

'Umma must have been asking older brother for some money,' said Pattumma.

Straightaway I said, 'Nothing of the sort!'

Umma got up and went off. Saying, 'What is it, umma?' they followed her.

So I sat there with some peace of mind. Once again I got Anumma to go and get a glass of tea. I drank it and then smoked a beedi.

Then I saw Pattumma's goat standing in the courtyard, straining to pick up with her tongue the match-box which was close by me on the verandah, so that she could eat it. I picked it up, took out the match-sticks and gave her the empty box.

Pattumma's goat ate the empty match-box with relish. Seeing that she then still stood there, I said, 'Look, beautiful, I need the match-sticks. I've got some more empty boxes, though.'

At that moment Pattumma brought it some rice-water. I said to her, 'Pattumma, your goat has eaten two of my books!'

Pattumma looked as if I had uttered some serious slander.

'Please don't talk like that—my goat wouldn't do such a thing,' she said. Then, very quietly, 'What about the earrings?'

I, too, spoke very quietly.

'I haven't forgotten!'

'Nobody need know!' said Pattumma very quietly, and she went off with her pot.

Meanwhile, Rashid and Subaida were in tears. As if in sympathy, Arifa, Saidu Muhammad and Laila had started to cry. Every so often, Laila made the statement, 'I shan't take mummy!' While all this was going on, along came Abu with a letter. After giving me the letter, he went off with his stick, shouting, 'What's all this?' Immediately they all stopped crying. The house was silent!

I opened the letter and read it. It is from Madras city, a long way from here. M. Govindan, Esq.'s wife, Dr Patmavati Amma, has given birth to a son. Mother and child are well.

I immediately wrote a reply conveying my best wishes to mother and son. I congratulated Bala on having a younger brother. I instructed the father to deposit two and a half rupees in the bank on her account. I praised him for the fact of Mr M. Govindan having become a worthy father for the second time. In addition to this I wrote that, if he saw A. Narayanan Nambyar, M.A., K.C.S. Panikkar, David George, Janamma, Parukkutti Amma, K. A. Kodungalore, K. P. G. Panikkar (Gopa Kumar), Sharat Kumar, Ramji, R. M. Manikkat and the rest of my friends in Madras, he was to let them know that I was living with my umma, and to tell them that I asked after them. Then, once again wishing all the best to father, children and mother, I brought the letter to a close, put it in an envelope, sealed it well, wrote the address, called Abu and gave it to him with instructions to post it without delay. It was then that I remembered something.

'Wait,' I said. 'I've been having serious complaints about you. You've been taking all the money in Abdulkhadar's shop and giving it as loans to others. You've taken the agency for all the monthly magazines you can find. You don't care a hoot for anybody. Is this true?'

In reply to all of this he said, 'Nobody can stand the sight of me.'

Before I could say anything, he went on, 'See how things are now you're here! Our sisters-in-law, our second sister, our eldest sister, along with umma, have swept the court-yard and compound, made a heap of the rubbish and burnt it, and made the place clean. I told them about it earlier, but nobody took a blind bit of notice. They all told me to sweep it myself. What's happening now? All this is work done so that they can touch you for some money. When somebody well-off came, they did all this to make him happy. Am I well-off? Have I any money? Elder brother, we must build a wall round the courtyard. We must put new beams in the roof and tile it.'

'What do you mean when you say "we"?' I asked.

'You must put up the money. Where do I have any ready cash?'

He had his meal and went off with the letter. Only after he gets to the shop can Abdulkhadar come home. As soon as he left, Hanifa came.

Hanifa had been a soldier. When that was over, he started a tailor's shop; he also had a cycle shop. Usually Hanifa is well turned out. Double dhoti and jubba, hair combed and face clean-shaven. Now he was only wearing a dhoti. He had something on his mind. I kept quiet. If I say any-thing. . . !

'Elder brother, I'm considering selling my place,' he said. 'I'll let you have it for a low price.'

'Why are you selling it now?'

'I've no money. If I had some, wouldn't I get a shirt made to wear?'

'What price do you want for the place?'

'As it's you, I'll let it go cheap. Give me ten thousand rupees.'

Ten thousand rupees! I knew what price he had paid for it. Changing the subject I asked, 'What are you giving now for household expenditure?'

Two or three years earlier, Hanifa's contribution for

household expenditure was two annas a day. For food and drink for him and his wife and two children. He didn't buy any bedding. He didn't buy oil or soap for bathing. That was all included in the two annas. Abdulkhadar would abuse him. He is shameless. If you pressed him on the subject, he would at once say, 'I shall go and join the army! The government needs me.'

Nevertheless, at that time, through my mediation, there were some adjustments. I made the two annas four annas. Gradually it was raised to twelve annas. As soon as I had gone, Hanifa cut it down. I remember hearing something about it being finally reduced to the original two annas. Hanifa fathered another child. That was an additional reason to make him pay more money. But the reply he gave had nothing to do with my question.

'Because of trouble from second brother, I can't live here,' he said.

'What trouble is there with Abdulkhadar?'

'He came into my shop with a bundle of currency notes. A lot of important gentlemen were sitting there. Next thing he said, "Hey, look at this!" and hit me in the face with the bundle of notes. Then, with the words "If you venture money, you'll make money!", he limped off. I was embarrassed. Don't I buy beedis for you every day? Don't I get you a box of matches every day? Why is it, that when I venture money, I don't make money?'

He is right.

But my reply had nothing to do with that.

'You've got Rashid as well now,' I said. 'What are you giving to buy food?'

He immediately said, 'I shall go and join the army. The government needs me.'

He got angry and went inside. After finishing his meal, he went straight to his tailor's shop.

While I was having my meal, Pattumma's goat came on to the verandah and got ready for a bit of 'inter-caste' dining. I shouted, 'Pattumma, come here quickly!'

Pattumma did so and got it to follow her into the compound.

'You should keep it tethered,' I said.

'Dear elder brother,' Pattumma replied. 'It doesn't like being tied up.'

At dusk Kochunni came. Sometimes he used to sleep in the house. Just by me. On the other side of me would be umma. On the far side of Kochunni would be Abu. Hanifa, along with his family, in the other room. Abdulkhadar, along with his family, in the main part of the house. On the verandah, inside a screen made of jute sacking, Sulaiman and his family. When he is not sleeping in the house, Kochunni goes off with his family. In front, bearing a lighted torch, will be Kochunni; in its light, just behind, Pattumma; close behind Pattumma, like a tail, the ten-year-old Khadija; just behind Khadija, the goat.

2)

The havoc caused by Pattumma's goat began in the morning. It would be about eight o'clock. I had rubbed oil on my head and body and put on my briefs and was doing my exercises, when I heard the children kicking up a din in the compound.

'Stupid twit! Stupid twit!'

'Grab its tail! Grab its tail!'

'Did you see it piddle! Did you see it piddle!'

'Grab the horns! Grab the horns!'

What was going on? I looked through the window. Nothing in particular. Pattumma's goat had eaten up the whole of the front part of Abi's shorts. It had caught hold of the rest of them also. Abi had his arms round the goat's neck. Pattukkutti was pulling at the tail. Saidu Muhammad had got hold of the horns. Arifa was standing there bewildered. Rashid and Subaida were sitting in the compound, sucking their thumbs and not paying attention to anything else. Laila was holding on to the goat's side and calling it bad names.

'Stupid twit! Stupid twit!'

I wrapped a bath-towel round me, passed from the room on to the verandah, went out into the compound and, catching hold of one of the goat's ears, freed Abi. The goat had eaten not only the front part of Abi's shorts, but also one of his pockets.

When I got the full story, Pattumma's goat was not at fault. There had been some rice-cakes in the pocket of Abi's shorts. He had taken one out and given a bit to the goat. Then, after stuffing the rest inside the front of his trousers, he had stood in front of the goat, telling her to eat it. The goat ate the cake and also the front part of the shorts. It had eaten what was in the pocket together with the pocket.

'Bapa will beat me!' said Abi.

'Shouldn't you have thought about that sooner? Serves you right!' I said. After a pause I added, 'Come on, there's nothing to be scared of. Nobody'll tell on you.'

I told Pattukkutti, Laila and Saidu Muhammad to keep it a secret. I also advised Laila not to call anyone a 'stupid twit'.

After finishing my exercises, I got ready to go and bathe in the river. I called Saidu Muhammad and Pattukkutti. Then Abi and Laila came too. They had not been to bathe with their father. They were standing waiting to go with me. There was no special reason. Laila had taken Abi's slate pencil and broken it into small pieces. For this their father took neither Abi nor Laila to bathe. Hanifa had given Pattukkutti and Abi a half anna to buy slate pencils.

I took them all to the river, gave them a bath and stood them on the bank. Then I dived down and splashed about. I was bathing like this, when I heard Abi call out, 'Uncle!'

I looked round. No-one had gone into the water. I swam to the bank and asked, 'What is it?'

'I've got no trousers!' Abi said.

He made clear what he meant. He had nothing to hide his nakedness. How could he go completely undressed along the country lane?

'You came like that, didn't you?' I said.

That was true enough. But Abi could now see a school-mate of his on the ferry-boat. He was wearing a dhoti!

I therefore gave Abi a towel to hide his nakedness. Then Pattukkutti also needed something to cover her. She, too, wanted a dhoti!

When I had finished bathing, I picked up my dhoti and put it on. Then I took off the towel, wrung it out and wiped my head. After that I dipped it in the water, wrung it out again and wrapped it round Pattukkutti.

Laila and Saidu Muhammad had not taken it into their heads to feel shy. If they had, what could I have done? I had only two towels with me.

When I got home, Abdulkhadar and Hanifa were there quarrelling. The cause of the quarrel was nothing in particular: Abdulkhadar had come to know the previous day that Hanifa gave nothing towards the cost of food for the house. Hanifa did not like that. So he and his family were going to leave!

'Come on out, Aishomma!' Hanifa shouted. 'Call the children also.'

He and his family were going to their banana-grove, where they would make a hut of palm-leaves. When I looked, I saw that the dhoti he was wearing was mine! He had pinched it. When I went to him and asked him, he said, 'I've no time to stand and talk, I've a lot of work to do,' and walked on. When he got as far as the gate, he said, 'It's got to the stage where I don't have any rights in this house.'

Hanifa went to his tailor's shop. I asked Abdulkhadar, 'Tell me, can't you save me from all this uproar? Can't you have another word with that inspector about moving out?'

'Don't you have everything you need here?' said Abdulkhadar. 'You have oil, ghee, milk, tea, beedis, matches, bananas, tomatoes, pineapples, plantains, jack-fruits, meals; and umma, me, Abu and Kochunni as company? What more do you want?'

Abdulkhadar was a schoolmaster. A great one for correct grammar, too. Long ago, he said to umma, 'Mater, kindly give me some pure water.' On that occasion umma beat him with the spoon she used for serving rice. Bapa consoled him.

'It's fair enough if you talk like that. What'll you call me?'

'Pater.'

On hearing that, umma gave him another one with the spoon. After that, he only called them 'umma' and 'bapa'. The cripple!

They started him and me at school together on the same day. In those days it was the 'Muhammadan School'. It was a devout man called Umbiyannan who got it built.

At that time Mr Pudusseri Narayana Pillai was the first-form teacher. He was the one who taught Abdulkhadar and me the 'ABC'.

Both in school and out Abdulkhadar was a proper rascal. I was well-behaved in school. He, on the other hand, got a lot of beatings from Mr Narayana Pillai.

Abdulkhadar used to kick the other children by swinging round his lame right leg while standing on the left one. He kicked me too in the same fashion. Then he would bring the sole of his right foot up to his nose and ask, 'Can you do that?'

Impossible! How could we? Are other people's legs that supple? This physical feat was beyond the capacity of others.

'In that case then, smell it!' The others had to smell the sole of the crippled foot. If not, he would punch them! If the other children moved to a safe distance, he would beat his chest and cry. Because of his lameness, people in general felt sorry for him. He exploited that to the utmost. No matter what he did, it was somebody else's fault. Children would stand there and let him punch them. I too have let him punch me. I have lost count of the number of blows I received. I had to carry his slate and books. I was the elder of the two. By rights, it is the younger brothers who should carry the older brothers' slates and books. But I had to carry his. If I did not, he would punch me!

I kept on getting beaten; I kept on carrying his books. The storm of protest raged within me. But what was I to do? He would place his slate and books on the road, stand near me with clenched fist and ask quietly, 'Are you going to take my slate and books?'

Every day I would say I didn't feel like it. Then I would argue about the rights and wrongs of it all.

'Aren't I your elder brother?'

'Are you going to pick them up or aren't you?'

'No!'

Then, standing on one leg, he would draw back, swing round and strike me full in the chest. Slightly stunned, I would fall down and lie there. He would stand back and order me, 'Get up and take them! Let's go. If you turn up late, the teacher'll beat you!'

I would lie there and think sadly: What justice is there in this, for a younger brother to deal out punches and for an elder brother to take them—and then to carry books and slate? I would lie there, and he would sit on my chest and ask, 'Do you want some more?'

'No,' I would concede. 'I'll carry them.'

So I would get up and carry his slate, books and so on. How often this happened! How many blows I got!

One day, while this state of affairs was continuing, I had a bright idea. Before he swung his arm round to punch me, I struck him, on his good leg!

There lay Abdulkhadar, flat out! On his back!

Straight away I jumped on to his chest. As if I had done him a great injustice, he asked, 'What's going on? Aren't I smaller than you? Is it fair to sit on my chest?'

I clenched my fist to punch him and he started to cry.

'Don't hit me! I'm your younger brother.'

Younger brother! Hm!

'Why didn't you think of that sooner?'

'From now on I'll always remember.'

'Right,' I asked, 'When we see a dog, who throws first?'

'You, elder brother.'

'When we bathe in the river, who is the first to dive in and go to the other side?'

'You.'

'When something is pinched from home, who gives you some?'

'You.'

'When the chalk is pinched from teacher Nara Pillai's table, who gives you some?'

'You.'

'So?'

'I shall carry your slate and books,' he said.

'You'll carry your own,' I said.

'Then who walks in front?'

'I do.'

So from then on Abdulkhadar knew his place as younger brother. He's the one I'm talking about.

The cripple!

'Hey,' I said, 'Couldn't you just have a word with that inspector and ask him to move out? Stuck in the middle of all the racket there is in this house, I'm having a hard time of it. This is something beyond your comprehension.'

'My dear elder brother, the man is looking for a place. The excise people, too, are looking for a place. Be patient and stay here for just a few more days.'

Supported by his iron stick, he hobbled off to his shop.

I had cut a pineapple in half and was removing the skin from one piece, when the goat turned up at the window and the children at the door. I mixed some mashed banana and ghee with some *puttu* (made from rice flour and coconut) and gave a knob of it to each of the children. One piece each of the pineapple too. On getting some puttu from me, the children would go off and make their usual noise. But unseen by any one of Abi, Pattukkutti, Laila, Arifa and Khadija, Anumma's son Saidu Muhammad would come and show his face. He would pretend to be just standing there, leaning on the pillar and singing. I would give him an extra-special knob of puttu. When this snack was over, I would give the banana skin and so on to Pattumma's goat. After that I would wash my hands and go and sit in a chair on the verandah with a glass of tea. At that time the school-children would be passing by. As usual the girls would be looking at me.

It was only later that I understood the secret hidden in this look. I shall tell you about it in due course.

On that day, Abi and Pattukkutti were going to school as usual. Before they set off, Abi, who was quietly hiding from the people in the house, beckoned me.

What had happened?

I went out. Pattukkutti was sitting quietly at the foot of a coconut tree. The moment I reached him, Abi said, 'It's the half-anna that bapa gave to buy a slate pencil. . . .'

'Half-anna?'

'It was in the pocket of my shorts!'

'What on earth are you talking about?'

'The pocket the goat ate!'

Hm! Pattumma's goat had also swallowed half an anna.

'Don't tell anybody about this,' I said. 'Keep it top secret. Let's see if there's any way to get half an anna.'

'If ummamma sees me, she'll beat me!' Abi reminded me.

'You hide there!'

I went and borrowed two annas from Pattumma, took half an anna from this to give to Abi and Pattukkutti, and sent them to school.

Pattumma's goat was standing in the courtyard. At any moment two quarter-annas were likely to fall out. I went and waited. But only very small droppings were coming out, and nothing the shape of a coin.

Was it not going to drop out? My eyes were fixed on the rear end of the goat.

Meanwhile, group after group of girl students were passing along the road, looking at me diffidently. I felt pleased. They would know who I was. It was for that reason that they looked at me as they passed. They would be carrying on a conversation among themselves (Please remember that this is all in my imagination!):—

The girl with curly locks: 'Do you know who it is lying in the canvas chair?'

The doe-eyed girl: 'As if I don't know! It's the well-known literary figure, Vaikom Muhummad Basheer!'

The girl with a voice like a nightingale: 'I'm going to get him to write in my autograph-book!'

The one with cat's eyes: 'It's not him. Don't you see the house? It's just a hut!'

The girl with a honey-sweet voice: 'Get away with you, cat's eyes! It is him. You want to see me get him to write in my autograph-book today?'

Cat's eyes: 'It's all right to talk! Let's see it!'

Well, on that day, on the way to school after their midday meal, they came to my house!

Then I remembered another incident. I was living in the other building at the time.

Having been informed that I had returned home, the High School headmaster came and told me that it was the school anniversary; I must make a speech. All I needed to do was give the children a bit of advice.

'I don't usually make speeches. Moreover, at that time I won't be here.'

'We'll print your name on the notice,' he said. 'You need come only if you happen to be here.'

They printed the notice; my name was on it. What was I to do? I had come here in order to be able to write something in peace and quiet! Hm!

While I was standing there among the plants, there was a pair of eyes between the bars of the gate! A girl with curly hair. I thought she might have come for some jasmine or something.

'What is it?' I asked.

'They've printed your name on the notice,' she said. 'You have to give us a talk. So be sure to come.'

'If I'm here at the time, I'll come.'

After that, she and the other girls would come up to the gate every day and call out, 'Be sure to come, won't you?'

But the day before the anniversary I took off! I went without luggage or bedding. Empty-handed. I told only umma. And the day after the anniversary was over, I returned. That very day, the curly-headed girl and the rest of them came and asked, 'Why did you do it?'

'Didn't I say I'd come if I was here?' I said.

'You're a fine one!'

That was the end of that.

I looked to see if the curly-headed girl was among those going by the gate. No; all of that group must have grown up by now. How quickly these girls grow up!

I considered getting a pen to write in their autograph-books. Then I thought: Wait; let them come and stand there for a little while.

They came. They did not even look at me! They went straight to the foot of the jambu tree, said something to umma and gave her something. Umma gave them a whole pile of jambu fruits that she had tied in a cloth. As they stood there eating one each, they looked towards the jambu tree with delight. Donkeys! The jambu fruits they were eating were tied up in umma's dirty cloth. I was clean. Couldn't they even look at me?

In a flash it all became clear. It was not me the girls had been looking at!

When they had gone, I asked umma, 'What was it they gave you?'

'An anna,' said umma.

'Have you been selling jambu fruits to those girls?'

'What else!'

'How many did you give for an anna?'

'Twenty.'

Fine! And to think of how many twenties I had fed to Pattumma's goat!

The indifference shown by those girls in not looking at me

made me sit and think. I asked umma, 'Who was it planted that jambu tree?'

'You grew it from a seed you brought from Taliyakkal,' she said.

There is a Jacobite family near here called Taliyakkal (which is also the name of the place where they live). There I have three friends, Thomas, Matthankunju and Kunjappan. *I* brought the seed from their place. *I* am the one who planted it. And those donkeys did not even look at me!

I jumped up and said to umma, 'Give me that anna!'

Umma gave it to me at once. I went and bought some beedis. Then I made my way to the river bank, where I sat down and puffed away thinking of the girls who did not look at me. What cheek!

After that, the girls looked at my jambu tree every day. Jambu fruits were hanging there in big bunches. I would say to myself, 'Donkeys, just you wait! It's my jambu tree. It was I who planted it. . . . Donkeys!'

How could I take revenge on them? I was waiting in the chair. These days I didn't go to lie down inside my room. That's how things were when they came! I got up and went and asked them scornfully, 'What do you want?'

'Half an anna's worth of jambus.'

'Give me the money!'

I took the money and twisted it in the edge of my dhoti. Then I picked out the smallest ten and gave them to the girls.

'What's this? They're all so small! If the lady's here, she gives us big ones.'

'This tree has nothing to do with that lady. That's why she gives so freely.'

Donkeys!

'Then give us one more!'

'I'm the one who took the trouble to grow this tree, and I say that's enough.'

I did not give even one more.

Those gluttons went off saying, 'What a man!' Greedy guts! They can't even look at me. But they are not bashful when it comes to looking at my jambu tree.

When I sold jambus like this, umma would come and ask for money. I would ask her, 'Why? What has this tree to do with you? It is the fruits of my toil. It is my drops of sweat that are hanging there as jambus. All those years you've been selling them! Where's all the money?'

Umma was standing there nonplussed. I did not stop at that.

'Then you ask for money for everything. Must buy this, must buy that. So much money! Who planted the tamarind tree?'

On one side of the compound there was a large tamarind tree. From the roots up, the whole tree was covered with bunches of tamarinds. Umma used to sell those also. Yet did I not plant that one too?

'It was planted by your bapa,' said umma. 'I have watered it a great deal.'

Then we do not have the rights of ownership over that one.

Umma got cross and went off.

I called Anumma and told her to get me some tea. Anumma went next door and got a boy to fetch some. While I was sitting there enjoying a beedi after drinking the tea, along came a lovely, dark-skinned girl! She would be around sixteen years old. It must be for jambus. Was she one of the quarter-anna lot? Or did she want half an anna's worth? I would give the donkey small ones only. But she did not look in the direction of the jambu tree. She came straight up to me and greeted me respectfully with folded hands. Then she said, 'I know you, sir. I have read all your books. My father told me you had come. That's why I am here. Would you please write something in my autograph-book and sign it!'

Oh, you dark beauty come to save my self-respect, my blessings on you!

'Tell me! What's your name?' I asked.

'Suhasini,' she said.

'What form are you in at school?'

'The sixth.'

'Who are you?'

'I am Madhavan the porter's daughter.'

The daughter of a labourer?

Long live labourers!

I went indoors to fetch a pen and wrote in Suhasini's autograph-book, 'To Suhasini: all good wishes.' Then, after signing it and giving it back to her, I asked Suhasini, 'Do you want to eat some jambus?'

'Yes please,' she said.

I fetched a large piece of paper, climbed into the tree and picked about fifty big red ones, which I wrapped up and gave to her, saying as I did so, 'Suhasini, I'm the one who planted this jambu tree.'

'Really?'

'Really!'

With folded hands, she took leave of me.

That night I heard a special bit of news.

'Pattumma's goat will soon be giving birth!' It was not just in kid, but about to give birth. Why was it that I did not know about this? It did not appear to be in kid. Sometimes its belly bulged out; sometimes it went in. Would that be the case if the goat was in kid? I asked umma, who said, 'It's about to give birth.'

Was it true? I had my doubts.

3)

So Pattumma's goat was about to give birth. Excellent. I was glad.

When Anumma came after sweeping my room, shaking out the bed and putting it in the sun, I asked, 'I say, did you give the goat anything?'

Anumma said she had given it some kanji-water.

'Just kanji-water's not enough. You must let it have some

grass. The best thing to give it is some oil-cake soaked in water.'

After giving these instructions, I let Anumma have a good lot of banana skins and a small banana to give to the goat. Anumma lovingly gave them to the goat before my very eyes. But it seemed to me that the women had rather mis-judged things. Women are the authorities on such matters. This I admit. Nevertheless . . . with regard to pregnancy, the women had in this case made a big mistake! I felt in-describably jubilant, because this goat that stood before me was not in kid. Its belly had gone in. The goat was eating the jambus that had fallen from the tree. Umma, too, was there. Umma was picking up the fruit.

There were jambus, like big red drops of dew, clustered thickly among the green leaves. Right in front of me, very close to the courtyard.

While I was sitting there, Pattumma turned up! What a surprise! There was a goat with her too; and Khadija. The goat that was with Pattumma, however, was in kid!

'What goat is this?' I asked Anumma.

'It's mine,' said Anumma. 'Elder sister gave it to me.'

Pattumma had given it to Anumma!

'It is the first kid that Pattumma's goat had,' umma ex-plained.

Then Anumma had a goat too! And it lived very close to me. Yet I didn't know. I was unable to tell one from an-other. They are both the same bran-colour. Later, when I look carefully, I notice that Pattumma's goat's eyes are ringed with black.

As soon as they arrived, the goat ran inside. I asked Pat-tumma, 'I say, Pattumma, why are you and the goat so late today?'

Pattumma explained. The grass that Kochunni brings (for the night-time) is insufficient for the goat, for it is in kid. So she went into some fields and other places and, before anyone else could do so, gathered the grass and gave it to the goat.

Pattumma went off and started grumbling at her sisters-in-law and her younger sister. It seemed that the kanji-water that had been kept for Pattumma's goat was not sufficient.

'She took it and gave it to her goat! Shouldn't you at least see that my goat has enough?'

I longed to hear a quarrel between sisters-in-law. I had never heard one either between sisters-in-law or between mother and daughter-in-law. All that could be heard was umma. She is a good hand at scolding people. Then Anumma's voice came through.

'I gave my goat only a little kanji-water. We drank a little. The rest we kept.'

I said nothing of the fact that Anumma's goat ate the banana skins I gave it.

'That'll do. You needn't say anything!' said Pattumma. Then she complained, 'Even umma doesn't like me.'

'You listen,' said umma. 'After eating tapioca, one must drink a little kanji-water. We drank only a little. The whole lot went to your goat!'

Did she say that after eating tapioca one must drink kanji-water? When do they eat tapioca? It was when I enquired, that I came to know a pitiful secret. Umma, Anumma, Aishomma and Kunjanumma—none of them eats rice regularly. That is to say that they do not get any. There is rice for the men and children only. The others live on tapioca. In the morning at eleven o'clock they pound the dried tapioca into a powder and make puttu with this instead of the usual rice-flour. They put a pinch of tea leaves (generally this is given by Sulaiman) into some hot water and drink it without sugar or milk. After that they work. They all have as much work as they can manage. The men come only when it is time to eat; it is the women who endure privation. This is not the case in my house alone. This is how things are in almost all middle-class homes. The women make great sacrifices; why are men unaware of this?

) 162 (

Abdulkhadar's wife Kunjanumma could be heard saying, 'Dear Pattumma, when the goat gives birth, don't forget us. You must give a drop or two of milk for Subaida.'

Hanifa's wife Aishomma asked, 'How about my Rashid? Do you think he can't swallow milk?'

Sulaiman's wife Anumma said, 'If Saidu Muhammad, too, drinks milk, it won't do him any harm.'

Though Pattumma is the elder sister, she is not so well-educated. So Pattumma said, 'That'll do! That's enough of your airs and graces!'

When, a little later, I went quietly into my room, there was Pattumma's goat with a couple of bananas from the top of my box in its mouth. It is Pattumma's goat without a doubt! The goat has come in through the door on the east side. Anumma has forgotten to close it.

'Anumma! Pattumma!' I called out. 'Come quick! Your goat is eating my bananas!'

Anumma and Pattumma ran up. Anumma was pleased.

'This is elder sister's goat,' she said.

'Never mind!' said Pattumma. 'I'll get a couple more for you. It's because it's hungry.'

'No matter what it eats,' said Anumma, 'it'll still be hungry. It steals my goat's grass and eats it.'

'That's enough of that!' said Pattumma. 'Your goat's grass!'

'That's neither here nor there,' I said. 'You must give goat's milk to all the children.'

'How can I do that? So many things are needed. We must sell the milk to repair the door of our house!'

What to do? The door of the house that Pattumma and Kochunni and Khadija live in is tied with string! It has to be repaired.

Before I go, I must give all the women in the house a good square meal at least once.

Where is the money for that? I do not have a single cent. What I had, I have shared out among them all. To say I have shared it out is a polite way of putting it. To tell the truth, they all just grabbed it and left me with nothing. When I think of it, I get angry. I have given so many things. I gave them money, I bought pots and pans for them, I bought tumblers, I bought head-cloths for the women to wear. In spite of this they all behave as if I have not given them anything. So I am extremely irritable. If someone so much as moves, I jump on them. I scold Abu, I scold Hanifa, I scold Abdulkhadar; I beat Hanifa's, Abdulkhadar's and Sulaiman's children. I do not beat Pattumma's daughter Khadija. That is because I never see her. I include all the women in my abuse. Especially the wives of my younger brothers. When I raise my voice like that, the house is quiet. So I sit there. Pattumma's goat is standing in the courtyard, eating dried-up jack-leaves. It is good that it eats plenty. When it gives birth, there will be a lot of milk. It will be nice if Subaida, Rashid, Khadija, Abi, Saidu Muhammad and Pattukkutti drink a little milk. In my house, however, no-one uses milk or ghee. I take ghee and drink milk. But mine is a special case.

Talking about ghee and milk in this way, I am reminded of an incident that took place some twenty-five years ago.

At that time, the only four children in the family were Abdulkhadar, Hanifa, Pattumma and I! I am not entirely sure whether umma had given birth to Anumma at that time. Abu certainly had not arrived.

There was a milch-cow at home and no shortage of milk and curds.

Bapa did business in small country boats along with dealings in timber. His practice was to have timber felled in the hills, make the boats on the spot, bring them along the rivers in groups, have them finished by Ulladars, who are skilled boat-makers, and sell them wholesale for a good sum.

During those days there was always ghee in the house. Ghee gold in colour and of the right texture. There it would be, a large glass jar full.

It was ghee from a cow nourished on the rich herbs of the

Kudayattur hills! I remember bapa saying this. Next to the jar of ghee, there was sugar in another glass jar. The two stood on a corner shelf.

We used to add ghee to the rice and snacks we ate.

At that time I used to get a lot of beatings from bapa. Abdulkhadar never got any! For me there were beatings in plenty. Sometimes the reason was plain; at other times it was not. Fathers beat children. So do mothers. Oh yes, ... my umma, too, beat me. She has beaten me with the wooden-spoon handle and chased me from the kitchen. Whenever I felt like a bite, I would go into the kitchen, grab hold of something and eat it. Abdulkhadar used to do the same thing. But no-one would believe it. Even though he stole something to eat, I got the blame and the beatings also.

One day, some time between morning tea and the midday meal, I seized my opportunity. I had begun to feel slightly peckish. It was the right time for a light snack. I made my way to the kitchen. Umma and the servant were there. The servant's name is Nangeli. This Nangeli used to beat me also. She has beaten me and chased me out.

I was supposed to be the young master. The servant should not beat the young master. But this sort of rule did not apply there. If I told umma, all she would say was, 'Serves you right! You took something, didn't you?' There was another justification: it seemed I had drunk milk from this Nangeli's breasts! [I have drunk a lot of women's milk, to judge from what umma and the others say.] After that I thought I would have a bite from a green mango. But there was no way of getting it. Nangeli would say, 'Stay hungry for a bit. You can have your meal soon. Or would you rather have a hiding?'

Hm! Without saying a word, I walked away. When I got inside the house, I made a new discovery. The ghee and the sugar were standing side by side; there were possibilities if they were mixed together. Hm! I did not wait long. Unseen by anyone I picked up a bowl. Unseen by anyone I made my way to the room where bapa slept. I slowly picked up the ghee jar and set it on bapa's bed. Slowly I removed the stopper, took some ghee with my nice clean hand and half-filled the bowl. Then I picked up the ghee jar and put it on the corner shelf. In the same way I put a lot of sugar, too, into the bowl. Both the jars were on the shelf. No matter who looked, they would not notice any difference. I had put them back just as bapa left them. With a spoon bapa used to just level off the contents of the jars. After doing the same thing with my hand, I sat on bapa's bed and mixed together the ghee and sugar. Then I put a little in my mouth and crunched away. It was hard-grained sugar and it had not dissolved well! Anyhow, I was eating it in fine style. Then softly, very softly, came a whispered question! I was startled. The person asking the question was Abdulkhadar. He was standing close by me. How and when did he enter the room? I had no idea. He asked softly, 'What is it you're eating?'

'Some medicine,' I whispered.

'I was just behind you. I saw everything. Give me some too, or I'll tell!'

As if it were a big secret I said softly, 'Tell me, you're my younger brother, aren't you?'

'In that case, give me some too.'

I gave him some. It was he who licked the bowl clean.

'From now on I won't take any,' I said, 'and you mustn't either.'

Having agreed on this, we went outside. We took the bowl back to where I had got it from and walked along as if nothing had happened.

It is the absolute truth that after that I never took any ghee or sugar. I did not know how nutritious ghee is. Just because there was nothing else, I had eaten some ghee and sugar. There were many things to eat in the house. There were ripe jack-fruits and mangoes. There was a jar full of fried meat in the cupboard. I turned my attention to these things. A few days passed like that. Then I found myself getting beaten for nothing, while Abdulkhadar was seriously ill!

The reason I got beaten was that somebody had been sticking his hand in the jar to steal the ghee. There were marks on the outside of the jar and on the bed. So I got beaten. It was Abdulkhadar's illness that was interesting. He had become as fat as a drum. He was always drinking water. He had no appetite.

'There's something wrong with the child,' umma and Nangeli said. Bapa went to fetch the astrologer. At that time the astrologer was the best physician available.

During this period umma would take Abdulkhadar on her knee and caress him sadly.

'Oh God, what has happened to my precious boy?'

'Oh Lord,' said Nangeli, 'let nothing happen to my darling.'

Without any expression, Abdulkhadar would sit there sick, fat and the centre of attention.

I looked him in the face, putting on an expression intended to convey the words, 'You thief! There you sit, you fat lump, after stealing and eating all the ghee!'

He did not flinch at all. The astrologer came. After that came Velan, another doctor. After that the Muslim elder came.

So the days passed. The ghee decreased. I got beatings as usual. Abdulkhadar was just like a drum. He did not take any medicine. He would throw it away without anyone seeing. Occasionally he would eat a little rice. Everybody would pet him because he was ill. Yet he was not in the least sick. He went about as usual.

I was sure that he was eating the ghee and sugar every day. But whom should I tell? If I said anything, nobody would believe me.

One day I gave him some fried meat I had stolen from the cupboard without anyone seeing. He took the meat and ate it.

'Look,' I said, 'you're my younger brother. Tell me

straight. It's because you ate the ghee and sugar that you are like a drum.'

'Please go away. Didn't they tell you I'm ill?'

How can I bring his deception to the notice of others? If I tell someone, who will believe it? Anyway, I told umma, and I also told Nangeli, that *he* was the big thief who was eating up the ghee and sugar.

It was as I said. Nobody believed me. It must have been because of my innocence that something happened. It was a Friday. Bapa had gone to the mosque for Jum'a, the Friday prayers. Umma was next door with some women, looking for fleas and gossiping. Among other things, they talked about Abdulkhadar's mysterious illness. After hearing all that, I came back to the house. Nangeli was asleep. Going to the kitchen, I had a bit of a look round. I picked up a few items and ate them. After that I came quietly through the house on to the verandah. I heard something in bapa's bedroom. The noise of someone crunching! . . . Quietly I looked in. I saw two legs under bapa's bed. One of them was a withered leg.

Abdulkhadar was eating ghee and sugar.

Quietly, very quietly, I went outside and ran to umma.

'If you want to see Abdulkhadar's sickness, come quickly!'

I brought them all and got them to stand quietly near the door. I squeezed inside and suddenly opened both doors fully.

Abdulkhadar was sitting under the bed, eating ghee and sugar from a bowl!

Having caught him red-handed, I brought him outside. Umma beat him right and left. Hearing the din, Nangeli woke up. On learning what had taken place, she too beat him.

I stood there watching that pleasing sight.

When bapa came, he beat him also.

When all this was over and we were alone, he asked me, 'I'm your younger brother, aren't I? Why did you do this to me?'

'You big thief!' I said. 'I've received so many beatings on
your behalf. Did you remember then that I was your elder
brother—you big thief!'

Recollecting all of this, I was laughing away to myself.
Then my dear old mother came up and asked, 'Why are you
sitting there laughing?'

'I was laughing about something that took place long ago,'
I said. 'You remember the time when Abdulkhadar stole
the ghee and sugar and became as fat as a drum—'

'You haven't forgotten that—eh?'

'No.'

'If you've got any money, give me five rupees or so. Pattumma's goat has smashed the pot we cook rice in!'

'It must have been Anumma's goat,' said Pattumma.

Anumma came up and said, 'It wasn't my goat; it was
definitely yours.'

'That'll do, that'll do,' said Pattumma. 'Don't you see
elder brother's here? Show a bit of respect. How did you
know it was my goat? Just tell me that!'

'I said that so that elder brother should know what's going
on,' said Anumma. 'If your goat comes, I at once take mine
inside and tie it up. Your goat steals my goat's grass and
eats it. The same with our tapioca puttu. It even steals our
unsweetened tea and drinks it. The children won't get
anything to eat. Your goat will eat everything!'

'That'll do!' said Pattumma. 'You and your goat that never
steals! Where did you get the goat from?'

'You gave it to me,' said Anumma.

'Then look here,' said Pattumma. 'In this world how many
elder sisters have given goats to their younger sisters? Just
tell me that!'

'Oh,' said Anumma. 'There are plenty of elder sisters who
give their younger sisters elephants! And you make so
much fuss about this miserable goat!'

Pattumma was furious.

'It's lucky for you elder brother is here!' she said. 'Other-

wise would I have let you stay? Don't say anything that
will displease our Creator. I had two goats. One of them I
gave to my dear younger sister. Just you remember that!'

Pattumma came up to me and asked in a low voice, 'Did
you forget about Khadija's earrings?'

I, too, spoke in a low voice.

'No.'

Softly Pattumma advised me, 'Nobody need know.'

At once Anumma came up to me and asked, 'What secret
is elder sister telling you?'

Pattumma ran up and said, 'I didn't tell him anything!'

'No!' said Anumma. 'I understand. Without any of us
knowing, you've told elder brother to give you something.'
Turning to me, she asked, 'What is it you've agreed to
give?'

Then from somewhere came the sound of two mysterious
voices in unison. They belonged to Abdulkhadar's wife,
Anumma, and Hanifa's wife, Aishomma.

'If it's gold or ornaments, we want some for our children
also.'

I have no idea where they got hold of this information. It
may have something to do with women's intuition.

But as soon as she heard that, Pattumma got furious again
and said, 'Come on, Khadija, call our goat and let's go.
This is the sort of rotten lot they are here. We mustn't set
foot in this house again!'

Anumma understood. She was pleased.

'Good God!' she said. 'So that's it! Gold!! What is it
you've said you'll give her?'

I said, or rather I proclaimed, 'Understand this, all of you!
It's a pair of earrings for Khadija. I have said I'll get them
made for her. And I intend to do so. Has anybody any
objections?'

'Dear elder brother,' said Anumma. 'I want a pair too!'

'That's enough of your jealousy, enough. Hasn't elder
brother said that when you move to your new house, he'll
buy you all the pots and pans you'll need there? Didn't he

agree to do that? I'm well aware of all this. Did you hear me, younger sister?'

How did Pattumma come to know this secret?

4)

Hearing an uproar, I went to the kitchen and saw all the women standing there somewhat bewildered. Umma was in charge of the proceedings. In the middle was Pattumma's goat. It had no head! That is to say that somehow, being greedy, it had put its head into a pot. And now it was standing there unable to get it out. When I say it was standing there, I mean that all the women were holding it there like that. How was the pot to be removed? That was the main concern.

I had now seen evidence of the way Pattumma's goat misbehaved. Pattumma felt it was something of a disgrace.

'Elder brother, it doesn't usually do this sort of thing,' she said.

With a small stone I broke the pot and set the goat free.

'We too could have done that!' umma said. 'A clever piece of work! Breaking a perfectly good pot!'

Ignominiously I returned to the verandah. Then Abdulkhadar's eldest daughter, Pattukkutti, ran up shouting, 'Uncle!' Some of her upper teeth were missing.

'Abi hit me!' she said.

Abi ran up and said, 'She hit me too.'

I sent them away with a warning that they were not to quarrel again. Then along comes Saidu Muhammad with another complaint.

'Uncle,' he called, 'Laila called me a stupid twit!'

Terrible! For a boy to be called a stupid twit—and that, too, by a girl!

'Laila!' I shouted. Laila came, her eyes filled with tears, and said as soon as she arrived, 'We won't take you with us!'

'Never mind that! Let me have a stick, boy!'

Saidu Muhammad brought some sticks from a tamarind

tree. I held them up to frighten Laila and then sent her off, after warning her never again to call anyone a stupid twit. Some hens, half running, half flying, and uttering terrible squawks, came and fell on me as I lay in the canvas chair. After that, also at a run, up came Pattumma's goat too! Nothing in particular, except that Pattumma's goat had broken a large kanji pot! I could hear the voices of the two Anummas (that is to say Anumma and Kunjanumma) and Aishomma, umma's scolding, the children's laughter, Pattumma's apologies. As if she knew nothing of all this, Pattumma's goat stood at the foot of the jack-tree.

When it was four o'clock, I went out for a stroll, which took me as far as the market.

Then I saw something which surprised me. Abi and Pattukkutti were sitting in the middle of a crowd with a small basket full of jambu fruits; like a couple of mice surrounded by thousands upon thousands of elephants. The two of them were conducting a sale. Abi was the salesman.

'One of my hands for a quarter anna. Both my hands plus one for two quarter annas!'

That is to say, a quarter of an anna for five. Eleven for half an anna. For Abi's hand has five fingers. I just stood there watching the transaction. They sold six annas worth. I took all the six annas.

That night I handed over eight annas to umma. Umma was pleased.

In the interval between supper and going to bed, I talked to their fathers about the way the children should be brought up. I said something on the subject of giving enough food to the mothers. I talked of the need to instil a sense of cleanliness into the children. I spoke about the necessity for keeping the house and its surroundings tidy. In reply to all of this, Hanifa said, 'I shall go and join the army.'

Abu said, 'You must be prepared to spend a little money. We have to replace the roof of the house and get it tiled. If you look into it, everything will be fine. Because you are here, the courtyard's all done.'

I had spent some money and made a good job of it. I had had a stone wall built.

'Never mind all that,' said Abdulkhadar. 'Everything'll work out great. Just wait till Pattumma's goat produces a kid!'

A few days passed.

Wham! Pattumma's goat had a kid!

I think the happy event was due to take place at noon. It was drizzling slightly. As soon as I heard the news, I became anxious. All sorts of things can go wrong. I recalled many cases of death in childbirth. I got more and more worried.

'Umma, please stand nearby!' I requested. Umma said nothing. I got really anxious. What was going to happen? What if I were to go and take a look? But I didn't have the nerve for it. Just the same, I had a peep. The only thing I didn't see was the goat. What I did see was a crowd of people. Umma, the two Anummas, Aishomma, Pattuk-kutti, Abi, Arifa, Saidu Muhammad, Rashid, Subaida, and, in addition to them, the women of the neighbourhood. It was like some big celebration. Everybody was happy.

Why does nobody feel concerned, I thought. I called umma and asked, 'Did you send for Pattumma?'

Pattumma was the person who really must be there. But they had not sent for her! As far as umma and the other women were concerned, there was nothing to it. It was then that I realised that to them this was no great matter. Each of them has borne children. Umma has given birth to quite a few. Umma's daughters Pattumma and Anumma have had children; Anumma and Aishomma, who are married to umma's sons, have had children too. When they hear about the expected birth, it is no great news to them! If they hear anywhere about a birth taking place, the only question they will have to ask is, 'Is it a boy or a girl?'

But I, who was not familiar with any of this, felt somewhat uneasy.

I was alone in a chair on the western side of the house. I was not getting any news. What was going on on the other side? I smoked my way through a good few beedis. I paced to and fro quite a lot. While I was walking like that, Abi and Pattukkutti came to where I was.

''Bi was the first to see it,' said Abi proudly.

'No he wasn't! I was the first to see it!' said Pattukkutti.

By that time Laila and Saidu Muhammad had arrived, and Saidu Muhammad said, 'I was the first to see it!'

Laila said, 'I won't take you, uncle! I was the first to see it!'

What was it that these young imps were the first to see?

I asked Abi, 'Hey! What is it that you saw first?'

With pride Abi said, 'The whole birth from start to finish. . . . 'Bi was the first to see it!'

'Has the goat given birth?' I asked.

'It has,' said Pattukkutti, 'and I was the first to see the whole birth, uncle!'

Wow! It had given birth. Without any difficulty. I felt relieved and went and had a look. On the verandah were mother and kid. The kid was beautiful and white. It lay there, coolly looking at this great universe.

I felt like asking that the mother be bathed in warm water and that milk be given to the kid. But where *is* the milk? There is some hot water. If I were to say anything, the women would treat it as a joke. Nevertheless, I asked umma, 'Did you give it something?'

They had not given it anything! After a while they would give it some special leaves, from a fig tree or something. That is what is usually done.

'Give the kid a mat to lie on,' I said. 'Is it just going to lie on the damp floor?'

I don't know whether they gave it a mat to lie on or not. I went off and fetched a large banana, which I gave to the mother. She ate it with gratitude.

The women all looked at me as if to say, 'What's all this?' Umma alone sat there smiling.

After dark, Pattumma, Khadija and Kochunni came. They said nothing when they heard the news that the goat had had a kid.

At bedtime I asked, 'Where have you put the baby goat?'

'In the kitchen,' said somebody.

'Won't there be a fire in the fire-place?' I asked.

'We've put it under a basket,' said umma.

Marvellous! They've put it under a basket!

'Anumma, won't it feel suffocated? Would you put any of your own children under a basket like this?' I asked.

'Then what do you want us to do with it?' There was an answer on these lines. I don't know who said it. I lay there quietly. There was no point in my saying anything in the midst of these child-bearers. When I was not there, they would get together and laugh about it. In the first place, I had never married. Then it was better not to talk on a subject I knew nothing about. I covered myself with the sheet, closed my eyes and just lay there.

The next morning, after I had got up and had my bath and so on, I asked Anumma as I sat there drinking tea, 'Did you give it anything?'

Anumma knew what 'it' referred to. It was Pattumma's goat.

'We gave it some grass,' said Anumma. That is to say, some grass that was there for Anumma's goat.

Pattumma's goat and kid were standing in the compound under the jack-tree. The mother might have brought its offspring to show it where their food came from. The kid, unsteady on its feet, fell down. All this walking was a bit difficult. I felt like picking it up and kissing it. Then in front of me appeared Hanifa. He was not dressed. He had just put on a dhoti.

'Elder brother,' he said, 'I need ten rupees. If I ask second brother, he'll look down his nose at me. Abu will join in and pull my leg. Look, if I had any money, wouldn't I be wearing a shirt?'

'Do you think I don't remember you got a double dhoti

and a shirt from me a few days back?'

'I?...I don't want a thing. I'll go and join the army. Even if nobody here needs me, the government needs me. Just remember that, that's all. The double dhoti and shirt that you gave me—'

I cut him short. 'Hold on a bit. It's not a matter of me giving them. When they came back from the wash, you just took them without asking me. Because I have only a few dhotis and shirts, I know how many there should be. When I had plenty, umma pinched them, and Abdulkhadar pinched them. Your wife Aishomma and Abdulkhadar's wife Anumma didn't take any.'

'Abu forced me to let him have a double dhoti and shirt,' said Hanifa. 'You see the state I'm in!'

'You mean to tell me that Abu, who's as thin as a lath, stole them from somebody as robust as you?'

'If you've any doubt about it, ask Abi—Hey, Abi!'

Abi came. It is he who in all cases is the sole witness for Hanifa. As soon as he came, he said, 'What dad says, 'Bi saw!'

At this juncture, Aishomma came through the half-open door carrying Rashid on her hip and said, 'What both bapa and son said is a complete lie. I heard him teaching the boy. Your double dhoti and shirt are in Abi's bapa's trunk!'

'You thief! You rotten thief! Do you remember the time you made me and Abdulkhadar collect coconut-leaf stocks?'

'I know nothing about that,' said Hanifa. 'I've got work to do. I work my fingers to the bone.'

'Then how do you come to own that banana grove?'

'I'll let you have it,' he said. 'If you give me ten thousand rupees, it'll be enough.'

I reckon he bought it for a tenth of that amount. The rotten thief!

I called umma and when she came asked her, 'Way back when I was a kid, didn't Hanifa steal five rupees? Straight-away he fancied himself to be a rich man and got me and

Abdulkhadar, his elder brothers, to spread out a pile of coconut-leaf stocks and dry them in the sun. He didn't do the job. Each day he'd pay us a miserable four chakrams each. It was only after six or seven days that bapa came to know. Thinking I'd stolen the money, bapa gave me a hiding. Do you remember, umma?'

'What Hanifa stole,' umma said, 'was not from bapa's box. In those days I used to keep a good lot of silver coins in my betel-nut bag. Do you know how he used to steal them? Never mind. I'd better not say. His wife and children will hear it.'

'Never mind, umma. Tell us just the same.'

The reason is that I was in the habit of stealing silver coins from umma's betel-nut bag. I would go and lie by umma's side. When I saw that she was just dozing off, I would take the betel-nut bag from where she had put it in the cloth round her waist, take a few coins and, without her being aware of anything, put the bag back where I had found it. I would then get up and go away.

'Even when he was quite big,' umma said, 'Hanifa used to come and suck at my breast. It was when he stood there breast-feeding that he stole the betel-nut bag and took the money. Once I caught him at it. I beat him and sent him off and put an end to his breast-feeding!'

'The rotten thief! Didn't Abdulkhadar steal any?'

'He too stole some. You alone didn't steal any.'

I was the virtuous one! It's a grand life!

'You see, you lot! Hanifa, Abi, Laila, Rashid! You see!'

'Umma, darling umma,' said Hanifa, 'your memory's at fault. Or otherwise you're making up a story for Aishomma, Anumma and second brother's wife to hear. Eldest brother, too, stole money from your betel-nut bag, umma! I remember it well, umma: he took me and second brother along and bought tea for us. Lots of times. On all those occasions it was silver coins that he gave. Where did eldest brother get such coins from in those days? Tell us, umma!'

I straightaway decided to change the subject.

'Not counting the money you've had from me on several occasions in fives and tens, you owe me about a hundred rupees. All those friends of yours—Christians, Nayars, Ezhavas—I'll have them all appear before umma as witnesses. Come on, give me my hundred rupees!'

'Dear umma, what is eldest brother saying? That I owe him money? I have bought bananas for him. I have bought him pineapples. I have bought him beedis without number. Okra, bitter gourd, sheep's liver, duck's eggs, fish, jackfruit—if I were now to get from him proper payment for all of these, it would come to about forty rupees. What I just asked for is ten rupees on account from that sum.'

'Oh yes, you have given me things. You gave me the unripe bananas that had broken off from the trees on your estate. Before bringing them, you softened them and changed their colour by smoking them. All the rest are what Abdulkhadar or Kochunni or Sulaiman paid for and gave to you. When you dropped by here, you just brought them along. You left them here under the pretence that you had bought them.'

As soon as he heard that, he shouted, 'Hey, Aishomma, come on, bring the children. Let's not stay here any longer. We'll make a hut of palm-leaves on our own bit of land and live there. Let's go.'

'Hold on a bit,' I said. 'You can go after sorting out that business of a hundred rupees. You hear, umma. It was the time when he had four bicycles. It's not all that many years ago. In those days, when I came here, I used to take one of his bicycles and ride around. Even if I brought it back after ten minutes, he'd say, "That makes two hours!" In short, he wanted the money for hiring it. You know what he used to do in those days? He'd come along with his Christian, Nayar and Ezhava friends to my place in Ernakulam. In the same way that he has taught Abi to tell lies on his behalf, he had taught them too. As soon as they came, their conversation would be about the unfortunate condition of Hanifa. Poor Hanifa, how badly off he was, and so on! It was after all this that his request for a loan would come. Eventually he'd ask for five rupees. It was supposed to be for him to buy something for the children on my behalf. I'd give him three rupees. He'd take one anna from that and buy sweets for the children. It was at that time that I bought a bicycle for three hundred and twenty-five rupees. Somehow he came to know of it. One day he came along with his friends. Including him, there were four of them. They came on three bicycles. As soon as they arrived, there was a sit-down strike. Hanifa wanted my bicycle. Only if he had it could his rotten bikes be hired out. I said I needed the bike very urgently. Then one of his pals said that Hanifa would pay for it. He'd barely finished speaking when Hanifa threw a bundle of notes into my lap. On counting them, I found there were two hundred and forty rupees. What about the rest? Oh, he would send it the moment he got home. His friends said they would make sure he sent it. Wouldn't it be all right if they stood surety for it? Even at such a moment as that Hanifa got a ten-rupee loan from me. Also three rupees to buy something for the children. Even after several months he had still not sent the balance of what he owed. When I came here, his friends would hide if they happened to see me. Come on, let's be having that money!'

'I'll go and join the army.'

'Bi's going to join the army too,' said Abi.

'I'm going to join the army as well,' said Laila.

'In that case,' said Aishomma, 'Rashid and I will come along too. We'll cook kanji and curry for the government.'

'That's enough of that! Who are you to poke your nose in and express an opinion on this! If elder brother hadn't been here, I'd have shown you what for! Clear off!' With that, he went off to his tailor's shop in the market.

Shortly after this, umma came up to me, carrying Rashid and Subaida with her.

'We're going for a bath. Just look after the bairns for us.'

I took charge of the children. Everybody had gone to

bathe. The two of them started to cry. In order to stop them crying, I fetched the kid and put it between them.

The two children made water. The kid did numbers one and two. Abu, that stickler for cleanliness, joined our little group and then asked, 'What's all this?'

Abu stopped the children crying. He did nothing special to achieve this. He glared at them. He made faces. He shouted. He punched and chased Pattumma's goat. He beat the cats. He ran after the hens.

I used this opportunity to remove the kid's droppings and urine. I lifted the kid up and stood it in the yard.

'See how the goat, the hens, the cats and the children—all of them together—have mucked up the yard and the veran-dah! Can't you stop them from doing this?'

'What do you want me to do?'

'Beat them!'

Abu, thin as a lath though he may be, is a great one for beating people and kicking up a row. Everybody is afraid of him. Neither umma nor the other women have what it takes to get him interested in looking after the children.

'Did younger sister say I stole a shirt and dhoti from you?'

I did not say whether Anumma had said it or not. He got angry and said, 'Every single one of them stole some. Not just me. Umma and sister each stole a dhoti. Did she tell you that?'

'Anumma didn't say you stole anything.'

'I stole a dhoti and a shirt. I'll say so to anybody. What have you ever given me?'

'The bed you lie on. It cost forty rupees. The blanket, mattress, pillows and bedsheet that are on the bed. The kashmir shawl you cover yourself with. That lot alone comes to fifty rupees. The Parker fountain-pen you strut around with clipped in your pocket—that cost forty-two rupees. Then the cash I give you whenever you come to me. I have lost count.'

'These were all old things, weren't they? Did you ever give me anything new?'

'They were new when I gave you them.'

'Please let me have twenty-five rupees.'

'What do you need it for?'

'I just do.'

Hanifa asked for money. Abu asked for money. What's so special about today? Abu is not one who has a great need for money. He has a score of shirts, dhotis and vests. A case full of sandals. From what umma said, they total about sixty.

When all the women who had gone to bathe returned, the men came to eat. As soon as Abdulkhadar came, he asked, 'Elder brother, I want fifty rupees. It's urgent.'

'Beat it!'

Hanifa once more reminded me about the ten rupees he had asked for.

I didn't say a word. An hour later I solved the mystery. As postman Kuttan Pillai came through the gate, he said, 'There's a money order for you, sir. For a hundred rupees.'

One of Kuttan Pillai's cheeks was puffed up as if he had a mango in his mouth. My eyes were on that as I asked, 'Did you mention this money order to anybody, Kuttan Pillai?'

'Sir, we all belong to these parts. I need Abdulkhadar and Hanifa for many things. They told me, sir, that when a money order came for you, I was to let them know first.'

'In that case, I don't want this money order. You take it, Kuttan Pillai.'

'Goodness me, sir, what do you mean?'

'How much does fifty and twenty-five, plus ten, plus three times five come to?'

'A hundred.'

'That's how it's been shared out.'

When I explained the whole thing clearly to Kuttan Pillai, he said, 'That's the way it goes, sir.'

Hm! That's the way it goes. What a frightful conspiracy! What a swindle!

I put my signature to it while Kuttan Pillai was in the middle of giving me the news of his daughter Saraswati and how she was at college. He handed me a hundred rupees in notes. At that point umma and Anumma happened, quite by chance, to come on to the verandah.

I offered a ten-rupee note to Pattumma's goat.

Kuttan Pillai asked, 'What are you up to, sir?'

'Let it eat it,' I said. 'It's Pattumma's goat. It had a kid only a couple of days ago.'

As Kuttan Pillai went off laughing, umma asked, 'How much is it?'

'Don't you know?'

And so, before the day was over, the whole lot had gone.

5)

That evening I got a tea at Hanifa's expense. Usually it is Abdulkhadar who pays for it and it is drunk in Hanifa's shop. On that occasion Hanifa paid!

Hanifa is a very stingy fellow. There is no lamp in his shop. Right next-door is Abdulkhadar's sheet-metal shop. Here there are ten or a dozen Petromax lamps. There is a gramophone. (He got umma to cry, so that she could get it from me.) The lamps are for hiring out. If there is work to do in the evening, Hanifa calls to Abu and says, 'Move that lamp this way a bit.'

It is with light provided in that way that Hanifa sews.

While I was sitting there, I remembered a story about Abdulkhadar.

He always sits very close to the fire. There is a blacksmith's forge in his shop. He is always hard at it. I mentioned earlier that his hair has become grey. On seeing him, many people have mistaken him for my elder brother.

He has to his credit a very bold action.

We studied together up to the fourth form in a Malayalam-medium school. Then I joined an English school. When Abdulkhadar passed out of the Malayalam-medium seventh form, I rather think I was doing nine months rigorous imprisonment in Cannanore jail. You can read about that episode in the book 'Recollections'. When I came home after all that was over, the whole of my family property was mortgaged to the hilt. There wasn't a bite to eat in the house. Abdulkhadar was a teacher in the school where Mr Pudusseri Narayana Pillai taught us our 'ABC'.

I went to Cochin to start a newspaper. Some time after, when I returned home, Abdulkhadar gave up his post as a teacher and went to work in a shop, rolling beedis.

With the leaves and fragments of tobacco and a pair of scissors beside him in a basket-work tray, he would sit there rolling beedis. He would roll a couple of thousand beedis and make between one and one and a half rupees.

When I came back on a later occasion, he had given up beedi-rolling. He had installed a blacksmith's forge in a small room in the market and busied himself with work on tin-plated metal sheeting. He can make anything with tin. Nobody has taught him how to do it. It is his own native talent and endeavour.

At that time—1936–1937—I had become a literary man and was living in Ernakulam. I did a lot of writing. I had nothing to eat. Nevertheless, I went on writing. I got things published in newspapers. All these I would cut out, arrange and keep in a safe place. When I was living like that as a writer, Abdulkhadar, supporting himself on an iron stick, came up to me one day with a big fat fountain pen.

'What's all this you've been getting published in the news-papers? Let me see it. I'd like to take a look at it.'

Proudly I took my literary creations and handed them over to him. Then I got him to let me have a couple of annas and went off for a drink of tea. I walked round for a short while. Let him enjoy reading it! Then I could ask him for a further loan of four annas. With the request coming from his elder brother who had created the world's greatest literary masterpieces, he would surely give it. With such thoughts in my mind I went back into my room. Imagine what I saw! On all the things he had read he had underlined things with his fat pen! What were these lines for? When I had lit a beedi and sat down in the chair, he called out,

'Elder brother, come over here!'

It must be something important. I got up and went and sat by his side on the mat. He gave me a very contemptuous look. Then he read out a sentence. It was a really first-rate sentence. But he asked me, 'Where's the predicate in this?'

I didn't understand. What predicate?

He spoke to me as if to a small schoolboy. He lectured me on the topic of grammar, telling me about subject, predicate, concord and a whole lot of stuff like that, with all sorts of clever words. In the course of the half-hour's conversation he made me out to be an ignoramus. Then he said, 'You should take lessons in grammar.'

And that was not all. He recommended the names of a few grammar books. I was furious and said, 'Clear off! Get up and get out! You and your grammar! You big thief! You stole and ate the ghee and then went around saying you were sick! Look, what I have put down in writing is the way I talk in conversation. What of it, if it doesn't have one of your silly predicates? Cripple!'

'You can abuse me as much as you like,' he said. 'I don't mind. There's just one thing: first spend a year reading the books I mentioned. Then, when you've learned to read and write properly, you can start writing for the public.'

'Get out of here,' I said. 'But tell everybody at home that I asked after them, especially bapa and umma. Tell them I have not started to get any money. That's why I don't send anything home.'

I didn't even ask him for the loan of a quarter-anna. I didn't have the nerve to ask. Him and his silly grammar!

Those days have gone. Now he's a most enthusiastic reader of my books. He also asks me to write a few stories about our relatives.

'All you need to do is write them. I'll see to the printing and publishing.'

He will take the money. The swindler!

The following day, as the girls were going by, their mouths watering as they looked longingly at my jambu tree, Pattumma came and took the goat to where she lived.

'No-one looks after it here, elder brother. Abu chases it. On top of that, from tomorrow it has to be milked. I've told a tea-shop that I'll let them have the milk.'

So that's the reason!

Pattumma went off with the goat and kid.

From then on, the goat and kid started coming at ten o'clock. The kid would gaily frisk and jump around. It would climb on my bed. It would eat along with the children. The mother goat had become very greedy. She would eat rice along with the children. There was a general din, uproar and tumult.

After a few days like this, there was laughter and uproar in the house. There was great joy. Abi, Pattukkutti, Saidu Muhammad, Laila, Arifa and so on are drinking tea with milk! Was that the reason for this laughter and uproar? I went to where it was coming from. The two Anummas, umma and Aishomma were drinking tea with milk along with their tapioca puttu! They were all laughing.

'Umma, what's all this laughter and uproar about?'

'Nothing!' said umma, laughing.

'You mustn't tell. We took the kid and tied it up.'

'So?'

'Will you tell?'

'What's going on?'

Abdulkhadar's wife joined in: 'We milked Pattumma's goat. We got a quarter of a measure of milk.'

'Umma, what's this I hear? Why should you milk Pattumma's goat on the sly like this?'

'It'll teach her a lesson,' said umma. 'She should have given us some.'

'Elder brother,' said Anumma. 'Don't tell! It would be a terrible disgrace for all of us.'

Disgrace or not, how could I allow this theft to take place before my eyes?

When Pattumma came, I said, 'Pattumma, be careful. They all got together and milked your goat and then drank the milk in their tea. Beforehand they took the kid and tied it up.'

Pattumma was furious.

'Have they no feelings! Will they take their own children and tie them up? Wait till I tax them with it!'

Pattumma ran to find them. When she did, umma, the two Annummas, Aishomma, Pattukutti, Abi, Laila, Arifa and the rest were standing there ready for her. All together they said, 'It was a good thing we did. We'd do it again. The goat and kid are fed here. It was through eating our tapioca puttu, the leaves from our jack-tree, our kanji-water and our children's rice that it became fat.'

Pattumma tried to set one against another.

'I say, Anumma, you're my younger sister, aren't you? Didn't I give you a goat? Umma, dear umma, you're my umma, aren't you? What is it that you let these unfeeling sisters-in-law do?'

'That'll do,' said umma. 'Your sisters-in-law, your umma, your younger sister—all got together and milked the goat. We all of us together drank the tea. It was delicious!'

'I'll never set foot in this house again,' said Pattumma.

Pattumma picked up the kid and kissed it.

'Darling, they stole your milk and drank it. Come, I'll give you some water.'

Pattumma came up to me with the kid.

'I'm going, elder brother. Let's see how they are going to milk my goat and drink the milk from now on.'

Pattumma went off carrying the kid. I was pleased. We'll see, shan't we, whether they milk the goat and drink the milk when there's no kid to start the milk flowing? Wow!

6)

Pattumma's goat would come at exactly ten o'clock. A little later Pattumma and Khadija would arrive. Was Pattumma nourishing any ill-feeling or not? She joined in conversation with her sisters-in-law, younger sister and umma. She did jobs around the house. She ate tapioca puttu. She drank black tea. She gave kanji-water to the goat.

When Kochunni came, I told him about the theft of the milk.

'That's what I told her,' said Kochunni, '—to give a little milk. Do you know what Pattumma went and did? She undertook to give milk to four households. And I too promised some in the tea-shop. She doesn't give me and Khadija a drop of milk for our tea!'

So that's the way it is! Then if necessary Kochunni and Khadija wouldn't hesitate to steal a little milk.

I asked Pattumma, why she was not giving a drop or two of milk to Kochunni and Khadija.

'Isn't it Khadija's bapa who takes the money I get from selling the milk?' said Pattumma. 'And then weren't they all drinking tea without milk so far? So why are they so keen to have milk now? Am I drinking any?'

'You've become very stingy, haven't you?'

'Khadija's bapa has joined a savings club. Doesn't he want money to invest in that?'

That was true also. While I was thinking about all this, Sulaiman brought three pineapples for me and said, 'This is a good variety. You'll like it.'

I cut one of them, and while I was eating it after giving a piece to each of the children, Abu showed up in all his glory.

'Ah . . . if one is a rich man, this is how it is!' he said. 'There's nobody to give me pineapples. Today they are making preparations to give you a feast.'

'What feast?'

'Bread, liver and tea.'

'Why don't you come along with me too?'

'Nobody has invited me. Do you know something? That miserly elder sister of ours yesterday sent some tea with milk to second brother and Hanifa.'

'Tea with milk?'

'Yes!'

'Didn't she give you any?'

'I'm sitting there under their very noses! For that reason I, too, got one.'

Amazing! Pattumma has given milk tea to Abdulkhadar and Hanifa, and to Abu as well! There must be something behind this!

'What's the reason for Pattumma providing this milk tea?'

'Elder brother Hanifa went on strike.'

'How do you mean, "went on strike"?'

'It is elder brother Hanifa who sews elder sister's kuppayam, Khadija's blouse, and then all their town clothes and so on. When Khadija came the day before yesterday or thereabouts to get something sewn, he sent word to say he wouldn't sew anything for them. That cup of tea was a bribe to ensure that he wouldn't say that again!'

'Why did she give Abdulkhadar some?'

'That's because eldest brother-in-law owes second brother some money. When he saw second sister, second brother said that, if he didn't get the money back right away, he'd file a suit! The first defendant would be eldest brother-in-law, the second would be eldest sister, the third Khadija. If that wasn't enough, he'd have the goat confiscated. So that glass of tea was an inducement to do nothing like that.'

So they are using Pattumma's goat's milk for bribing people!

'Kuttan Pillai is coming,' said Abu.

It was true. Kuttan Pillai, the postman, came through the gate and gave me a parcel, which I duly signed for. Even when Kuttan Pillai had gone, I did not untie the parcel to see what was in it. Umma asked me, 'Hey, what is it, in that bundle?'

'There are ten copies of my new book,' I said. 'The publishers have sent me them as complimentary copies. Are you satisfied?'

Umma had to know something else. 'Would you get any money for them if you sold them?'

'Why don't you leave me alone? Money, money, money!'

For my part, at that time I did not have even a quarter of an anna. I had an idea. When umma went, I called Abu quietly and asked him, 'Will you sell these books in the market somewhere?'

Right away he asked, 'What commission will you give?'

Saying that I would give him a commission, I untied the parcel, wrapped nine books in a sheet of paper and sent Abu off with them. After that I waited.

This is my home town, I thought. Will anybody pay money for books that I wrote?

An hour or two passed. Abu came back. We were in luck. He had sold all the books! I gave Abu the full price of one book. While I was counting the rest of the money, umma came and asked, 'Hey, what did you get?' I felt extremely angry that she had seen the money. I picked up a glass that was standing by me and flung it with full force against the wall. The glass broke into ten thousand pieces. The house became silent. I felt much relieved. Umma, without saying a word, swept it all up, wrapped it in a piece of paper and threw it away. Then she came back and without a word sat down directly in front of me and turned her face away from me.

I picked up the remaining copy of 'The World-famous Nose' and held it out to Pattumma's goat. It came up to me eagerly.

'What are you doing?' asked Abu.

'Pattumma's goat ate "Childhood Friend" and "Sounds" with relish,' I replied. 'On that occasion I said that I had one more book that I'd give her. Let her taste "The World-famous Nose".'

'Don't let her eat it,' said Abu. I took the book and put it in my box. When Abu left, I gave half the money I got to umma.

'How much was one of those books?' she asked.

I told her the truth. After some time, when Abdulkhadar came to have lunch, he took the one book that was left with me.

'Wasn't it a big parcel ?'

'Yes, there were ten copies. I got Abu to sell nine of them.'

'Where's the money ?'

'I gave the price of one to Abu. Half of what was left I gave to umma.'

'And nothing for me ?'

'You sell that book and keep the money.'

'Umma !' he called and went inside. There was some commotion there.

'I'm the one who sees to all the household expenses, not you !' I heard Abdulkhadar say. After some time he went out looking happy. When I saw umma's face, I realised that Abdulkhadar had taken away whatever she had with her.

By four o'clock Kochunni and Khadija came and invited me. I took Abu along.

Kochunni's bapa, umma and sisters are in his house. Abu said that they had made a small hut for Pattumma, Kochunni, Khadija, Pattumma's goat, its kid and some hens to live in. 'Elder sister said that you shouldn't know about it. You must see it,' Abu told me confidentially.

We had our fill of pattiri and liver curry. We drank tea with milk. We saw Pattumma's house.

'Why did you come here, elder brother ?' Pattumma asked sadly. Pattumma's house was a pitiful sight. It was a small room with mud walls and a roof of palm-leaves. Its door came from some old house or other. It was tied up with rope. It had no lock.

'Such a disgrace,' said Pattumma. 'How can I go on living after this ?'

'Don't worry,' I said. 'I'll give you the money to repair this door.'

'You don't have to do that. I'll sell my goat's milk and make some money.'

'There's no need; I'll give you the money.'

That night after dinner I was sitting at home on a chair. Kochunni, Sulaiman, Pattumma—everyone was there.

Abdulkhadar said to Hanifa, 'We must go early in the morning. As soon as the court opens, we'll file the suit and come away.'

'What suit?' I asked.

'A civil action. There is an immediate confiscation. I had postponed this suit. But there have been further developments. I cannot put it off any more.'

'What further developments?'

'When they made pattiri, dipped it in coconut milk, stacked it on a plate and gave it to everyone, they didn't think of us. When they made liver curry and gave people bowls full, they didn't think of us. For us a glass of tea each! For others pattiri and liver curry!'

'Umma, sisters-in-law and I were sitting in this house with our mouths watering,' said Anumma. 'They didn't think of us either.'

'How about me then?' said Sulaiman.

'Sulaiman,' said Abdulkhadar, 'you're the first witness.'

'How many people I should be afraid of!' said Pattumma. 'Umma, my sister-in-law, my younger sister, second brother, Hanifa, Abu, my husband! And now Sulaiman!'

'Nobody need be afraid of me!' bawled Abu.

'That's enough of that!' I said.

'Second brother,' said Pattumma. 'I'll give everyone liver curry, bread and tea. Be patient for just a few days.'

'How many days?' he asked.

'I'll let you know. Hey, Hanifa! How could you do it? You sent it back through Khadija without sewing it.'

'Do you think I must do free sewing for everybody?' said Hanifa. 'I'm always having to sew shirts for Abu. I have to sew for everyone in this house: does anyone pay me for it?'

Abdulkhadar joined in.

'I have to pay you for sewing your wife's kuppayam. I have to pay you for sewing Laila's skirt and blouse. I have to pay you for sewing Abi's coat and trousers. What do you think of that!'

Hanifa was hurt.

'Nobody need give me anything. I'll go and join the army. This very night!'

Then I remembered something.

'Look!' I said. 'You can go and join the army in about half an hour. Remember how, when you were in the army, you used to come to me in Ernakulam when you were going back after being home on leave? On those occasions you used to borrow money in fives and tens. You used to say that whatever you had, umma took or Abdulkhadar took. You never returned any of it to me. Let me have all of it now!'

Straightaway Hanifa called Aishomma.

'Come on, bring the children also. We don't need to stay in this house any more. They're always getting at us. We'll go and live in a hut made of palm-leaves. Come on, Abi, get up.'

'Tell me,' I said. 'Do you owe me money, or don't you?'

'That was long ago, elder brother,' he said. 'Who remembers all those things?'

'Now it's clear that you do owe me some. That's great.'

I went and lay down. Early in the morning, at four o'clock, I was awakened by the noise of Pattumma, Kochunni and Khadija leaving. While I was still lying there, umma asked, 'Are you up?'

'No,' I said, 'I'm lying down. What is it?'

'If you have any money,' said umma, 'give me a rupee. Nobody need know.'

'Didn't I give you some yesterday?'

'Abdulkhadar took all that. It is he who looks after all the expenditure here. There are so many to be taken care of. Just think how much money is needed every day.'

'Just leave me alone. If you say anything, I'll go away from here right now!'

Umma did not say anything. I lay there quietly. Then I remembered an incident that took place when I arrived some time previously.

In those days I lived in my small house.

) 192 (

I came in a taxi. When they saw the taxi coming and stopping in front of the building, people gathered. Everyone saw me counting out rupee notes to pay the taxi driver.

That night, after dinner, when I was about to go to bed, Abdulkhadar, umma and Hanifa came in. As soon as they came, Abdulkhadar said, 'Elder brother, if you have any money, don't keep it here. Some thieves will come. And when they do, they'll beat you to death. Better let me have it!'

I counted five hundred rupees in front of umma and gave it to him! Let the thieves come and beat me to death; at least the money will be saved. Everyone went away satisfied. I lay there in a peaceful frame of mind and lit a beedi. Then I felt there was someone in the house. A little bit afraid, I asked, 'Who is it?'

'It's me,' said umma softly. 'I came in without anyone seeing.'

'What for?'

'Look, there's no need for it to get around,' umma said. 'You must give me twenty-five rupees. Nobody need know.'

After all, it was umma. I gave her twenty-five rupees then and there. I slept in a peaceful frame of mind. From the next day on, there was a regular procession of borrowers. Mostly women. Not all of them were Muslims. But I had been breast-fed by all of them! 'Have you forgotten that? Give me two rupees.'

I started giving two or three rupees at a time. When the total had reached a hundred rupees, I came out with the statement, 'No, I wasn't breast-fed by anybody!' Meanwhile, something else was going on. Umma would bring Abi and Pattukkutti and say, 'Give something to these little ones. Don't give any coppers!'

That was not all.

'Look, now you have come to stay. Your friends will come to see you. What shall we let them eat from?'

'Banana leaves!'

'That would be a disgrace. We need some plates and bowls and glasses.'

'I don't have any money.'

'Then I'll go to that Anapparambil's shop. I'll say it's for you and get some.'

And she would have done it, too. Varkkikkunju Anapparambil has a big stationery shop, and he's a friend of mine. If umma had gone there, she wouldn't have hesitated to bring all that was in the shop. So I said, 'You needn't go, umma. I'll go and get some.'

I went and got a man to bring one head-load of crockery. I had peace for some days. Then umma came and said, 'Look, now you have come here to stay. If your friends come, where will they sleep? You must buy some mattresses and pillows.'

'Leave me alone.'

What was the point! To put an end to being bothered like this, I went and bought them. Then umma wanted a copper pot! We could use it for boiling rice or for heating water for bathing.

I said to myself: After copper pot it will be bullock-cart! Then maybe a car! Hm!

I went away with my suitcase and bedding. I went through Varkala and all round Madras. I came back and went again. Now I have come back again. It's not like Hanifa saying he'll go and join the army. If I say I'll go, I go. So umma was lying there, still and quiet. I got up and opened my suitcase, brought the rest of the money I had, gave it to her and said, 'You don't need to be afraid any more. Even if I say I'll go, I won't be able to go. I don't have any money for the fare. You can take care of me from now on.'

So the days went by.

Then a remarkable thing happened. The two Anummas and Aishomma together milked Pattumma's goat and put the milk in their tea! It was done without the kid. They did it not just once, but every day. Pattumma was living peacefully and quietly in the belief that the goat's milk would not flow without the kid!

They tried to make Abi and Pattukkutti act as the kid, but it did not work. In the end they tried it with Subaida and Rashid and succeeded. Pattumma came to know about this remarkable thing. She beat her breast and wept.

'Are you human? To do such a thing! Please don't do it. I'll give you some milk.'

From the very next day, Pattumma started sending home half a bottle of milk.

Subaida, Rashid, Abi, Arifa, Laila, Pattukkutti are all happy. The two Anummas, Aishomma and umma started having milk tea.

Now, along with the goat, the kid also comes. Along with them, Khadija and half a bottle of milk.

So we get two kinds of milk at home; one that they steal and the other that Pattumma gives. Poor Pattumma!

One secret I have not been able to fathom as yet. Which of the women was the first to have this brainwave?

GLOSSARY

That a good number of words listed here may be considered to
have been, at some point in time at least, partly or wholly assimi-
lated into the vocabulary of English is shown by their appearance in standard dictionaries. We have thought it useful to draw
attention to such words (and to some not entirely unfamiliar
proper names) by the use of the following abbreviations:

> C = Collins Dictionary of
> the English Language, 1979
> O = The Oxford English Dictionary, 1933
> W = Webster's Third New International
> Dictionary of the English Language,
> 1961
> B = Encyclopaedia Britannica, 1974.

al-Alamin, see *Rabb al-Alamin*.

Ali (C,B) = Ali ibn Abi Talib, a cousin of Muhammad,
whose daughter Fatima he married. He reigned as the
fourth caliph (successor to Muhammad) from 656–661.

Allah (C,O,W,B) = the name of the Deity among Muslims.

Allah akbar = 'God is great'.

anna (C,O,W) = formerly (i.e. before decimalisation) a
unit of currency in India, being $\frac{1}{16}$ of a rupee.

As-habus (B) = the Companions of Muhammad—those of
his followers who had personal contact with him.

ashram (C,O,W) = a place of religious retreat.

Asr = afternoon, the third of the five daily congregational
prayers in Islam.

as-salamu alaikum = 'Peace be upon you', the customary greeting among Muslims.

aviyal = a kind of vegetable curry.

bapa = father; a term used exclusively by Muslims in Kerala.

bayt = a couplet, the basic unit of Arabic poetry (approximately corresponding to the line in English verse).

beedi (W; *biri*) = a cheap smoke made of fragments of tobacco wrapped in a leaf.

begum (C,O,W) = a Muslim queen, princess, or lady of high rank.

betel (C,O,W,B) = a climbing pepper (*Piper betle*), the leaves of which, in combination with scrapings of areca-nut and lime made from burnt coral, are widely used in South Asia as a masticatory.

betel-box (O) = a box in which a ready supply of betel-leaves, betel-nut and lime is kept.

betel-nut (C,O) = areca-nut, obtained from the palm *Areca catechu*.

bibi (W) = lady; used as a term of respectful address.

biriyani = a rice dish, coloured and flavoured with saffron and turmeric and consisting of alternate layers of rice and rich meat or vegetable curry.

bismillah = 'in the name of God', the opening words of the Koran and the formula by which a pious Muslim precedes every daily act or special undertaking.

brahman (C,O,W,B) = a member of the highest caste of Hindu society.

chakram (W) = a small silver coin formerly issued by the state of Travancore (the southern part of Kerala). Its value was $\frac{1}{32}$ of a rupee.

coir (C,O,W,B) = stiff, coarse fibre from the husk of a coconut, used for making ropes, matting, etc.

dhoti (C,O,W,B) = man's lower garment, consisting of a length of cloth. A double dhoti is made of finer cloth, is twice as long and is worn double.

Dhualfiqar (B) = a magical sword, said to have been

originally the property of an unbeliever but to have come into the possession of Muhammad after the battle of Badr in 624. Muhammad gave it to his son-in-law, Ali, with whom it is always associated in Islamic mythology.

fakir (C,O,W,B) = Muslim religious mendicant or ascetic.

fala = a sequence of syllables used in incantation; no semantic content.

Firdaus = one of the Islamic terms for Paradise.

ghee (C,O,W,B) = clarified butter, usually made from buffalo milk; an essential and valued element in Indian cuisine.

Hajar al-Aswad (B) = the Black Stone. A stone (or rather three large pieces of stone and some fragments) built into the eastern wall of the Ka'ba, the small shrine near the centre of the Great Mosque in Mecca. Every Muslim who makes the pilgrimage to Mecca will touch and kiss this stone. Said to have been given to Adam when he was turned out of the Garden of Eden, the stone is held to have been originally white, but to have turned black through contact with the impurity and sin of mankind.

haji (C,O,W; *hadji*) = a Muslim who has made the pilgrimage to Mecca; often used as a title.

hajj (C,O,W; *hadj*) = the pilgrimage to Mecca prescribed as one of the religious duties of Muslims.

hala = a sequence of syllables used in incantation; no semantic content.

halal (C,W) = 'lawful'; flesh of animals slaughtered according to ritual and so fit for consumption by Muslims.

halqat = earring of the sort worn in the upper part of the ear by Muslim women and girls in northern Kerala.

hamkin = donkey-like, stupid, ignorant.

Iblis = the Islamic name for the devil, the representative of the powers of evil.

ifrit (W,B) = a class of powerful and cunning evil spirits, a subset of the *jinn*.

ikkakka = elder brother; a term used exclusively by Muslims in Kerala.

imam (C,B) = the head of the Muslim community.

iman = 'faith', the theoretical part of the religion of Islam, its doctrines, as opposed to the practical course that a believer must conform to in his life.

ins = mankind.

Isha = late evening, the fifth of the five daily congregational prayers in Islam.

islam = submission (to the will of God), entering into peace—the dominant idea in the religion of Islam.

jaggery (C,O,W) = an unrefined brown sugar made in India from the sap of certain kinds of palm.

jambu (O,W) = a tall tree (*Eugenia jambolana*), common in Kerala, that bears a dark crimson fruit.

jinn = the plural form of *jinni*.

jinni (C,O,W,B) = one of a class of spirits in Muslim demonology; lower than the angels, they are said to inhabit the earth and to have the power to assume different forms; generally malevolent, they are held to be responsible for accidents and diseases.

jubba (C,O,W,B) = long outer garment with long sleeves worn by Muslim officials and professional men.

Jum'a (B) = Friday of the Muslim week, and hence the special noonday service that takes place in the mosque on that day, 'the day of congregation'.

Ka'ba (C,B; *Kaaba*) = the small rectangular shrine near the centre of the Great Mosque at Mecca that is the most sacred spot on earth for Muslims. Circumambulation of the Ka'ba is an essential part of the *hajj*. See also *Hajar al-Aswad*.

kafan = the Muslim three-fold shroud.

kafir (C,O,W,B) = infidel, one who is not a Muslim; commonly used disparagingly.

kalan = a vegetable curry, prepared from pumpkin cooked with curd.

kanji (O,W; *conjee, congee*) = rice boiled in a large amount of water until it becomes soft, a kind of gruel.

kanji-water = water in which rice has been boiled.

khatib (B) = preacher, the one who gives the *khutba* or sermon at the beginning of the special Friday midday worship. See *Jum'a*.

Koran (C,O,W,B) = the sacred book of Islam, regarded by Muslims as the word of Allah that was revealed to Muhammad.

kuppayam = long-sleeved, long-waisted blouse worn by Muslim women in Kerala.

la ilaha illallah = 'There is no god but Allah', the opening words of the creed of Islam.

lakh (C,O,W) = 100,000.

Maghrib = the period immediately after sunset, the fourth of the five daily congregational prayers in Islam.

mahout (C,O,W) = driver of an elephant.

malak = angel.

Mayyadin (B) = Muhyi ad-Din (1165–1240), a renowned Muslim mystic and philosopher.

muezzin (C,O,W,B) = the official who proclaims the call to public worship at a mosque.

mundu = woman's lower garment, consisting of a length of cloth.

murral (W) = a predatory freshwater fish (*Ophicephalus striatus*) of the family Ophicephalidae (Snake-heads).

muqri = reader; one who recites the text of the Koran at festivals and at mosque services.

Mushaf = a collection of written pages; one of the names by which the holy Koran is known.

Nabi = prophet; the most usual epithet of Muhammad.

Nikah = the Muslim marriage service.

ossan = the barber who performs the operation of circumcision on Muslim boys.

pallatti = a small freshwater fish (*Etroplus coruchi*) of the family of Cichlids.

pandal (O,W,B) = a temporary pavilion with open sides, made of upright poles supporting a roof of plaited coconut leaves or bamboo matting.

pandit (C,O,W) = a teacher or scholar, more particularly

one versed in Hindu philosophy and religion.

papaya (C,O,W,B) = the fruit of the *Carica papaya* tree.

Parasuraman (B) = the sixth incarnation of the Hindu god Vishnu and the legendary creator of Kerala.

pattiri = a type of unleavened bread made from wheat flour.

portia tree (O,W) = a medium-sized flowering tree common in South India (*Thespia populnea*).

puttu = a food made from rice-flour and ground coconut.

qissa = a tale or story (an Arabic literary technical term).

qiyamat = the rising of men at the resurrection on the Last Day.

Rabb = God, the Nourisher to Perfection.

Rabb al-Alamin = God, the Fosterer and Nourisher of all creation.

Ramaẓan (C,O,W,B; *Ramadan*) = the ninth month of the Muhammadan year and a month of strict fasting during the hours of daylight.

rasul = messenger, a great prophet.

ruhani = a spiritual being; sometimes used as a cover term for both angels and *jinn*, but more commonly to mean evil spirit.

rupee (C,O,W) = the basic monetary unit in India.

sahib (C,O,W) = master, lord; used as a term of respect.

salam = to greet a fellow Muslim in the conventional way (see *as-salamu alaikum*).

salam alaikum, see *as-salamu alaikum*.

sambar = a mixed vegetable curry flavoured with tamarind and asafoetida.

sanduq = a Muslim coffin.

sanyasi (B) = a Hindu religious ascetic.

sari (C,O,W,B) = Indian woman's garment consisting of a long length of cloth; not traditionally the dress of Muslim women.

satyagraha (C,O,W) = non-violent civil disobedience or passive resistance with a view to exerting pressure for political or social reform.

Sidrat al-Muntaha = a tree in Paradise, called in the Koran 'the *sidra* (lote-tree) which marks the boundary'; it is believed to bear as many leaves as there are inhabitants in the world and on each leaf a name is written. On the middle night of the eighth month the tree is shaken and those whose leaves fall will die during the following year.

sloka (O,W) = a couplet or distich of Sanskrit verse.

Subh = dawn, the first of the five daily congregational prayers in Islam.

suh = a syllable used in incantation; no semantic content.

sundari = Malayalam for 'beautiful woman'; used also as a proper name.

Sur = trumpet, specifically that sounded by the angel Israfil on the day of Judgment.

swamiji (C,O,W,B) = lord, master; used as a form of respectful address to a Hindu religious teacher. *-ji* is an optional honorific suffix.

takbir = 'magnifying the greatness [of God]'; the utterance of the creed *Allah akbar*.

tali (W) = a thread, of gold where possible, tied round an Indian bride's neck by the bridegroom.

tawba = repentance, an act of penance.

umma = mother; a term used exclusively by Muslims in Kerala.

ummamma = grandmother; term used exclusively by Muslims.

uppuppa = grandfather; term used exclusively by Muslims.

Vaka = in the Hindu epic *Mahābhārata*, a demon who tyrannised a town, forcing the citizens to send him every day a dish of food by a man whom he always devoured at the end of the meal; hence symbolises an insatiable appetite.

wa alaikum salam = the response to the customary Muslim greeting, *as-salamu alaikum*.

wa'z = sermon.

wuzu = (partial) ritual ablution.

zakat (W,B) = an annual alms tax required of all Muslims;

one of the five pillars of Islam—along with the profession of faith, prayer, fasting and the pilgrimage to Mecca.

Zuhr = midday, the second of the five daily congregational prayers in Islam.